Wicked IN A KILT

Hot Scots, Book Two

ANNA DURAND

JACOBSVILLE BOOKS JB MARIETTA, OHIO

ISBN: 978-1-934631-86-7 (paperback)
ISBN: 978-1-934631-87-4 (EPUB ebook)
ISBN: 978-1-934631-85-0 (Kindle ebook)
ISBN: 978-1-934631-82-9 (audiobook)
Library of Congress Control Number: 2017955865

Manufactured in the United States.

Jacobsville Books
www.JacobsvilleBooks.com

Publisher's Cataloging-in-Publication Data
provided by Five Rainbows Cataloging Services

Names: Durand, Anna.
Title: Wicked in a kilt / Anna Durand.
Description: Lake Linden, MI : Jacobsville Books, 2017. | Series: Hot Scots, bk. 2.
Identifiers: LCCN 2017955865 | ISBN 978-1-934631-86-7 (paperback) | ISBN 978-1-934631-87-4 (EPUB ebook) | ISBN 978-1-934631-85-0 (Kindle ebook) | 978-1-934631-82-9 (audiobook)
Subjects: LCSH: Man-woman relationships--Fiction. | Scots--Fiction. | Chicago (Ill.)--Fiction. | Michigan--Fiction. | Romance fiction. | BISAC: FICTION / Romance / Contemporary. | FICTION / Romance / Romantic comedy. | GSAFD: Love stories.
Classification: LCC PS3604.U724 W53 2016 (print) | LCC PS3604.U724 (ebook) | DDC 813/.6--dc23.

Praise for Anna Durand's Books

"An enthralling story. [...] I highly recommend the writing of Ms. Durand and *Wicked in a Kilt*, but be warned you will find yourself addicted and want your own Hot Scot."
Coffee Time Romance & More

"Durand's Hot Scots series has been loads of fun to read, and [*Irresistible in a Kilt*] is no exception. [...] The author's action-packed and suspenseful plot keeps the reader on their toes, and the grown-up sizzle never disappoints."
Jack Magnus, Readers' Favorite

"[*Lethal in a Kilt* is] full of hot sex, adventure, and so much laughter. I found myself laughing-out-loud at the antics of the Witches of Ballachulish (Logan's sisters) and the hilarious flirting and sexy banter between Serena and Logan. [...] Recommend highly!"
Sharon Clayton, The Eclectic Review

"[*Insatiable in a Kilt*] smokes from the very first pages... Durand's characters are a delight and seeing how they mix business with their increasing attraction for each other is entertaining indeed. [...] Durand's Hot Scots family saga just keeps on getting better."
Jack Magnus, Readers' Favorite

"I loved the Scottish in Ian and the strength of Rae, but the love of one little girl makes [*Notorious in a Kilt*] something to behold."
Coffee Time Romance

"*Gift-Wrapped in a Kilt* is a marvelous continuation of the author's MacTaggart family saga. Durand's story has an entertaining plot, and her steamy interludes are well-written...a celebration of healthy relationships between loving adults written in a tasteful and compelling manner."
Jack Magnus, Readers' Favorite

"I have enjoyed this whole series, but Emery and Rory [from *Scandalous in a Kilt*] have stolen my heart and are now my favorites!"
The Romance Reviews

"There's a huge hero's and heroine's journey [in *Dangerous in a Kilt*] that I quite enjoyed, not to mention the hot sex, and again, not to mention the sweet seduction of the Scotsman who pulls out all the stops to get Erica to love him."
Manic Readers

Other Books by Anna Durand

Dangerous in a Kilt (Hot Scots, Book One)
Scandalous in a Kilt (Hot Scots, Book Three)
The MacTaggart Brothers Trilogy (Hot Scots, Books 1-3)
Gift-Wrapped in a Kilt (Hot Scots, Book Four)
Notorious in a Kilt (Hot Scots, Book Five)
Insatiable in a Kilt (Hot Scots, Book Six)
Lethal in a Kilt (Hot Scots, Book Seven)
Irresistible in a Kilt (Hot Scots, Book Eight)
One Hot Chance (Hot Brits, Book One)
One Hot Roomie (Hot Brits, Book Two)
One Hot Crush (Hot Brits, Book Three)
The Dixon Brothers Trilogy (Hot Brits, Books 1-3)
Natural Passion (Au Naturel Trilogy, Book One)
Natural Impulse (Au Naturel Trilogy, Book Two)
Natural Satisfaction (Au Naturel Trilogy, Book Three)
Fired Up (a standalone romance)
The Mortal Falls (Undercover Elementals, Book One)
The Mortal Fires (Undercover Elementals, Book Two)
The Mortal Tempest (Undercover Elementals, Book Three)
The Janusite Trilogy (Undercover Elementals, Books 1-3)
Obsidian Hunger (Undercover Elementals, Book Four)
Willpower (Psychic Crossroads, Book One)
Intuition (Psychic Crossroads, Book Two)
Kinetic (Psychic Crossroads, Book Three)
Passion Never Dies: The Complete Reborn Series
Reborn to Die (Reborn, Part One)
Reborn to Burn (Reborn, Part Two)
Reborn to Avenge (Reborn, Part Three)
Reborn to Conquer (Reborn, Part Four)

<h1 style="text-align:center">Chapter One</h1>

I marched down the hallway toward the swinging double doors that led out into the main part of the nightclub, pausing inches from the doors to consider my mission—track down a wayward male stripper. Seriously. My cousin Tara had begged me to "please-please-please" find the exotic dancer who was supposed to be the highlight of tonight's entertainment. Modern bachelorette parties, Tara had assured me, must include a striptease. And our entertainment was late.

She'd neglected to mention my maid of honor duties involved corralling the star of the show.

Just call me Calli Douglas, stripper wrangler.

Behind me, the cheering and laughter of female voices sifted down the hallway. The bridal party had gathered inside a private back room of the club, Dance Ardor, for a wild girls' night before the wedding tomorrow. The room's closed door couldn't fully contain the raucous sounds of revelry.

I glanced back, sighed, and pushed through the doors, out into the club. Thumping bass beats vibrated through the floor and my body. Strobe lights in shades of violet, indigo, and scarlet crisscrossed the cavernous space, once a warehouse but now an underground club. Their beams stroked across the dance floor and out onto the high tables arrayed around the floor atop a raised platform.

A draft chilled the bare skin of my back, shoulders, and arms. The neckline of my emerald-green halter dress plunged low enough to expose the entire inner slopes of my breasts. The dress hugged my hips, flaring out partway down my thighs but stopping well above my knees. Tara had insisted on buying me a new dress for tonight as well as the matching strappy heels I wore.

Rubbing my arms, I wondered how to find the man I sought. Maybe I should've run through the club yelling "here, stripper-stripper-stripper."

I discarded that plan and headed down the semi-circular platform that surrounded the dance floor, passing table after table occupied by laughing groups and cuddling couples. On the floor, more couples writhed and thrust their hips, arms raised above their heads or hanging loose at their sides in displays of wanton abandon. One woman had plastered her body to her slender partner, who clasped her buttocks to keep their hips locked together.

This wasn't my kind of scene. I would've rather stayed home in the woods of far northern Michigan, playing with my two six-month-old puppies. But I wouldn't miss Tara's wedding, no matter how much I disliked parties.

Scanning the club, I hunted for a man who looked like a stripper. Trouble was, every male in here could've qualified—the women too. My dress, the sexiest I'd ever worn, seemed downright dowdy next to the barely there attire of every other female in the place. I halted, raising onto tiptoes to get a better view of the opposite side of the club. All the men over there had partners, whom they were kissing or fondling amid the shadows, while the strobes swept over them in a dizzying blur of colors.

Swerving my gaze away, I started off again.

And slammed into a hard body.

With a yelp, I flung my hands up. They landed on a massive chest sheathed in a cobalt-blue shirt. The sight of tanned skin revealed by two open buttons riveted my attention. Muscles flexed under my fingers as the stranger laid his warm palms over my hands.

"Well now," the stranger drawled, his voice deep and husky, "I've been looking for a bonnie lass, but I didn't expect to literally run into one."

His accent. It was…Scottish? I stumbled backward, out of his grasp, and blinked rapidly. He wore a kilt fashioned from a blue-and-green tartan laced with orange lines. His shirt clung to his muscled torso, and the short sleeves hugged his impressive biceps. Honey-brown leather boots, stylishly scuffed, covered his large feet.

I swung my gaze to his face, and my heart stuttered. Eyes the color of sapphires watched me, glittering in the pulsing lights. His gaze traveled the length of me, his eyes narrowing and then widening as he took in my dress and everything it exposed. My strappy heels boosted my height by a few inches, but I still had to tilt my head back to meet the Scotsman's eyes.

He brushed a lock of hair away from my face. "Your dress brings out the green of your eyes. But this lighting can't do justice to your beautiful red hair."

My voice had abandoned me at the sight of him and those muscle-bound legs revealed below the kilt. Too bad the kilt concealed his thighs, because I would've bet the entirety of my meager savings they were thick and strong too.

But who wore a kilt in a nightclub? He had to be the stripper. But why was the entertainment hitting on me? Maybe this was part of the show. I'd never met a stripper before, so I had no idea.

I couldn't tear my gaze away from the view of his powerful legs, all sinew and sun-kissed, golden skin dusted with fine brown hairs a shade darker than the chestnut hair that curled around his ears. The wavy locks, longish but not too long, glistened in the strobing lights. My fingers twitched, anxious to dive into those locks and discover their silky softness. *And God created man for woman to lick.*

Oh. Dear. Lord. I was turning into a sex-crazed bridesmaid, just like the rest of them.

He angled his head to study my face. "You're the one I've been looking for, I think."

I smoothed my dress, cleared my throat, and lifted my chin. Had to, in order to meet his gaze. The man was enormous.

"Are you looking for the party?" I asked.

His lips slid into a wicked grin. "Aye."

No idea what that meant, but it sounded like assent. I bit my lip, eying his kilt. Tara had mentioned wanting a "hot fireman," but she'd let her ditzy friend Sienna arrange the entertainment. Sienna must've gotten the order wrong.

"You're not a firefighter," I said.

His forehead crinkled in the most disarming way. "I didn't realize American women are so specific about what they want."

"As long as you look good without your clothes, you'll do."

Chestnut eyebrows shot up over his blue eyes. "You're direct, aren't you? Yes, I've been told I look quite good naked."

"Naked?" I glanced down at his kilt. "Please tell me you're wearing a G-string under that thing. That's the protocol, isn't it?"

"A G-string protocol?" He laughed, shaking his head. "You're adorable, but I'm beginning to think you're off your head."

"Are you calling me crazy?" When he opened his mouth to answer, I raised a hand palm out to silence him. "Never mind. Come with me."

I turned away, crooking a finger to beckon him to follow.

"Ah, lass," the Scot all but purred, "I'll follow ye anywhere, even if ye are a bampot."

"Whatever, just hurry up." I headed for the doorway to the club's inner sanctum, Scot in tow. I swore I could feel his gaze on my back, appraising me with sultry interest. My stomach fluttered again as if it had grown wings and desperately wanted to fly to my new friend. Latch on. Take a nibble. I glanced back at him, pushed by an irresistible urge. Those lustrous eyes zeroed in on mine, and my mouth went dry. *What is wrong with me?*

He smiled, slow and sensual. "After the party, may I buy you a drink?"

"I don't drink. Not morally opposed or anything, but I've never tasted an alcoholic beverage I liked."

"Water is a drink, you know." He peered down the hallway past me. "Where are we headed?"

"The party, of course." I scrunched my eyebrows, wondering why he asked. Didn't the agency tell him what he was in for tonight? Well, they might've omitted the part about a gaggle of lustful, liquored-up women. Realizing he'd slowed down, falling a few paces behind, I waved for him to pick up speed. "Come on, they're waiting."

"They?"

"It's a party." I tried not to sound sarcastic, but really. Was he gorgeous but utterly dense or what? "Just come along, will you?"

"Aye." He strode up alongside me as we pushed through the swinging door. His hand drifted up to my arm and skated over my skin, forging a tempting trail up to my bare shoulder. "I'm yours to command."

"Um…" I stumbled to a halt, helpless to look away from him. My breaths had grown labored again. I couldn't think, my senses overpowered by the scent of his dark, spicy cologne. Sex in a bottle, that stuff was. I lifted my face to stare into his shimmering, curious eyes. His fingers caressed my shoulder with a feather-light touch as he leaned in ever so slightly, his lips curved up at the corners, his eyes searing into mine. All the pertinent parts of my body tightened, ached, or tingled. No, it wasn't the cologne. *He* was sex incarnate.

I cleared my throat, shaking off his hand. "Where were you, anyway? I've been looking everywhere."

His brows rose as his lips parted. "Have ye, then?"

"Yes." I seized his arm—my breath caught at the feel of his warm, pliant flesh and the hard muscles beneath it—and tugged. "Get a move on."

His confusion melted into a bright smile, as if he were a teenager given the keys to the adult bookstore. "Lead on, lass. Lead on."

I hauled him straight to the private room where the bridal party waited. At the door, I released his arm and hesitated, my hand on the knob. "I hope they're not too disappointed you aren't a firefighter."

"Is it really that important to every American woman?"

"Never mind." I couldn't resist taking one last peek—okay, a long, lingering look—at him.

Shoving the thought away, because that always worked with unbidden thoughts, I flung the door open and gestured for him to enter. Feminine whoops exploded out of the room.

"He's here!" someone hollered, and the whoops began anew.

The Scotsman drew back, his eyes widening. I slapped a hand on his back and gave him a little push. He stumbled inside, caught himself, and straightened. The whooping mutated into cheers and catcalls. The Scotsman halted two steps inside the room.

I took a step across the threshold, and from my sidelong vantage, I glimpsed his shocked expression. I tracked his line of sight to the spectacle that had stopped him. Across the room, one of the ladies had just stabbed a paper penis onto the cartoonish image of a naked man. The first round of Pin the Junk on the Hunk had commenced.

The bridesmaid whipped off her blindfold and her attention snapped to the solitary man in the room.

"Wooo!" she hollered, pumping her fists in the air. "Time to get the party started!"

A throng of champagne-addled women surged toward the stripper, whose face went ashen.

"Take it off, baby," Sienna said, her black hair flailing as she jumped up and down. "Show us what you got."

The Scotsman staggered backward, smack into me. My heels tripped me up, sending me tumbling to the floor outside the doorway.

"Shit!" The expletive burst out of me at the same instant the kilted dancer hustled out of the room backward, tripped over my legs, and hopped sideways to avoid crushing me. He threw a hand out to brace himself on the wall, preventing his own fall.

Inside the room, someone shrieked. Tara rushed to the doorway, eyes wide, face blanched. "Calli, are you okay? What happened?"

Pushing up onto my elbows, I blew my hair out of my face. "The exotic dancer trampled me."

The Scotsman stared at me, his jaw dropping.

My elfin cousin offered me a hand. I grasped it, letting her lever me up off the floor. The second my right foot contacted the linoleum, pain scorched through my ankle. I hissed and grabbed the doorjamb for support, frowning at the man in plaid. "What's wrong with you? A stripper ought to be used to being pawed by salivating women."

Tara aimed a chastising look at him and slipped an arm around my waist. Her head barely reached my shoulder. "Yeah. What's your damage, Kilt Boy?"

His palm still flat on the wall, Kilt Boy gaped at us.

"I'm getting a refund," Tara said. "I don't want a nutso stripper, even if he is wicked hot."

"Refund for what?" the Scot asked. He looked first at Tara, then at me, with utter confusion. "Did you call me—You women are cracked. Ahmno a stripper."

Chapter Two

Tara huffed. "Of course you're a stripper. We paid for you."

"Paid?" He moved away from the wall, straightening to his full height. "I donnae take my clothes off for money."

"Who else but a stripper would wear a kilt?"

His jaw tensed, a muscle ticked there. "A man from Scotland would."

I hobbled between my irate cousin and the offended stranger, holding up a hand to each of them. "Let's all calm down. This was obviously a huge misunderstanding, and that's my fault."

Tara pointed at my ankle. "He broke your leg."

"Don't be so melodramatic. I twisted my ankle, that's all."

The Scotsman glanced down at my ankle and grimaced. He rubbed the back of his neck, rolling his eyes up to look at me. "I'm sorry. Didnae mean to hurt you."

"She needs medical attention," Tara pronounced. "I'm calling nine-one-one."

"No," I said. "A twisted ankle is not an emergency. I need to sit down, that's all."

Tara eyed me warily. "You sure?"

"It was an accident, and I will be fine." I raised my hand palm out. "I swear it."

The doors to the club proper swung open and a man in a firefighter outfit sauntered down the hallway toward us. He held a boombox on one shoulder. Pouting like a male model, he nodded at me. "Hey babe, where's the bachelorette party?"

I hooked a thumb over my shoulder. "In there."

The real stripper pushed past me. I tried to sidle out of the way, but my ankle gave out and I staggered into the Scotsman. He caught me by my shoulders, steadying me against his firm body with both of his big, strong hands. With no conscious thought whatsoever, I turned my gaze up to his.

"Thanks," I whispered.

Whoops and catcalls erupted inside the party room once more. Music started up too, full of pounding bass and electric guitars.

My Scotsman leaned closer to be heard above the din. "You need to rest your ankle. Let me help you find a place to sit."

Tara lingered nearby, but her focus was on the festivities inside the room. She bit her lip, casting me a sideways glance.

I waved the Scot away. "Go on, I'll be fine. I appreciate your concern, but you must want to be out there. Don't let me disrupt your plans." To Tara, I said, "You go on too, get to your party. I'll be right there."

Tara squinted at my new friend, who kept his hands on my upper arms. "I can't leave you alone with a stranger."

"I'm not a stranger," the Scotsman said. He proffered a hand to me. "Aidan MacTaggart. There, now you know me."

I settled my hand in his warm, callused palm. A man who worked with his hands, perhaps? My mind flew to fantasies of his hands on my—Oh no, not going there. I coughed and said, "I'm Calli. Nice to meet you."

"Enchanted to meet you." He lifted my hand to kiss it. "But I feel responsible for your injury. Please let me take care of you."

Warmth shivered through me. "No need. I can get my own butt into a chair."

The corners of his mouth twitched as if he struggled to restrain a smile. "I'm sure you can, but a gentleman offers aid to a lady in distress."

"That's sweet, but—"

"I'll see you to a chair and leave you be." Aidan placed a hand on my back and spread the other arm wide, indicating the doorway to the party room. "After you."

Kicking off my shoes, I started to reach down for them, but he snatched them up and offered me his arm like a Victorian gentleman escorting a lady. I hooked my arm under his, curling my hand around his forearm, letting him guide me toward the doorway. My limping improved with each step.

At the threshold, I released his arm. "Thank you, but my ankle is feeling much better. You can go back out there and find a hot chick in a slinky dress to occupy your time."

His gaze traveled the length of me, down to my toes and back up to my face. "Donnae need to go anywhere to find that. You are exceptionally hot, and your dress is slinky enough to capture any man's interest."

My stomach fluttered, my skin tightened. Men had paid me compliments before but never had anyone described me in such a sensual way.

"Let me have a look at your ankle," he said, "to make sure I haven't wounded you grievously."

He spoke like no other man I'd met, his words intelligent and precise. Of course, he did occasionally spout a bizarre word unknown to the American lexicon.

"I'm fine, really," I said. Seeing the determined look on his face, and considering he seemed unwilling to budge until I entered the room, I shuffled across the threshold. "See? I can walk all by my itty-bitty self."

"You aren't itty-bitty." He appraised me from head to toe once more, paying special attention to my breasts and my lips before aiming those brilliant eyes at me. "You're a full-grown woman with soft, inviting curves in all the right places."

Wow. This guy knew how to entice a woman. I wanted to jump into his arms and crush my lips to that luscious mouth.

Instead, I told him, "Thank you for helping me. And I'm really sorry I thought you were a stripper."

He shrugged. "I suppose it's a compliment. My offer to buy you a drink after the party is still open, even if you want to sip apple juice."

"I'll probably be too tired later, but I appreciate the offer."

"Come find me if you change your mind." He took my hand and kissed it again. "Till we meet again, Calli."

Aidan strode down the hallway and out the swinging doors.

I joined the party, but my thoughts kept wandering back to the man in a kilt.

While the stripper gyrated his hips and the other bridesmaids cheered, I glanced at the clock for the dozenth time. Twenty minutes had elapsed since I left Aidan MacTaggart. Twenty minutes since he'd kissed my hand and bid me farewell like an old-school gentleman. Twenty minutes since I'd resisted, through a Herculean effort of willpower, throwing myself at him in the most literal way. Only a matter of seconds had passed, however, since the last time I wished I hadn't resisted the impulse.

This was crazy. I did not kiss men I'd just met. Maybe the wild vibe of this party had influenced me, or maybe years of not dating had affected me more than I realized. Since I couldn't get involved with anyone, maybe a little dalliance in a club was exactly what I needed.

Oh man. Somewhere between a game of Pin the Junk on the Hunk and running into a hot Scotsman, I'd gone totally insane. Still, it couldn't hurt to check if Aidan was still out there. Just to say good night.

I leaned toward Tara and said, "I need a drink. This water isn't doing it for me, think I need something stronger. Like Pepsi."

"Don't burp too much." She squinted her hazel eyes at me with knowing suspicion. "You're going out there to find your Scottish dreamboat, aren't you?"

"No." I wriggled in my seat, uncomfortable lying to her. "Maybe."

"Before you go, I need to ask you something." Tara scrunched up the corner of her mouth and bent toward me. A lock of her long blonde hair spilled over her shoulder. In a quieter voice only I could hear, she said, "Am I crazy for doing this? Divorced at twenty-two, walking down the aisle again at twenty-four?"

I clasped her hand, squeezing lightly. "First time didn't count. He wasn't the right one for you."

"You're right." She sat up and squared her shoulders. "Blake is the one for me. I know it."

"He's a great guy, Tara. And he makes you happy, which is all I want for you."

"Knowing you like him makes me feel better." She leaned back in her chair and waved a regally dismissive hand. "Go ahead, abandon me to get your groove on with Kilt Boy."

"Thank you, Tara." I kissed her cheek. "You are my favorite cousin."

"I'm your only cousin."

"Then obviously, you'd be my favorite."

She rolled her eyes. "Go find Kilt Boy. I want you to be happy, and that guy lit you up like nothing I've ever seen before."

Lit me up? I hadn't realized anyone else noticed my reaction to him. *Ugh.* That probably meant *he* had noticed it.

"You've been hiding in the woods too long," Tara said. "Time to get back out there."

"I've only lived in the woods for a year and a half."

"But you've been hiding for a lot longer and you won't tell me why."

She was right. I couldn't explain, though. Couldn't risk implicating her in my mistake.

I patted her arm and rose, wending my way through the throng of bridesmaids. They ignored me, their attention fixated on the stripper. The guy had gotten down to his G-string, which was stuffed with dollar bills that flapped every time he thrust his hips.

Once the door clicked shut behind me, and the pounding beat of the stripper music was muted, I suddenly found myself unable to move any farther. What was I doing? Chasing after a strange man. So what if he was hotter than the pavement on a summer's afternoon. So what if I had felt lit up inside when he smiled at me. So what if—

I gave myself a mental slap and a command to stop dillydallying. I didn't have to do anything other than talk to him and maybe dance with him.

Straightening, rolling my shoulders back, I marched through the double doors into the club. The lights pulsated all around me in sync with the throbbing beat of the music, a slow and steamy tune that inspired every couple to cling to each other as they shared glossy-eyed looks. I glanced around, not really expecting to find the Scot.

My gaze landed on Aidan MacTaggart.

He stood at the bar, an empty glass beside him, frowning at the scene around him. When his gaze intersected with mine, his mouth curved into the most brilliant smile I'd ever seen.

And I lit up again. *Damn.*

Warmth flowed through me, softening everything inside my body, as an electric tingle swept over my skin. I watched Aidan saunter toward me, his kilt shifting with every swing of his powerful hips. He approached like a Celtic god risen from the earth itself, imbued with the innate sensuality of a sex deity, his lips kinked in a closed-mouth smile that made me dissolve in the most wonderful ways.

He stopped so close to me I swore I could feel his body heat and slanted his head down toward mine. "This is a lovely surprise. Thought I wouldn't see you again."

"Here I am." Why was I here? Why was I gazing into his blue eyes, longing to drown in them?

"Aye," he said, and settled his hands on my upper arms, sliding them down to my elbows. "I'd love to spend more time with you."

"I'd like that too."

"What about a private booth?" He pointed down the short hallway that led to curtained booths. "I promise to take no liberties without your express consent. Will you come with me?"

Take no liberties? There he went again, talking like a man unaffected by trends, like a man who cared about treating a woman like a lady. Standing there, so close to his muscular body and those enormous biceps, I could do nothing except nod.

He took my hand and guided me down the hallway, toward a booth with its curtains open, revealing no one inside. He ushered me into the empty booth, pulling the curtains shut behind us. The lush, purple velvet billowed.

I stared at the semicircular table, at the plum-colored velvet of the curved sofa behind it and at the plum tabletop with a thick, flickering candle at its center. Wax gathered within the candle's concave top, forming a lava-like pool in its center and dribbling down the sides. On the ledge that backed the sofa, I noticed a small bowl, deep purple in color and filled with…I blinked. Filled with condom packets.

Aidan placed a hand on the small of my back. "Have a seat."

When I didn't move, he seemed to track my gaze to the bowl. Wincing, he said, "Didn't know about those. I swear, I didn't."

"I believe you." And I did, because I got the feeling he'd never been to this club before. "First time at Dance Ardor?"

"Yes. Have you been before?"

"No. Came for my cousin's bachelorette party."

Lowering onto the sofa, I shimmied sideways until I was behind the table with the bowl of rubbers behind me. At least then I didn't have to see them. To realize the true purpose of these booths.

Which didn't matter to me. I'd found Aidan so I could wish him farewell. Again.

He slid in beside me, draping an arm across the sofa's back behind my shoulders. The scent of him, a mix of sweat and spicy cologne and pure maleness, enveloped me. His body surrounded me. The purple shades of everything in this booth surrounded me too, somehow more decadent than the condoms in the bowl behind me.

Smoothing out my dress, I cleared my throat. "Sorry I shoved you into that room with all those ravening bridesmaids. They're actually nice ladies, but they've had a little too much champagne tonight."

"Have you been drinking?"

"No. Told you I don't drink."

"Thought maybe you were desperate enough to try it after being in a room with those bampots. Are you the one chosen to drive everyone home?"

"I'm not the designated driver," I said, squirming a little with him so near me. "We came in a van with a professional driver."

"Hope he's not in this club getting jaked." I must've looked confused, because he explained, "Getting drunk."

"No, *she* is waiting in the van watching TV on her phone."

"Ah." He glanced down at my feet. "How's the ankle?"

"Okay. Hurts a little when I walk, especially in these heels."

"May I have a look? I'm no doctor, but I've had my share of injuries."

I gnawed my lip, trying to think of a reason to say no when my body wanted me to say yes. Wanted to feel his hands on me. Wanted… "It's not necessary. Really."

"Humor me?" he said. "I won't bite. Unless you want me to."

His grin was devilish, and it did things to my body I couldn't explain. Marvelous, stimulating things. I leaned back against the plush cushioning and raised my foot. He clasped it in both hands, bringing my leg up and onto his lap with everything from the knee down in contact with him. Nothing but the kilt separated our skin. The warmth of him suffused me, transmitted through the plaid and from his hands on my naked flesh.

Aidan slipped my shoe off and set it on the table. Though the air chilled the bottom of my foot, the rest of me had grown hot. The roughness of his hands excited my skin more than the softest silk as he ran his hand over my sole and down to my toes. He rubbed the ball of my foot with leisurely strokes, his fingers roaming over my flesh, kneading in a hypnotic rhythm.

"It's my ankle," I said, fighting against the way my voice wanted to go breathless, "not my toes."

He smirked, and somehow, the expression made him even sexier. "Aye, but I thought to check your whole foot to be sure. All right?"

"Okay."

Keeping his hand on my sole, rubbing and rubbing, he placed his other palm on my heel and glided it up to my ankle, his strong fingers fondling my flesh. The combination of massage and exploration had my body tensing, my breath hitching, and a wetness flourishing between my thighs.

"Oh..." I lost my train of thought as those sure, masculine hands mapped out every contour of my ankle and foot.

His hands went still. "Is this uncomfortable?"

"No." Uncomfortable was not the right word for how I felt. Aroused, for sure. But uncomfortable? Far from it.

"I've been looking for a woman like you," he rumbled, his voice too soft and seductive for my sanity. "A woman with substance and heart and sensuality."

"You don't know me. Maybe I'm obsessed with my looks and never pick up a book, except to prop open my bedroom door for the long line of men waiting for their turn."

He chuckled, his fingers plying the sensitive flesh of my sole. "You aren't like that. I can tell."

"Exactly how can you identify my character traits after a few minutes in my presence?"

"The way you talk is one clue." His hand wandered from my sole to the top of my foot, smoothing his finger up my skin from my toes up my ankle and down again, while his other hand continued massaging my ankle in lazy strokes. "The way you carry yourself is another clue. You're a real woman, not a silly girl."

Maybe I should tell him I was a virgin, so he'd give up and go away. But then he'd stop touching me. I wasn't at all sure I wanted to give up this lovely feeling quite yet.

He let go of my foot, moving it off his lap, and edged closer until his bare knees brushed my bare knees. My foot had fallen back to the floor, the coolness of it sending a wonderful shiver through me. His kilt tickled my thigh. He braced one hand on the sofa behind my head, the other hand floating down to settle on my thigh. His face hovered inches from mine, his heated breaths whispered over my lips.

Aidan leaned in close, his breaths hot on my ear. "I want to kiss you."

I stopped blinking. Stopped breathing. Tried to avert my eyes, but my gaze remained fastened to his, captured by those crystalline eyes that regarded me with keen interest. He dragged his tongue across his lower lip, his eyes going hooded, as if he were imagining sampling my lips.

He slanted his head, eyes locked on my mouth.

I should've moved. Should've told him to stop. Should've…Thoughts disintegrated when he paused with his lips millimeters from mine, his breaths tickling my skin. His eyes rolled up to meet mine again, the naked hunger in them stealing my breath. This man wanted more than a kiss. If I let him do this, I wasn't at all sure I had the willpower to end it after one touch of his lips.

One of his palms cradled my nape. He tilted my head back a little, enough to raise my mouth to his and expose the tender flesh of my throat.

He pressed his lips to mine, softly, sweetly, brushing them back and forth.

My lips parted on a soft gasp. God, how I craved more.

Aidan withdrew a few inches. "May I kiss you?"

Hadn't he just been doing that? No, not quite. My body confirmed it, the way my lips burned for his and my sex grew wetter every second.

I whispered, "Yes."

That mouth—so hot and sensual, yielding yet demanding—claimed mine in a hard crush of lips against lips. I dissolved into him with a tiny, soft whimper. Damn, was that me making such a pathetic, needy noise? His hand clasped my nape a little firmer as his tongue flicked out to explore the seam of my lips. I grasped the lapels of his shirt, my fingers crooking into the fabric, and opened my mouth to him, all but pleading for him to devour me.

And he did.

In the instant his tongue thrust inside my mouth, his free arm came around my waist to bind me to his rock-hard body. I clung to his shirt, my breasts mounded against him, and surrendered to his swirling, seeking tongue as it urged mine to respond. I coiled my tongue around his, desperate for the flavor of him, for the feel of his slick flesh gliding over mine. His mouth was hot and soft and—*Oh God.* I moaned as he slid his hand down from my nape, along the bare skin of my back, following my spine to the edge of my dress.

I arched into him as we ravaged each other's mouths with more and more frantic lashes of our tongues. He tasted of liquor and man and sex.

Aidan groaned low in his throat.

My body thrummed with a strange need. My panties had grown damp, plastered to my groin, and my nipples tingled as if yearning for his mouth on them. I wanted him. Christ, I wanted him like I'd never wanted any man. Could I really do this? Lose my virginity in a private booth inside an underground club?

This isn't me, not me at all.

I scrambled off his lap, banged my hip on the table, floundered to get out of the booth. Tripping on my own heels, I grabbed for the purple curtain to stay my fall.

Aidan reached for me, clearly intending to help.

Steadying myself, I shrugged away from his outstretched hand. The last thing I needed was this man laying hands on me. If he did, I might—

"I'm sorry," I said, shaking my head, as confused by my behavior as he seemed to be, given his furrowed brow and open mouth. "I can't do this."

Without waiting for his response, I fled the booth.

Chapter Three

I slouched in a chair beside a wall of floor-to-ceiling windows inside the Gingko Room at the Morton Arboretum, gazing out at a glassy pond surrounded by greenery. The wedding had been a fairytale affair set on Thornhill Lawn beneath a clear blue sky, with Tara like a princess in her flowing gown and Blake the perfect groom in his elegant tux. I'd stood by my cousin, as both maid of honor and best friend. And yep, I cried through the whole thing.

My sentimentality had good reasons behind it. Though only twenty-four, Tara had been married once before. She'd said "I do" to her first husband in college, but he'd turned out to be a manipulative jerk who constantly berated my sweet little cousin for her looks and her brains. I'd wanted to run him over with my car. Luckily, I hadn't needed to resort to violence, because she'd dumped the cretin after fourteen months of marriage.

Now she had Blake. He seemed like a great guy. Kind, considerate, loving, protective without being overbearing. Everything a husband should be. I hoped she really had found the right guy this time.

Across the room, the newlyweds mingled with their guests. The band started to play a slow, romantic tune and Blake took Tara's hand to guide her out onto the dance floor. I watched them gliding across the shiny wood floor, smiling at each other with genuine happiness and love. I sent out a silent prayer that Tara had found her soul mate this time. She deserved a happy ending.

While they danced, the perfect fairytale couple, I sat alone in the corner brooding about last night.

The man in the kilt. Our searing kiss.

My cheeks heated at the memory of how wantonly I'd behaved with him.

My encounter with Aidan MacTaggart had knocked me off balance—he'd literally knocked me off my feet—which might explain my lapse in judgment. Make that my string of lapses that culminated in the most outrageous moment of my life. Making out with a strange man inside a velvet-draped booth next to a bowl of condoms.

Oh for heaven's sake, forget about him.

Yes, I had to put that crazy night behind me. Go home, somehow sort out my messed-up life, and move on.

I was staring out the windows again when Tara approached, amid a flurry of swishing satin, and plopped onto the chair beside me.

She pointed at the half-eaten meal on the plate in front of me. "What are you brooding about?"

"I'm not brooding." I fiddled with the waistband of my bridesmaid dress—a long, mint-green chiffon number that draped over one shoulder and featured a side slit that revealed a portion of my thigh. Tara had picked the dress, of course. She had good taste, in everything, and I trusted her judgment more than my own at the moment. I admitted, "I'm distracted. Confused."

Her lips puckered as she tried to quash her knowing smile. "You're thinking about him, aren't you?"

"Who?" My attempt at seeming clueless fell flat, and we both knew it.

Tara shook her head. "Kilt Boy. He made quite an impression on my cousin and you made quite an impression on him. When you came running back into the party, with your cheeks all pink and your lips looking just kissed, I knew you had it bad for the non-stripper."

I'd returned to the melee only to ask Tara if she minded me leaving, so I could go back to the hotel and rest up for the wedding.

"Last night," I said, "you thought Aidan might be a psycho."

"Gotta be careful with my maid of honor." She leaned in to pat my knee. "But I changed my mind about him. He's a sweetie."

I stiffened, the hairs on the back of my neck lifting. "Why does it sound like you've talked to him?"

"Because I have."

"When?" I clenched my fingers in my dress.

Tara shrugged one shoulder. "After you left the club, he came to see me. And boy, he was so polite, knocking on the door and waiting to be invited in. He was worried about you and, well, we got to talking."

My stomach churned as a sinking feeling had me gripping my chair. "What did you do?"

She gave me a look of overdone innocence.

"Come on, Tara," I said. "I've known you all your life and you can't fool me. You've done something I won't like. Tell me and get it over with."

"Well…" She smoothed the skirt of her gown, squaring her shoulders. "I invited Aidan to the reception."

My mouth dropped open but only sputtering came out. After a couple seconds, I managed to croak, "You did what?"

"I invited him. He's here." Tara surveyed the room with narrowed eyes until she found what she was looking for, then she smiled and waved at someone. "And he's coming over."

Speechless, I watched as Aidan MacTaggart separated from a group of wedding guests and strode toward us. Dressed in a dark-blue suit with a crisp, white shirt, he moved through the crowd with ease, his wavy hair glistening in the sunlight that also shimmered in his blue eyes. When he caught sight of me, he shot me the most brilliant smile, as if he'd stumbled onto the lost treasure of Atlantis.

I squirmed in my seat, straightened, and ran my hands over the skirt of my dress, suddenly wishing I had a mirror to check my makeup. Not that I cared what he thought of me. Not that it mattered what I looked like.

"You're beautiful," Tara said, "so relax and enjoy yourself."

With that, she rose and sashayed back to her husband.

Alone, with acid burning in my gut and a strange excitement zinging through me, I struggled to look like I didn't give a damn, picking up my fork to shift food around my plate.

The Scot halted beside the chair Tara had vacated. "May I sit with you?"

"Um…sure."

He lowered his big body onto the chair, settling one arm on the table. Our shoes almost touched, and our knees were uncomfortably close, but he seemed not to notice. I crossed my right leg over the left.

Aidan's gaze snapped to my right thigh. His tongue darted out to moisten his lower lip.

I glanced down—and froze. The slit in my dress exposed nearly all of my leg. I dropped my right foot back to the floor, yanking the dress to cover my leg, and crossed my left leg over the right. No slit on the left side. Had my subconscious driven me to flash Aidan an outrageous amount of skin? No, of course not. It was an accident.

His gaze met mine, those eyes simmering with interest.

My body responded, softening like butter in the sun, and my thoughts went fuzzy.

Nuts. Maybe my subconscious had done it after all.

"Calli Douglas," Aidan said, his brogue rolling the words into a sensual phrase. "I was hoping to get you alone again."

I folded my hands on my lap. "We're not alone. We're in the middle of a packed wedding reception."

"Everyone else is over there." He waved a hand toward the other side of the room where the rest of the party loitered. "And we are over here."

How on earth did he make that phrase sound dirty? Maybe it was my fevered brain, still on fire from last night, that kept molding his every word into a come-on.

My mind finally realized what he'd said a moment ago. "How do you know my last name?"

"Your cousin told me."

Tara. My cousin had a nasty habit of meddling in my personal life, a hobby she shared with my older brother, Gavin. They both did it out of love and a desire to improve my life, but it still annoyed me.

I pointed at Aidan's slacks. "No kilt?"

"Don't wear one every day."

"Only at nightclubs?"

"Ah…" He scratched the back of his neck, grimaced, and mumbled, "Bloody Lachlan."

"Is that some kind of Scottish cocktail?"

"No." He sighed. "My brother, Lachlan. He told me every Friday is kilt night at the club. Now I'm thinking he said that so he could get his revenge on me."

"Revenge?" I asked, slanting forward in spite of myself. "What did you do to him?"

Aidan cleared his throat, shifting in his seat, but soon a smirk tightened his lips. "At Lachlan's wedding last fall, I tried to trick his bride into repeating a Gaelic phrase. She's American and didn't know the language."

Oh, I could guess where this was going. "What did you get her to say?"

"An toir thu dhomh pòg." His smirk widened into a grin. "It means will you give me a kiss. Lachlan, the uptight man he is, warned her before she said it. Erica's a bonnie lass and I really don't see how he can blame me for trying."

I sighed, shaking my head. "You are a wicked one, aren't you?"

"Noticed, have you?"

Leaning back in my chair, I tilted my head to study him with a touch of suspicion. "What exactly are you hoping to accomplish here?"

"Have a good time. Drink mediocre whiskey." He gazed into my eyes, his face the picture of sincerity. "Dance with a beautiful woman."

Dance with Aidan? My skin tingled at the memory of his touch last night, how the simple brush of his fingers could inflame me and the way his tongue in my mouth had driven me to the brink of madness. Coughing, I gestured toward the throng of people, many of them female. "Plenty of pretty girls to choose from."

"Only interested in one." He stroked the tabletop with his fingertips. "Dance with me, Calli. Please."

"I think you've gotten the wrong impression of me."

His smile was sweet. "You're a bonnie, sexy lass who's well-spoken and charming. Am I mistaken?"

"Well-spoken?"

He sat forward, hands linked between his knees, expression earnest. "I heard your speech at dinner this evening. You're eloquent, entertaining, and clearly love your cousin very much."

"Oh." He'd listened to my speech, the one Tara begged me to make. I'd assumed no one actually paid attention to wedding speeches. Yet Aidan listened. Really listened. "I still think you might have the wrong idea about me. Despite my behavior last night, I'm not the kind of girl who makes out with strangers in nightclubs."

"I never thought that." He glanced down at the floor, then looked up at me with a sheepish expression. "I don't normally take so many liberties with a woman."

I stared at him. "You don't?"

"No."

Right then, music began to emanate from his pants. Sounded like bag-pipes. I pointed at his slacks and said, "I hope that's your phone."

"It is."

Mouth crimped, growling a sigh, he extricated the phone from his pock-et, upside down, and tried to flip it over. He lost his hold on it, and the phone flew through the air, plopping down smack on my lap.

Without thinking, I picked it up. A text message from someone named Jamie filled the screen. It read, "Have you found your quarry, Don Juan? Expect details about American fling."

I tossed the phone at Aidan.

He caught it in both hands and glanced at the screen. Grimacing, he let out a long groan.

Planting both feet on the floor, I tugged my dress to ensure it covered all of me. "So, Don Juan, am I right in assuming I'm your quarry? The hapless American you tried to lure into a fling?"

"It's not like that." He sank back in his chair, shoving the phone in his pocket. "My brothers and sisters have a strange sense of humor. They call me Don Juan because I like women, but I don't use them and I'm not out shagging a different woman every night."

The way he pronounced everything, with that silken brogue reshaping the vowels, it affected me in strange and enticing ways. I flashed back to last night in the booth, immersed in a full-on sense memory of our kiss. I needed a couple seconds to reassemble my scattered thoughts. "Shagging? What a funny word for sex."

His eyes took on a teasing glint. "I could've said fucking. Would that be more acceptable?"

"Normal people call it having sex."

He smiled, chuckling softly. "I've never been accused of being normal. But why does the word fuck fash you?"

"Why does it what me?"

"Fash." His lips tightened, and he sighed. "Sorry. Fash means bother. Why does 'fuck' upset you?"

"I—The word doesn't offend me, but could you please stop saying it?"

"Dance with me and I will." He offered me his hand, palm up. "Otherwise, I'll have to remind you about our time in the club."

"Blackmail, hm?"

"Anything to get you in my arms again." He rose, still offering his hand. "Please, Calli. One dance. I promise to behave. Mostly."

I considered his hand, callused and rough as if he worked outdoors, an assessment supported by his tanned skin. I wanted to ask what he did for a living, but the answer hardly mattered since I would never see him again after the reception. I'd fly home to Michigan, he'd fly home to Scotland or wherever he'd come from, and that would be the end of our acquaintance. Why not take my cousin's advice and enjoy myself?

"One dance," I said, slipping my hand into his. He closed his fingers around my hand, the warmth of him suffusing my flesh, spreading through every cell of my body and melting me down to my core.

"Aye, one dance," Aidan said, leading me toward the dance floor. He flashed me a mischievous smile over his shoulder. "But I will make the most of the single dance I have with you."

Hand in hand, we weaved through the couples twirling across the floor in time with a sedate instrumental played by a small string ensemble. I bumped into Tara, shoulder to shoulder, as she danced with her new husband. Blake and Tara both grinned at me and Aidan, and my cousin winked at me. Giving her a fake scowl, I let Aidan propel me onward until we found a spot. He raised our joined hands, snaked his other arm around my side to spread his palm over the small of my back, and tugged me close. My heels boosted me up a few inches, but he still towered over me. The fragrance of his cologne enveloped me.

As he began to sway his hips and shuffle his feet, a tingle swept over my skin and settled between my thighs. Though not unseemly, his movements did things to me I couldn't explain. My breasts brushed against his chest. His palm on my back and our linked hands anchored me to him, while his hips compelled mine to move, matching his rhythm. The rest of the room seemed to fade away, leaving only the soft strains of the music and the feel of this man cradling me in his brawny arms.

He bent his head to whisper in my ear. "Couldnae stop thinking about ye. All night, all morning, every second till I found ye here."

Spinning us around the floor, deftly maneuvering between other couples, he kept his mouth near my ear. The room whirled around us, blurring into an abstract painting, my focus telescoping down to our bodies united in swirling, exhilarating motion.

"Did you think about me?" he purred into my ear.

"Yes." Why the hell I said it, I had no clue. My mind had shut down, rationality a long-forgotten concept.

"Good." He pulled me into him, our bodies pressed together, my breasts mashed into his torso. "I went too far last night. I'm sorry."

"I gave you permission to kiss me. Which makes it my fault, not yours."

"You're not angry?"

"No." Lustful. Confused. Intrigued by this odd and sweetly enticing man. But not angry.

"The party's almost over," he said. "Spend the evening with me."

"What?" I drew my head back to meet his crystalline blue eyes. "I don't know you."

"Get to know me, then." His hand on my back skated upward, then back down, his fingers teasing the upper curve of my buttocks through my dress. "I want to know you. Give me the rest of tonight, please."

"I'm flying home to Michigan in the morning. Have to pack and get some sleep."

"Can't you stay an extra day?"

"Why are you so determined? We're essentially strangers."

"Been told I'm impulsive and you are the most captivating woman I've ever met." He lifted our hands to his lips, feathering a kiss across my knuckles. "When I see what I want, I donnae give up easily."

Captivating? Sounded like a line to me, the kind a player would lay on a gullible girl to get her in the sack. But something about his manner made me wonder if he might be genuine.

Doesn't matter. You're leaving the state, remember?

Movement caught my attention, and I glanced over to see Tara waving at me. She mouthed, "It's time."

I disentangled my hand from Aidan's. "The bride and groom are heading out. I have to see them off, so please excuse me. It was nice meeting you."

His mouth opened and then shut again as he tracked my journey across the dance floor away from him. I sensed his gaze on me, somehow knew he was watching, and with a great effort prevented myself from stealing one last glimpse of him.

Chapter Four

I stood beneath a tree, its branches a canopy over my head, gazing out across a glassy pond. Tara and Blake had climbed into a taxi, headed to the airport for their honeymoon trip to Hawaii. I'd stayed at the arboretum to take in the view one last time before I went back to my empty hotel room and, tomorrow, my home in Michigan. Sleep seemed unlikely tonight, since my thoughts kept circling back to a certain Scotsman who made my mouth water whether he wore a kilt or a suit.

Laying a hand on the tree trunk, I shut my eyes and relived the entirety of my acquaintance with Aidan MacTaggart. A case of mistaken identity. His hands on me. One outrageously hot kiss. And to cap it off, a dance and a plea to spend the evening with him.

"There you are."

With a yelp and a jump, I whirled on the speaker.

Aidan smiled. "Did I scare you? Sorry. I've been looking everywhere for you and finally spotted a red-haired woman in a green dress out here, looking melancholy."

Despite the ten feet or so between us, I swore I could feel the heat of his skin on mine. A sense memory from last night, I supposed. I could shake it off if he weren't here. Watching me. Looking so good.

He strode closer, narrowing the distance to an arm's length. "I was hoping for a real goodbye."

"I said goodbye."

"No," he said, "you excused yourself and told me it was nice meeting me."

Rats. He was right. But I hardly owed a virtual stranger a formal goodbye, whatever that might entail. I offered him my hand. "It was nice meeting you. Goodbye, Aidan."

He slid his hand into mine, his long fingers grazing the underside of my wrist, sending a warm current up my nerves. "I'd like to kiss you goodbye."

My pulse accelerated at the suggestion, at the vivid fantasy it inspired. "On the cheek."

"On the lips." He drew me closer until he held our joined hands to his chest. "Please. One last taste of you before you go."

I shouldn't consent to this. It was crazy. But the naughty little voice in my head whispered to me. *What harm can come from another kiss?*

Well, it wasn't like we could have sex right here in a public place. Stragglers from the reception loitered inside the Gingko Room, perhaps thirty feet away, with nothing but floor-to-ceiling glass between us and them. And yet, I wanted the kiss. Despite the people who might see. Despite the fact that I'd never done anything like this, kissing a stranger—not once, but twice. If I said yes this time. I ought to say no.

What harm can come from it?

Anticipation chased over my skin like a delicate caress. "Okay."

He moved forward, easing me backward until the tree shielded us from the windows of the Gingko Room. My palms were clammy, my breaths short and fast. He backed me up to the tree, his body inches from mine, his hand clasping mine to his chest. His other hand cupped my cheek, his thumb rubbing across my lips. I parted them without thinking and the tip of his thumb dipped inside for a split second, just enough for the flavor of his skin to tease my senses. My eyes drifted half shut as I exhaled a long breath. My shoulders sagged, my body went limp against the tree.

Aidan swept his hand up my cheek into my hair, cradling my nape. I couldn't tear my gaze away from his, away from those sapphire eyes and the fire raging within them. Beneath my hand, his heartbeat thumped hard and fast.

"Thank you," he said in a low, rough voice.

"For what?"

"This."

His mouth brushed across mine, exciting my skin, triggering every hair on my body to shiver erect. He took my upper lip between both of his, pulling it into his mouth, licking at it with swift, light strokes. As he released my lip little by little, he shifted his hand on my nape to angle my head back. Eyes closed, I burned for more, for the passion we'd shared last night—but he only nipped at my bottom lip and swept his tongue over the seam of my lips. Without realizing what I was doing, I rocked my hips forward. My body nudged his erection, hard and big inside his slacks.

Aidan groaned, long and low, the feral sound resonating in his chest.

I thrust my free hand into his hair, clawing at his scalp, desperate to drag him in for a real kiss.

He seized both of my hands, pinning them to the tree above my head. His body pressed into mine, firm enough to hold me in place but not so forcefully that I felt endangered. No, threatened was not how he made me feel. Not in the least.

For a heart-stopping moment, he stared into my eyes with a naked hunger that left me breathless. Then, just when I feared he'd changed his mind, he adjusted his hold on my hands to take both my wrists in one of his hands and skimmed his other palm down my bare arm and across my exposed shoulder to my collarbone. He danced his fingertips up my throat to my chin. With light pressure from his thumb, he urged me to open my mouth wider.

And I surrendered to him.

His hand fell to my hip, curling around it. His mouth covered mine in an open-mouth kiss, his tongue diving deep to ravish me with possessive strokes. My clitoris throbbed, and I writhed against him, rubbing my breasts over his chest, rolling my hips into his rigid cock. His erection scraped over my belly as he groaned into my mouth. The vibration of it shot lust through me and I ached to wrap my arms around him, to grind myself into his hard shaft, but he kept me bound to the tree with his body. A frustrated noise burst out of me. His kiss grew wilder, scorching hot, his tongue tangling with mine and our lips mashed together. A need pulsated through my sex, squeezing a whimper out of me.

Aidan peeled his mouth from mine. Breathing hard, eyes glossy, he let his head fall forward until our foreheads touched. "Let me see you again. Please."

"I live in another state."

"And I live in another country." He freed my hands, stepped back a half step, and held my face in his palms. "May I visit you sometime?"

"I guess so." The words tumbled out before I regained the ability to think clearly. Too late to take them back, but anyway, he had no idea where I lived. Besides, I wanted to see him again.

He bent to press a tender kiss to my lips. "Meant to give you a simple kiss, but I lose my mind when I touch you."

"I liked it. Both times."

Aidan reached into his pants pocket, withdrawing his cell phone. "May I have your number?"

I bit my lip as I considered my answer. Since I had only a cell phone, not a landline, he couldn't really track me down that way. Could he? And that stupid, naughty part of me wanted to hear from him. To hear his voice. Deep and sexy, telling me I was bonnie and well-spoken and captivating.

"Sure," I said, gesturing for him to give me his phone. When he did, I found the address book and typed in my number and name, then I handed the phone back to him. "There you go."

His smile melted me again—but my heart this time, not my body. He looked so adorably thrilled to have my number.

Before I could do anything else dumb and reckless, I pushed away from the tree, smoothed out my dress, and said, "Well, it's time for me to head out. Goodbye, Aidan."

He lifted my hand to his mouth and brushed his lips over my knuckles. "Till we meet again, Calli Douglas."

God, I loved the way he said my name. I muttered something unintelligible and tried to walk purposefully away from him, but I stumbled over a tree root and wound up half staggering back toward the building. Times like this, I really wished I was a drinker. At least it would give me an excuse for my behavior. My only viable excuse was that five years of self-imposed exile, five years of staying true to a false vow, had made me ripe for a freak-out. I could never have predicted what would come of doing a seemingly innocent favor for someone I'd considered a friend.

If I could've talked about it publicly—or told anyone about it, even in private—maybe I wouldn't feel quite so trapped. But I couldn't tell anyone. Not Tara. Not my brother, Gavin. Definitely not the sexy Scot who tempted me to do things I'd never imagined I was capable of doing. If he knew my secret, maybe he'd lose interest. He seemed like a decent guy. Only a total sleaze would want to be with a married woman.

Especially one guilty of marriage fraud.

Chapter Five

The next morning, as I finished packing and headed out for my flight home, I wondered what on earth had possessed me. Why had I given Aidan an invitation to call me? And worse, why had I offered to let him visit me at home? If he called, I didn't have to talk to him. Right, and I didn't have to kiss him either. Aidan MacTaggart affected me in ways I couldn't explain, couldn't control, and wasn't sure I wanted to stop. It felt too damn good.

As I dragged my wheeled suitcase toward the door of my hotel room, someone knocked.

I froze, staring at the door. Visions raced through my mind of the door bursting inward and cops flooding in with guns drawn. They'd throw me down on the floor, handcuff me, read me my rights. *You're under arrest for marriage fraud*, an authoritative voice would declare. I'd be hauled through the hotel. Shoved into a police car. Whisked away to jail and, eventually, prison.

Maximum sentence: five years. Maximum fine: $250,000.

I swallowed back the bile burning up my throat, surging into my mouth. *You're being paranoid*, I reminded myself. But I couldn't shake the cold sliver of dread wending its way through me.

A fist rapped on the door again.

Shaking my head at my own silliness, I grasped the knob and swung the door open.

My husband smiled at me. In his Croatian accent, lightened by many years in America, he said, "You requested my presence. Here I am, Calli."

Sure, I'd called him yesterday—but not to invite him to my hotel room.

I looked straight into his dark-brown eyes. "How did you find me?"

"Caller ID told me you were calling from this hotel." He leaned one shoulder against the doorjamb, and the light from within the room painted a sheen on his short black hair. "The man at the desk was kind enough to tell me in which room my wife was staying."

Rade Vukoja was my husband, technically. He could produce the marriage certificate if he wanted, since he'd kept possession of it. Most likely, the desk clerk had simply believed him, and besides, most people were trusting and Rade was charming. For two years before we'd married, we'd been good friends. The hardest part of all this mess was that I still liked him, though not in any romantic way.

"I asked you to call me, Rade, not show up at my door." I kept my hand on the handle of my suitcase, ready to go as soon as he left. "I have to get to the airport."

"You wanted to serve the divorce papers." He patted his chest. "Here I am."

I hissed out a sigh. "Honestly, you know I can't serve the papers myself. The law says someone unconnected to the case has to do it. That's why I sent a process server, over and over and over again. You dodged him every time."

"Yes, I do apologize for that. I have been very busy."

I glanced back at the bedside clock, seeing I had to leave in less than five minutes. "Listen, you know I have money problems and it costs me at least a hundred dollars every time the server tries to track you down. He's made six attempts in the last ninety days. Now I'll have to file for a second summons, which means more money spent on trying to serve you."

"There's a simple solution." He smiled that congenial smile, the one that made me feel like a jerk even when I was in the right. "Come live with me. I will pay your debts as I did before and help you find work."

"We've been through this how many times? You promised to give me a divorce six months after you got citizenship, and that happened over a year ago."

His steady gaze locked onto mine. "I know we entered into a marriage strictly to evade immigration laws, but I'd hoped we could find common ground and forget the divorce."

"I don't love you. Why would you want to stay married to me?" I swung the door wide, intending to squeeze past him. "Let it go, Rade. Please."

We both knew I meant more than letting me out the door. He needed to let me go, let me move on with my life.

Though he stepped aside, he laid a hand on my arm. "Please, Calli, let's talk over this divorce matter."

"We had an agreement. I honored my end. Time to honor yours."

"I don't want this divorce." He released my arm but gazed at me with a strange longing. "Please."

For a moment, I wondered if he was trying to tell me he'd developed romantic feelings for me. For five years, we'd lived apart. Before that, he'd never given the slightest hint he might feel more than friendship. He couldn't have developed a deeper attachment to me.

"You knew this was how it would end," I said as I dragged my suitcase across the threshold and shut the door. "I did you a favor and the least you could do is honor your promise. Next time I send a server, be there to accept the papers. If you really care for me at all, you'll do the right thing."

I hurried down the hall, my suitcase's wheels rumbling across the floor, and got into the elevator before Rade had time to catch up to me. As the elevator made its way to the first floor, I sagged against the wall. I'd had to go for a do-it-yourself divorce since I couldn't afford a lawyer. Yet even when Rade finally accepted the divorce papers, I had a long road ahead to free myself of my worst mistake. Marrying a guy so he could stay in the country? That was marriage fraud. Marrying a guy I didn't love? That was hell on earth.

Sometimes I wished Rade was a creep I could hate. That might make this easier to take. But he'd always been respectful and even kind to me. Never tried to claim his husbandly rights, so to speak. He knew I didn't have those kinds of feelings for him.

Why, then, was he holding on so tightly to our phony marriage?

The elevator doors rolled open.

I wheeled my suitcase out, heading for the desk to check out, but I hesitated when the door to the stairs burst open.

Rade jogged out and made a beeline for me.

I hung my head, muttering a few choice words under my breath.

He stopped a few feet away, panting from exertion. "If you send another server, I will take delivery of the papers. However, this does not mean I accept losing you. I plan to fight for us, Calli, because I know we can be a genuine couple."

I glanced up at the ceiling, seeking divine intervention or a modicum of patience. The roof probably blocked me from reaching the heavens with my plea. "Why would you want a wife who doesn't love you? I'm not attracted to you either."

"Please." His tone of voice matched his pleading expression.

"We both know you can slow down the divorce if you want to," I said, "but you can't stop it. Eventually, it will go through. Make it easier on both of us and give up the idea of staying married. I don't want to be with a man I don't love. I've known you for seven years, Rade, and I still don't feel that way about you."

His entire body seemed to sag. His face went slack as he turned his gaze down to the floor.

"That's just the way it is," I said. "I'm sorry it's not what you want to hear."

I walked away, suitcase in tow, once again feeling like a jerk for no good reason.

My husband didn't follow me.

Chapter Six

My flight landed at the Houghton County Memorial Airport at a little after one p.m., and I picked up my car to drive home—er, back to the place where I was living. Not home, not exactly. Somebody else owned the place. I paid rent. If the owners knew about my criminal behavior, they might not have rented to me.

Shadows and light alternately slashed across my car as I navigated down the seasonal, two-track road toward the one-story log house nestled in the middle of nowhere. Another car sat parked in the driveway, next to where I always parked. Through the window beside the front door, I glimpsed a white shape springing up and down, and doggy ears flapping. When I clambered out of the car, barking greeted me.

The front door flew open. A figure rushed out, and my house sitter slammed the door behind her.

"Never again," Judith Landau declared, hurrying past me with a frazzled expression, her blonde hair flying wild around her head as she shook it. "I am never babysitting for you again. Your babies are demons."

"They're not that bad."

She flung her hands up to the heavens as if praying for patience. "They leaped on the bed at five o'clock and started licking my face while jumping around like insane rabbits."

I had warned her about my rambunctious puppies, but she'd sworn she loved dogs. "Thanks for taking care of them for me. I'm sorry they were such a handful."

She smiled ruefully. "They can be really cute when they're not pooping everywhere."

"They were stressed about me being gone. I've never left them before. I'm so sorry."

"It's not your fault, Calli."

"Still feel bad about it. They know you and I thought they'd be okay."

"Relax. I'm not mad, just frazzled." Judith gave me a quick hug. "Welcome home. How was the wedding?"

"Beautiful. Romantic. I met a lot of new people." A vision of Aidan flared in my mind, but I tamped it down as best I could. Yeah, that worked.

"Glad you had fun." Judith started toward her car. "Gotta get home. Talk to you later, okay?"

"Sure."

I watched her get into her car and waved as she drove off down the road. Judith and I had worked together at a gift shop until three months ago when the owner had let us both go due to financial reasons. Judith had found another job, but I hadn't. The difference between us was that she'd lived in this area her whole life, while I was a newcomer who'd moved here a year and a half ago. My first job—as a librarian at a public library, the job I'd moved here for—had evaporated for similar reasons as this one. Despite having a master's degree, I couldn't get a job that paid more than minimum wage.

Now I couldn't get a job, period. When my savings ran out in a month or two, I'd probably have to move in with my brother in Minneapolis. He'd invited me to stay with him when he learned I'd lost another job.

The barking inside the house grew more frantic. Through the living room window, I spotted a second, smaller body leaping up to peer out at me while the larger body kept boinging up and down as if mounted on springs.

I trudged into the house, hauling my wheeled suitcase behind me. I'd barely shut the door and let go of the suitcase's handle when two furry bodies launched themselves at me. Mandy and Misty, my all-American mutts, struggled to get high enough to lick me, but their paws reached only to my belly. At six months old, they possessed a level of energy I often envied. I scratched Misty behind her floppy ears and patted the smaller Mandy on top of her head. They whined and whimpered, too excited to hold still, their tails wagging furiously.

Misty resumed leaping side to side through the air, almost flying in her glee. Little Mandy ran circles around me, her tail wagging so hard it shimmied her whole back end. The two of them resembled a cross between a beagle and a Labrador, their pale golden coats splotched with brown.

I managed to shamble down the hallway to my bedroom despite the puppies scooting around my feet. As I passed the open door to the guest room, where Judith had stayed, I wondered if the poor woman would ever set foot in this house again after spending three days in the company of my wild-and-crazy puppies. I didn't bother unpacking my suitcase but simply stripped naked and crawled under the covers, desperate for a nap after a sleepless night at the hotel.

The moment my head hit the pillow, my phone rang. Grumbling, I flailed a hand out to grab the phone. "Hello?"

"You sound sleepy. Did I wake you?"

Words deserted me at the soft rumble of Aidan's voice.

"Are you there?" he asked.

"Yes." Here, yes. Able to converse, no.

He cleared his throat. "Is it too soon to ring you?"

"No, I guess not." I pushed up, braced on one elbow, and rubbed my eyes. It was afternoon, not early morning, and I should've been more conscious. "You don't waste any time, do you?"

Aidan sighed and chuckled. "Impulsive, remember?"

Impulsive and determined. Having a man so intent on spending time with me was flattering, but these days a woman had to be careful. Particularly a woman with a husband intent on mucking up the divorce. Which begged the question of why I'd given Aidan my number. *Not a clue.*

Lying to myself wouldn't help anything. I'd given him a way to get in touch, encouraged him to do so, because I liked him. I wanted to see him or at least talk to him.

"What are you doing?" he asked, sounding casually interested.

"Not sleeping." It came out a little bitchy, so I added, "Sorry. I get grumpy when I'm tired. Exhausted from the trip."

"Tell me one thing before we say goodbye."

"What do you want to know?"

"Are you with anyone? A husband, a boyfriend, a lover?"

I pondered how to answer without exposing my secret. "I'm not interested in starting anything."

"Hmm." He paused, then said, "You seemed interested at the club and again after the wedding."

My thoughts wound back to the moment in the velvet-encased booth when I'd been dangerously close to compromising myself. Did Aidan think I was an easy score?

"I'm not having sex with you," I said.

"Sex? Didnae mention that. I meant seeing each other as in dating." His voice dropped to a husky whisper. "But if you'd rather skip straight to the good part..."

"No. I wouldn't rather." I slapped a hand on my forehead, praying for some of my usual composure. The universe ignored my pleas. "I have to go. To sleep. Not with you, just to—Oh forget it. I'm exhausted and I have no idea what I'm saying."

"I'm sorry for disturbing you, but I'd love to see you again. I'm tired of the city, hired a car for a drive…anywhere." He cleared his throat and said, in a hesitant tone, "May I come to see you?"

Visit me? A warm little shiver rushed through me and I couldn't stop the words from tumbling out. "Well, we could meet in a public place. When will you get here?"

"I could be there tomorrow. Mid-morning."

"Okay. Meet me at the beach." I gave him directions to my favorite beach, punctuating my words with a yawn.

"Better let you go," he said. "Get some rest."

"See you tomorrow."

I shouldn't have invited him. I shouldn't have acted like I was free to hang out with a man who wanted to pursue me. Maybe if I told him about my husband, Aidan would flee back to Scotland on the first flight out. Why hadn't I told him already? Telling Aidan might make him some kind of accessory. I didn't know for sure and I couldn't take the risk—the same reason I hadn't told my brother or Tara. Yet here I was, courting disaster with a stranger.

Mandy and Misty leaped onto the bed as if they sensed I needed comforting. As they licked my face, tails wagging, I gave up trying to sort out why I was drawn to Aidan. He'd made me feel like a human being again after so long in solitude, but more than that, he made me feel alive again.

The puppies settled down on either side of me and we all fell asleep. What they dreamed of, I had no idea. But I dreamed of a man in a kilt whose smile melted the shell I'd constructed around myself.

I could enjoy his company, then send him on his way. One day of pretending. Nothing more. One day with Aidan MacTaggart.

Then goodbye.

I stood before the full-length mirror affixed to the back of the bedroom door, considering my outfit—the tenth one I'd tried this morning. Aidan had texted me two hours ago to report he would arrive by eleven o'clock. Since it was a quarter past ten, I had only fifteen more minutes to decide on my wardrobe before heading to the beach.

Mandy and Misty sat nearby watching me with intense interest.

Spinning in a circle, I asked them, "What do you think? Appropriate for a date—a meeting with a stranger I met in a nightclub?"

Misty chuffed. I took that as agreement.

I kept assuring myself I didn't care what Aidan thought of my outfit or if he liked my looks. Why, then, had I spent the better part of an hour scouring my closet for the right outfit?

I faced the mirror, studying my ensemble. Tan shorts that stopped a third of the way down my thighs. A tank top in bright pink, with sparkly red flowers over my chest. A loose, partially transparent shirt with short sleeves. Tennies and white ankle socks completed my outfit.

My gaze dropped to the neckline of my tank top. It dipped rather low, but not so low I'd feel like a slut. Just enough to hint at my cleavage.

Not that I cared if Aidan noticed my cleavage. My clothes were comfortable and appropriate for a warm, late-spring day. His approval meant zilch to me.

I winced. This was probably what they called protesting too much.

The two canines seated to my right thumped their tails.

I glanced at Mandy and Misty. "How do I look, girls?"

Misty panted and thumped her tail some more. Mandy eyed me with her head canted.

"Don't look at me like that," I said, wagging a finger at her. "I'm going to a public place, which means I have to look respectable. But I can still wear something attractive."

Like the bikini I'd put on under my clothes, in lieu of lingerie, just in case I wanted to go for a swim. With Aidan. I imagined him in swim trunks, rising out of the lake, water sluicing down his chiseled chest.

"Tell me, puppy babies," I said. "Have I turned into a raging slut? I mean, I practically begged a total stranger to visit me. Not to mention the way I made out with him twice. Sheesh, this could be a huge mistake." I glanced at the dogs. "What do you think?"

Misty sneezed. Mandy swished her tail, swaying her whole back end.

Oh jeez. I was discussing my love life with puppies. Maybe I had spent too much time sequestered in the woods.

I stopped, reflecting on my own thoughts. Love life? No, this had nothing to do with love or even dating. Pure lust. An indulgence that would go no further than flirtation. And maybe some kissing. Possibly a swim.

Groaning, rolling my eyes at my reflection in the mirror, I snagged my purse from the dresser and hurried down the hallway with the puppies nipping at my heels—literally. Well, Mandy nipped at the heels of my tennies. Misty preferred to jam her nose into the backs of my knees.

I shooed her away, and she hopped up, all four feet in the air.

My phone rang. I dug it out of my purse, answering with a hiccupping hello as Mandy shoved her snout into my butt.

"Calli, how are you this morning?"

Sighing, I laid a palm on my forehead. "Rade, why are you calling me?"

"To check on my wife. I worry about you, all alone there in the forest." He paused for a second, then added, "And to ask when your server might come by."

I'd called the process server this morning, so at least I had an answer for him. "Tomorrow. At your house, around two o'clock."

"I will make sure I'm at home." He paused again, his breathing audible. "Though I would still prefer to forget the divorce."

"What's going on with you?" I asked. "You promised after you got your citizenship, we'd wait six months and then get divorced. You swore you'd initiate the proceedings, but you never did. I'm paying for all of this and you damn well better accept the papers this time."

"I will. You have my word."

"Keep your word this time. You got what you wanted, now give me what you owe me."

Except I owed him far more than I could ever repay and we both knew it. Tens of thousands of dollars, in fact.

"I don't have everything I wanted," he said, sighing wistfully. "I don't have you."

"You never did have me."

"Give me a chance to show you we can have a good marriage."

I shoved a hand into my hair, scraping my nails on my scalp. "It's time to move on with your life, Rade."

When I punched the button to disconnect the call, the clock appeared on the phone's screen. Unless I left right this minute, I'd be late for my meeting with Aidan at the beach. A picnic with a stranger. With another man from a foreign country. Aidan seemed to have a lot in common with my husband. Sweet, attentive, empathetic. Today, I would tell him the truth—the parts I could tell him, without possibly involving him in my crime—and he would lose interest. He had to.

Yes, that was a good plan. Scare him away with the truth.

I dashed to the kitchen to retrieve the plastic cooler I'd packed with supplies for a picnic lunch. Then I patted the puppies on their heads and hurried out the door.

"Sorry, puppy babies," I told the mutts as I shut the door. "You have to stay home. This is grown-up time."

Chapter Seven

Wispy white clouds slid across the blue sky as gentle waves lapped at the golden sand on the beach, the water shimmering a pale aqua blue. The four-foot cliff behind us jutted out at our right, sequestering us from the beachgoers frolicking on the long, straight stretch beyond. Sitting cross-legged on a beach towel, I tried to concentrate on the gorgeous view of Lake Superior, but my focus kept drifting back to the gorgeous Scotsman reclining on the beach towel adjacent to mine.

Aidan rested on his side, propped up on one elbow. His tight jeans and T-shirt showed off his muscular physique while leaving enough to the imagination that any hapless females passing by—and okay, me—couldn't resist gawking.

"You like me," he said in a casual tone, as if it were an obvious truth. His chestnut hair glistened in the sunshine and a delicate breeze ruffled the locks.

I had the overwhelming urge to thrust my fingers into that hair, to find out if it was as silky and soft as I imagined. Maybe the truth was obvious, but I couldn't help saying, "You have no idea what I think about you. And vice versa."

He gazed at me, his bright eyes locked on mine, his lips quirked with secret amusement. His voice flowed over my senses as smooth and decadent as melted milk chocolate. "If ye donnae like me, why would you bring me to a private place?"

Why, indeed. I'd met Aidan in the parking lot, where he'd been chatting with an elderly couple, the three of them smiling and laughing like old friends. Damn, he really had a knack for ingratiating himself. Maybe I was a little envious of his social aptitude, but that did not explain why I led us down the beach, past the groupings of people scattered along the main stretch of shoreline, around a bend to a spot where trees shrouded us and only the occasional passersby wandered past us. Mostly teenage girls. Who drooled. At Aidan. I swore I'd seen actual saliva dribbling from their hanging tongues.

Not jealous.

"I'm starting to think," Aidan said, "you have lascivious intentions."

Yeah, it sure was a mystery why he'd think that. I'd only shoved my tongue down his throat back at Dance Ardor. Still, I aimed for nonchalance when I said, "I like the shade. Too much sun makes me feel sweaty and icky."

"I like a sweaty lass. Watching the drops of perspiration run down between a woman's breasts makes me want to lick it away."

A quick glance reassured me I did not have sweat trickling between my breasts or anywhere else. The day was warm but not too warm, and the breeze kept things temperate. The shade of the trees ensured I would not get hot, at least not from the weather.

I fiddled with the lid of the plastic cooler I'd stocked with provisions for a picnic. "Do you want to eat yet?"

"In a bit." He settled a palm on the sand between us, moving his fingers in a petting motion. "First, I'd like us to get to know each other better."

"Okay, but we need to be perfectly clear on a few things before we share our life stories or whatever."

"Such as?"

Wriggling my butt on the towel, I adjusted my position so I was turned partway toward him and looked straight into his eyes. "You need to understand the rules I live by."

He pushed up into a semi-erect sitting position, still on his side, held up by one hand flat on his towel. "Tell me your rules, then."

I bit my upper lip, reminding myself that no man would appreciate my rules, and since I couldn't tell him why I lived this way, I couldn't expect him to understand. Inhaling a deep breath to fortify my nerves, I plunged ahead. "These are my rules. No sex, no love, no marriage."

His brows crinkled, cinching together over his nose. His smile turned bemused. "I don't understand. Not wanting marriage, that's not too unusual. But no love? Giving up sex is one thing but—"

"I haven't given up sex."

Those luscious lips parted, and his knit brows lifted. "You just said—"

Holding up one finger, I silenced him. "I said exactly what I meant. Don't make assumptions about what you think it means, take it at face value."

When he still looked baffled, I sighed and my shoulders crumpled. Time to clarify and accept the consequences. "I've never had sex, therefore I can't give it up. I am a twenty-five-year-old virgin."

He shrugged. "Are you thinking I'll be shocked? I'm not."

I folded my arms on my knees. "No one in this day and age believes a person over the age of eighteen could be a virgin unless there's something terribly wrong with them."

He leaned forward to touch my arm. "I've been with virgins older than you."

"They must've been nuns, right?"

"No. Each had her reasons for staying innocent and I'm sure you have yours."

"I'm not innocent."

He stared at me for several seconds. "You are a confusing woman. How are you not innocent if you're a virgin?"

"You're making assumptions again." I tried to ignore the way his fingers caressed my skin, but it sent a continuous, tingling current through me. Sidling away from him, beyond his reach, I faced the lake again and stretched my legs out, leaning back to brace my hands on the towel behind me. "I've never had sexual intercourse with anyone, but that doesn't mean I'm ignorant of all sexual knowledge."

His gaze roved up and down my body, from my sneaker-clad feet and bare legs exposed by my shorts to my low-cut T-shirt, and finally, to my face. "You're very comfortable with your body, aren't you? Not embarrassed to show it off."

"I don't usually dress this way. Sweats and baggy T-shirts are my M.O." Though the trees still shaded us, I grew hot from head to toe. "What does my clothing have to do with the topic at hand?"

"You say you're not innocent and I'm noticing how you're at ease with your sensuality. But I could use a wee bit of help connecting the dots here."

"Tell me," I said, evading his gaze even as he sat up to look at me, "what do you think being a virgin means? In terms of sexual experience?"

The endearing little crinkle between his eyes, over the bridge of his nose, returned. "Means no experience, of course."

"Not for me." My stomach had begun to roil, the closer I got to confessing the truth. I'd never told anyone about it before. Shutting my eyes, I made myself utter the words. "Just because I've never been touched by a man doesn't mean I have no idea what pleasure feels like. There are other ways to, um…have orgasms."

I winced, eyes still firmly shut, and awaited his reaction.

He chuckled, low and soft and sexy as hell. "You masturbate."

Opening one eye only, I peeked at him.

He was grinning, his body still quivering with contained laughter.

Both eyes open now, I made a face at him. "You think it's funny?"

"No." He brushed the backs of his fingertips down my cheek, his laughter dying and his grin morphing into a sweet smile. "I think it's charming."

Now my brows snapped together. "Charming? I intend to stay a virgin for the foreseeable future, but meanwhile I—do naughty things to myself in the privacy of my bedroom. How can you not think I'm demented?"

He shrugged one strapping shoulder, his eyes alight. "I knew you were a passionate woman the night we met. And I was right."

"It's not passion when you're alone."

"Of course it is." He leaned in close to murmur in my ear. "I plan to take full advantage of your secret passion."

"Remember the rules, Aidan. No sex, no love, no marriage."

Lingering too close, his breaths fanning over my ear and cheek, he murmured, "Ye cannae stop from falling in love."

"Yes I can." I sat forward, clasping my hands on my lap. "I can control my feelings, the same way I control my behavior."

He shook his head. "Emotions are uncontrollable. You can't keep from feeling."

"I disagree."

"Maybe you are daft," he said with a teasing smile. "But since you can't control your behavior, that doesn't bode well for your no-love plans."

"What do you mean I can't control my behavior?"

"The other night. At the club." One corner of his mouth lifted. "You molested me."

"I did not—Well, maybe I did. But you started it, begging to kiss me like that."

"Guilty. I wasn't begging, though." He moved back enough to see my face—and so I could see his. "You've been honest with me about your rules. I should be honest with you about what I want."

"Okay," I said slowly, unsure if I wanted to hear this.

"I came to America to find a wife."

"Don't they have women in Scotland?"

"Been dating in Scotland since I was fifteen, but I've never met the right kind of girl."

I drew my knees up, wrapping my arms around them. "Doesn't explain why you came all the way to America."

"Ah..." He bowed his head briefly, then gave me a tight-lipped smile. "My brother Lachlan found an American wife. Met her at Dance Ardor. If it worked for him, why not for me?"

"Let me get this straight." I tapped my fingers on my crossed arms. "Your brother, the one who told you every Friday is kilt night at the club, met his wife in that very same club."

"Aye."

"Was he, by any chance, wearing a kilt at the time?"

Clearing his throat, head down, Aidan peeked up at me through his long lashes. "Yes. It was kilt night then, which is why I believed him when he said every Friday was for kilts."

"I see. And what will you do with this American wife once you find her? Do you plan on kidnapping her back to Scotland?"

"Not kidnapping anyone." He made a scoffing face. "And I don't know. Haven't thought that far ahead. Find a wife first, talk about living arrangements later."

"Uh-huh. A good, specific plan."

"Everything can be worked out when I find the right woman." He slanted toward me again, his mouth temptingly close to mine. "I knew the moment I saw you, Calli, you could be the right one for me. Give me four weeks to convince you, and if I can't, I'll go away and never pester you again."

My suspicious side decided to speak up. "Why four weeks? That's an awfully specific timeframe. Most people would say a month."

He scratched behind his ear, his expression pinched. "Lachlan spent four weeks with Erica."

I threw my head back, groaning at the heavens before I returned my attention to Aidan. "I don't want to participate in a reenactment of the epic love affair between the Amazing Lachlan and Erica the American Wonder-Wife."

"Ahmno trying to—" He scrunched up one side of his mouth, then exhaled a long breath and his features relaxed. "Forget about Lachlan and Erica. Please, Calli, give me four weeks."

"To do what, precisely? You'll never convince me we belong together."

A sly smile crept across his face. "I mean to seduce you. If I can tempt you to break your first rule, the rest will follow."

"The rest meaning love and marriage." My stomach churned once more, the sour taste of bile rising in my throat. I might have confessed my naughty little secret to him, but I dreaded sharing the reasons behind my eschewing of romance. "You can't make me fall in love with you."

With total seriousness, he said, "I can, and I will."

I snorted.

He slid a fingertip along my jaw, down my throat, over my collarbone. When his finger teased the upper curve of one breast, I sucked in a breath.

"You like me," he said, "otherwise you wouldn't have invited me to visit you or brought me to a secluded beach. You want me, otherwise you wouldn't have kissed me twice—with breathtaking passion and sensuality." He coasted his fingertip down the valley between my breasts until it collided with the neckline of my T-shirt. "Those facts give me hope you will fall for me. Ye willnae be able to stop it."

"Because you're so irresistible."

"That's not the main reason." He withdrew his hand but kept his mouth near mine, our gazes glued to each other. "It's because I'm lovable."

Laughter bubbled out of me—the light, girlie kind that made me feel silly, even though I'd never been labeled silly in my life. Weird, yes. Serious, for sure. Never silly.

"You are bonnie all the time," he said, "but when you laugh, you're the bonniest of the bonnie."

"Thanks."

He studied me for a moment, as if entranced by my bonnie silliness. Then he glanced over at the water, squinting at the sunlight glancing off it. "What is Calli short for?"

"Nothing. It's my name. Calli Bethany Douglas."

"A good Scottish name, Douglas."

"I'm American." I stretched my legs out again, wiggling my feet to iron out the kinks in my ankles. "Is Aidan short for something?"

He shot me that grin—wide and brilliant and full of exuberance yet heated by an underlying sensuality. "Aidan the Magnificent. It's my full, Viking name."

"Thought you were Scottish."

"Vikings came to Scotland, you know. I've probably got at least a wee bit of Norse blood in me."

Well, that might explain his ruthless determination to seduce me into bedding, loving, and wedding him. No, it wasn't ruthless. It was...sweetly determined.

"What part of Scotland are you from?" I asked.

"Ballachulish. A village in the Highlands, on the shores of Loch Leven." He gazed out across the blue waters of Lake Superior. "Maybe I'll have a swim. The water's making me sentimental."

"Did you bring swim trunks?"

"I don't need them." He sprang to his feet, lifting his shirt as if to shed it.

"What have you got on under those jeans?"

He paused with his shirt partly lifted, revealing half of his six-pack abs. "Skin."

For a couple heart-pounding seconds, I couldn't breathe or blink or tear my gaze away from his belly, away from the narrow trail of cinnamon hair bisecting his abs and vanishing beneath his waistband. No boxers or briefs under there. Nothing but skin. Touchable, lickable skin.

Aidan lifted his shirt a little higher.

I shook off my fantasy and held up a hand. "Hold up, Flipper. That water is frigid. Why do you think we didn't see a single person swimming or wading? It comes straight from the depths of Lake Superior, which is very deep and cold. They don't call it an inland sea for nothing."

He flattened his lips into an *oh please* expression. "I'm Scottish. Chilly water doesnae scare me."

"Maybe you should dip your toes in first to test how cold it is." When he continued to scoff and rolled his eyes, I said, "Trust me. You don't want to swim this early in the year unless it's an inland lake or a protected bay. Even then…Well, trust me. Okay?"

Grumbling, he let his shirt fall back down and nodded. Stripping off his sneakers and socks, he rolled his pant legs up to his knees. While he ambled toward the water, I leaned back, braced on my arms, to watch his muscles flex underneath his clothes. He did have a fine body. Unbelievably fine. Better than fine, actually.

I let my head loll to the left and moistened my lips, all my attention riveted to his ass and its sculpted muscles shifting inside his jeans.

Aidan waded out into the gently lapping waves without stopping until the water reached his knees. He froze there, his shoulders bunching and his curled fingers snapping out straight and stiff.

Though he faced away from me, I could imagine his expression. I'd seen it before, on tourists who thought they could handle the frigid water.

"Ah!" he hissed, backing out of the water in quick time. "*Bod an Donais*!"

I slapped a hand over my mouth to stifle a laugh.

Aidan spun around and dropped onto his beach towel, rubbing his feet furiously. "You think it's funny? I've probably got frostbite."

"I warned you." Canting my head, I couldn't help smiling as he gave an exaggerated shiver. I recalled his exclamation and asked, "What was that you said a minute ago? Sounded like another language."

"Gaelic. I was cursing at the bloody freezing water."

"What does it mean? The phrase you said."

"*Bod an Donais*. Means the devil's penis."

This time, I couldn't hold back the laughter. It erupted out of me and wouldn't stop until my stomach muscles ached from the exertion and my eyes watered. Aidan watched me with a half smile, half frown until I wiped my eyes and caught my breath.

"You think that's funny too?" he said. "It's a legitimate Scottish curse. Though I could've said *bod a' chac*, which means shit's penis."

I burst out laughing again and collapsed onto my back on the towel, hands clutching my belly. I was in serious danger of suffocating due to an inability to stop laughing.

My giggles died away when Aidan reclined beside me, his head supported on one hand, his focus squarely on me. "I can teach you plenty of dirty Gaelic phrases—starting with the ones about sex."

Gaelic sex talk? Spoken in his soft, husky voice, the one he used when he wanted to get me worked up? A delicious little shiver rippled through me. I liked the idea way too much.

"Let's eat now," I said, as if he hadn't just offered to talk dirty to me.

"Not yet," he murmured, tipping toward me, his face suddenly positioned over mine and the masculine scent of him wafting over me. "First, I want to kiss you."

"No sex. Rule number one."

His mouth twisted into a half-suppressed smirk. "You keep assuming I'm wanting sex, which makes me wonder if you're the one who can't stop thinking about it."

Good point. Not that I'd admit it. "No comment."

"Let me kiss you." His eyes had gone hooded, his gaze intent on mine. "Unless you're afraid you can't keep from fucking me, right here on the beach."

Naturally, a vivid image of just that flared in my mind, complete with sound effects and phantom sensations. I clasped my hands more tightly over my belly, feeling a heaviness there spreading lower. My lips tingled from the memory of our previous kisses, and dammit, I itched to slip my hand inside my shorts and ease the ache growing in my clitoris.

Aidan's slow smile made me wonder if he could read my mind. "Ready to break your first rule?"

"No." I squirmed, adjusting my position, but the damp ache lingered. "But we can kiss. Only kiss. No clothing will be removed and no parts of you will sneak under my clothes to touch parts of me. Understand?"

"Aye. I willnae stroke your *boicionn* unless you beg me to."

"My what?"

"*Boicionn*." He swept a hand down my body, hovering it a bare inch above me, and halted it over my groin. "Your sweet, pink, slippery folds. The ones I'll lick and stroke when I finally have you naked under me."

"Never going to happen."

"We'll see."

"Are you going to kiss me or what?"

He laid a hand on my cheek, his thumb drawing circles on my skin, grazing the corner of my mouth. Slanting closer, he hovered his lips millimeters from mine. "Desperate for me?"

"Patience is not my forte. When I decide to do something, I want to get it done right away."

"I like that about you."

His voice had gone deep and gravelly, his breaths tickled my skin. Blue eyes darkened with desire, he commanded my focus. I let my lips drift apart as if I might take his breaths inside me and revel in the flavor of him. My mouth watered at the idea of it.

"I like everything I've learned about you," he rumbled. "Even your rules."

Before I could mutter a single syllable in response, he swept his lips across mine—once, twice, three times. His mouth skated over mine, delicate as a breeze, teasing me until I had to fist my hands in the towel beneath me to keep from shoving them into his hair and dragging him in for the kind of deep, unbridled lip-lock we'd shared before, the kind I burned for this time.

When he darted his tongue out to flick it across the seam of my lips, back and forth, a hot bolt of lust ripped through me. My rational brain shut down, and for once, I didn't give a damn about rules or propriety. I wanted him. His mouth, his tongue, everything. Letting out a long, low moan, I seized his head in both hands and pulled him in to meet my waiting, hungry lips. Our mouths fused, I sank my fingers into his hair and opened my mouth wider, beckoning him to take control.

A groan resonated in his chest and throat. His tongue dived into my mouth, lashing and coiling around my tongue, starved for the taste and sensation of him inside me, taking and giving with equal measure, overpowered by the pleasure of kissing him.

When we came up for air, both breathless, we could do nothing but gaze into each other's eyes for a long moment. His blue eyes were glossy and half-closed, and I imagined mine looked the same way. I felt the way he looked—dazed and lustful, craving more.

I'd just reclaimed my breath when he bent down for another kiss.

Placing a hand on his chest, I managed to keep him at bay. "Listen, you need to accept I won't ever love you. I do not fall for men called Don Juan."

He rubbed his eyes with his thumb and forefinger. "Bloody Jamie. Little sisters can be a trial, that's for sure. When you've got five brothers and sisters, you get used to being called all sorts of sarcastic names. Doesn't your brother annoy you that way?"

"Gavin prefers to annoy me by meddling in my life."

Aidan nodded. "Overbearing brothers. I sympathize."

"Ditto. But about this Don Juan thing…"

"I am not a Don Juan. I like women and I like to flirt, that's all."

My hand still flat on his chest, I could feel the heat of his body. "How many women have you been with?"

"Seven."

I couldn't stop my eyebrows from shooting up. "Seven? That's it? Doesn't sound very Don Juan-ish to me."

"Told you, I'm not like that. Jamie's exaggerating."

Aidan laid his hand over mine, slowly peeling my palm away from his shirt. "I'd like another kiss now, please."

"Okay."

He set my hand on my bare thigh, his fingers grazing my skin, and bent his head closer to mine. Closer. Closer. Breaths whispering on my skin. Lips millimeters from mine. Closer. Closer.

His phone warbled a bagpipe melody.

Muttering what sounded like another Gaelic curse, he rolled away and dug the phone out of his pants pocket. Whatever he saw on the screen made him flinch.

"Have to take this," he said. "Won't be a minute."

I had no time to say anything, because he sprang to his feet and trotted a little ways down the beach to answer his call. Though he faced away from me, I could see his anxiety in the tightness of his shoulders and the way he clasped one hand to the back of his bowed head.

He paced a short length of the beach, head down so I couldn't make out his expression, though he shook his head and gesticulated with one hand as he spoke to the other party.

I couldn't look away from Aidan, my curiosity mounting with every passing second. What kind of call would make him so agitated? What secrets did he hide? I didn't really know him. Maybe I'd indulged in the fantasy we had some kind of connection, a purely physical one, but Aidan Mac-Taggart was a stranger. I ought to rethink this…whatever it was between us. Inviting him to visit me. Making out with him on the beach. Confiding my secrets to him. *Insanity.*

Aidan ended his call, stuffing the phone back in his pocket. He stalked back down the beach to me. Settling onto his towel beside me, Aidan reached for the cooler. "Let's eat."

"Yes," I said, rubbing my hands together and licking my lips. "I'm famished."

Head down, he peeked up at me. "I know. You are always famished."

The suggestive tone of his voice shivered a thrill through me. Why I should like his flirtatious talk and erotic ways baffled me. But I couldn't have sex with a man I'd met two days ago. A man from another country, an ocean away. A man who explicitly stated his intention to seduce me.

A man who wanted a wife.

Though I was still married, I didn't think I could use that as an excuse to stay away from Aidan. I had filed for divorce, after all, which meant eventually I'd be an ex-wife and free to marry again. Unease slithered through me. Marry again? Risk being trapped again? I didn't know if I had the courage to try it.

Chapter Eight

While he brought out plastic-wrapped sandwiches and bottles of water, I struggled to rationalize my behavior with him. I was lonely, nothing more. Ever since losing my job, I'd spent three months alone in the woods in a secluded cabin with only puppies for companions. Even before that, I'd avoided getting friendly with men because of my unwanted, illegal marriage. The idea of hanging out with Aidan, engaging in strange and oddly enjoyable conversations with him, made me feel almost normal again, not like a fugitive from the law.

I could enjoy kissing him. Talking to him. Basking in his sensual aura. Didn't mean I'd be tempted to sleep with him. Certainly didn't mean I'd fall for him. No way. In a week or so, the novelty would wear off and I'd send him on his way. No harm done.

You will fall for me, he'd said. *Ye willnae be able to help it.*

Aidan handed me an unwrapped sandwich. Our fingers nudged each other when I accepted the sandwich, and awareness shimmered through me.

Okay, I was attracted to him. Wildly, hotly attracted. But I had self-control. Really, I did.

No sex, no love, no marriage.

I should've told him to take a hike. Should've gone back to my hermitage. Why couldn't I tell him to give up and go away?

Maybe I couldn't speak the words, but I did have a way to discourage him.

"Listen," I said after swallowing a bite of sandwich, "there's something else I need to tell you about me."

He bit off a chunk of his sandwich, chewing with deliberate slowness, swallowing and dragging his tongue across his lips. "I'm listening."

I picked at the crust of my sandwich to avoid looking at him. "Even if I wanted to marry you, which I don't, I can't do it. I'm already married."

Daring to glance up, I found him still as a boulder, eyes unblinking. He held the sandwich an inch from his mouth.

"What?" he asked. "But you don't wear a ring. And you're a virgin."

"I am married, Aidan. Filed for divorce, but still married."

"Filed for divorce?" He set down his food. "Then you're separated. Legally."

"There's no such thing as legal separation in Michigan. But yes, I started the divorce process." I flashed back to my conversations with Rade in the hotel and on the phone earlier. "My husband has been trying to delay the proceedings."

"Are you still in love with him?"

"I never loved him."

"Donnae understand." He glanced at his sandwich, his lip curled, and he set it down. "You don't love him, and you've never slept with him. Why did you marry the man? Why not get an annulment instead of divorce?"

"It's a long story." I held up a hand when Aidan opened his mouth to speak. "Please don't ask any more questions. That's all I can tell you, for your own protection."

He squinted at me, lips pursed. "Protection? Why would I need to be protected from knowing about your relationship with your husband?"

"It's complicated."

"Has he abused you?"

"No, nothing like that."

"All right." Aidan picked up his sandwich and devoured another bite. The playful gleam had returned to his eyes. "Then we can kiss and I'm free to seduce you, since you're not really another man's wife anymore."

"Maybe you should go home. I'm bad news."

"You've already been good for me. I haven't had this much fun in a long time."

I stared at him, still holding my sandwich. "Aren't you worried I'm a criminal wanted by the FBI? Or that I'll try to con you into murdering my husband for his life insurance?"

Aidan laughed, shaking his head, and went back to eating his lunch.

If he wouldn't take me seriously, I had no other option except to order him to go away. But I still couldn't make myself say it. Didn't want to. Because I hadn't had this much fun in a long time either.

"Tell me," Aidan said, "can your husband stop the divorce?"

"No. Michigan is a no-fault state, which means the divorce will happen. He can argue about the terms and bring in his team of lawyers to slow things down, but it will go through eventually."

"His team of lawyers?" Aidan's brows lowered. "Is he wealthy?"

I absently drew lines in the sand, my gaze on the lake. "Yeah, he's rich. Inherited a fortune from his parents."

"Does he want to keep you from getting any of his money?"

"No." I dived my fingers into the sand, sinking the tips down through the warm top layer into the cool, damp sand beneath. "I already told him I don't want any more of his money. I want nothing from him except a divorce."

"Any *more* of his money?" Aidan asked. "He's given you—"

"Yes and no. It's complicated, please don't ask me to explain."

"If that's what you want." He stroked the back of one finger along my upper arm, a faint smile on his lips. "Speaking of what you want…Since I don't want to overstay my welcome, would you rather I go back to Chicago tomorrow?"

My head wanted to say yes, but the rest of me longed to say no. *What the hell,* urged my mischievous inner voice, *have a little fun.* For five years, I'd denied myself anything close to fun out of fear and guilt. About time I took Tara's advice and cut loose.

I would not sleep with Aidan. Couldn't fall for him, not in the short time I had in mind.

"Okay," I said, "stay for a week. We can reevaluate at that point."

Aidan smiled, lighting up his face and igniting a brilliant flare inside me.

I might regret my decision later, but for now, I planned to enjoy the warmth he engendered in me. I planned to enjoy the company of a sexy man who made me feel wanted.

"Have dinner with me," Aidan said.

My reply came without any hesitation. "I'd love to."

I rested my hands on my lap, spreading my fingers over the floral fabric of my sundress as I surveyed the restaurant around me. Picture windows overlooked the Portage Canal and the lift bridge, with its two blue towers spanning the narrow waterway. Though it was seven o'clock in the evening, the sun still glowed in the teal sky.

Aidan had received another mysterious call just as we walked into the restaurant, but he'd dismissed the caller with a gruff "can't talk now."

Seated across the table from me, Aidan relaxed in his chair, his focus on my face and a faint smile on his lips.

I fidgeted, a bit unnerved by his undivided attention. "You look pleased with yourself. Are you concocting some sort of plan to get me into bed?"

"No." He picked up his water glass and took a sip, but his gaze stayed on me. "Just wondering how long you'll keep pretending we're not dating."

"We aren't. Dating implies a desire to advance the relationship." I plucked at my dress, resisting the urge to chew on the inside of my cheek. "There will be no advancement."

His eyebrows lifted, his smile ticking up a little higher. "We share meals, we talk about our lives and our plans, and we kiss. That's dating."

I growled my frustration. "We. Are. Not. Dating."

"What are we doing, then?"

"Hanging out."

Shrugging one shoulder, he swallowed another mouthful of water. "Call it whatever you like, if it makes you feel better."

"Thank you. I will." Did I sound like a person desperately denying the truth? Maybe I did. Hardly mattered, though, because I could not go down that road. A change of topic was in order. I wrapped my hand around my glass of fizzing pop, the cold firming up my resolve. Sort of. "You've mentioned having five siblings, brothers and sisters. How many of each?"

Aidan leaned back, eying me with curious amusement. "Are you sure you want me to answer? This sort of question might lead to accidental dating—or sex."

"Very funny." I gulped a mouthful of pop and set my glass down a little too hard. It thunked on the tabletop, splashing the fizzy liquid inside. "I'll risk it. Hearing about your family won't make me wild with desire for you."

"In that case, I have two brothers and three sisters."

"Wow, big family. Do you get along with them?"

"Aye," he said. "Lachlan used to be the most uptight person you'd ever meet, until Erica softened him up. He's annoyingly happy these days. My brother Rory has always been serious, but he hasn't found a woman to loosen him up yet. My sister Catriona is the most American of us because she went to university here and came back to take a job at a museum. Fiona's a spitfire and Jamie doesn't know what she wants yet."

The affection in his tone told me he loved his family.

A pang pierced my heart, triggered by memories of events I'd tried not to think about for years, memories of my own family. I swallowed against the thickness in my throat.

"My parents," he went on, sitting forward to brace his elbows on the table, "they're embarrassingly in love after forty-five years together."

The start of tears burned in my eyes. I cleared my throat, sucked down a third of my glass of pop, and coughed at the sudden onslaught of carbonation.

Aidan stretched a hand across the table to clasp mine. "What's wrong? You look unwell."

"I'm fine." I took a slower sip of my drink, allowing his hand to warm mine despite the unsettling intimacy of it. "I drank too fast, that's all."

His fingers caressed my skin, more comforting than any words. The memories faded into the background of my mind, supplanted by the presence of this man.

"I blethered on and on about my family," he said. "Should we talk about something else?"

"Actually," I said, my stomach fluttering at the sensation of his fingers on my hand, "I'd like to know more. Like who's the oldest and where you fit into the hierarchy."

"Make us sound like a royal family." He sat back, withdrawing his hand and the lovely warmth it imbued into me. He rested an arm on the table. "Lachlan is the oldest. He's forty-two. Rory's next, and he acts eighty even though he's thirty-eight. Then there's Fiona who's thirty-five, followed by Catriona who's thirty-one. I'm the youngest son, but Jamie's the baby of the family at twenty-six."

"How old are you?"

"Twenty-eight." He tapped one finger on the tablecloth. "Tell me about your family."

I shifted in my seat, suddenly feeling like I'd sat on a rock. "I have one brother, Gavin. He's eight years older and very overbearing at times."

"You don't get along?"

"Oh no, we do. He's bossy because he loves me and all we've got is—" I clutched my glass in both hands, but the cold no longer calmed me. It chilled me to the core. Unable to look up at Aidan, I stared at the bubbles in the liquid. "All we've got is each other. Our parents died in a car accident five years ago."

Aidan wrapped his hand around both of mine, still clamped around the cold glass. "I'm sorry. Cannae imagine how awful that must be for you."

"Not like it happened yesterday."

He peeled my hands away from the glass, enveloping them in his own. "But it still hurts, I can see it in your eyes."

"Sure, it hurts once in a while. But it was a long time ago and I'm okay with it." I'd recovered from the body-slam shock of their sudden deaths, but the secrets exposed afterward still haunted me. Then there was Rade and his role in the aftermath.

"Is there more?" Aidan asked gently.

"Yes, but I'd rather not talk about it." I slid my hands out from between his. "I hardly know you. Need a little more time before I share all my secrets."

He nodded, seeming not the least bit irritated. "Maybe one day you will tell me. When you feel comfortable enough with me."

I studied him for a moment, my nosiness rearing up again. "May I ask you a personal question?"

"Ask anything you like."

"Why are you really here? In America, I mean. You say you're looking for a wife, the way your brother found his, but my intuition tells me there's more to it than that."

His gaze drifted to the windows and the view beyond them. The smile faded into a somber expression. "I need to change my life."

"Fleeing to another country seems a bit excessive. You could've changed your life in Scotland."

"Had to be somewhere else." He sank into his chair, still staring out the windows. "I've been selfish, and that has to change. I have to change."

I had no idea what to say. He'd confided more than I'd expected, so much that I wasn't sure I should respond. My insatiable curiosity pushed me to ask how he'd been selfish, but I couldn't pry into his secrets when I refused to let him pry into mine.

He looked straight at me. "I took a hard look at myself and realized what I really want. It's what my parents have. Love, commitment, family—children, I mean. I'm looking for the right woman and the moment I saw you I knew you might be the one I need."

Stunned, I couldn't move or blink. When my eyes began to sting from dryness, I finally blinked again. "Aidan—"

"We're virtually strangers, I know." He fiddled with his napkin, gaze downcast, then raised his eyes to look straight into mine. "I trust my instincts. And they tell me you could be the one I've wanted. I'm only asking for a chance to find out if you are."

This conversation had gotten way too serious.

I straightened, stretching my fingers out on my lap. "So, what do you do for a living?"

He picked up his fork and twirled it around his fingers like a gunfighter practicing his quick draw. "I have a company. General contracting. I like the work and I like being in control of my own destiny."

"What's your company called?"

"MacTaggart Construction. Afraid I'm not very imaginative."

I leaned back against my chair. "Oh, I suspect you have plenty of imagination when it counts."

He smiled, setting down the fork. "With you, I'll harness every bit of my creativity."

An inventive man with a roguish streak? I might be in deep trouble here.

"Are you the boss in the office," I said, "or a hands-on type of guy?"

"Hands on," he said, steepling his fingers. "Always."

I'd guessed as much from his hands—the strong, callused hands of a man unafraid of hard labor. Skilled hands, capable of much more than hammering nails.

"What about you?" he asked. "What do you do?"

"Nothing exciting. I'm a librarian, got a master's degree and everything." A useless scrap of paper, my degree.

"Librarian?" He bent forward, moistening his lips. "A bonnie, sexy one for sure. Where are you working? I saw a library a few streets over."

"Haven't started my next job yet." Because I didn't have one. Maybe I should've confessed, but I didn't know him very well. Besides, I'd been trying to steer the conversation to lighter topics.

"You haven't told me," he said, "if you'll give me a chance to find out if you're the woman I've been looking for."

Elbows on the table, I dropped my face into my raised hands. "Aidan, please, stop wasting your time here. I'm way too damaged to give you any of the things you want. Go back to Chicago or Scotland or wherever and find a girl who's right for you. I am not."

I heard rustling and the scrape of his chair as he moved around. When I lowered my hands, he was beside me, having realigned his chair to sit next to me.

He laid a hand on my forearm. "Let me decide if I'm wasting my time."

"You are so pigheaded."

He smiled, his hand lingering on my bare skin. "Lachlan told me the same thing when I said I wanted to come to America. He tried to talk me out of it, but I'd set my mind to it." He bent closer, his eyes twinkling in the sunlight. "I've decided this too. I want to spend time with you. Give me four weeks, it's all I ask."

"I agreed to one week, with the potential for extensions."

"Make it four weeks. Please. You can always boot me out after the first week."

I gazed into his blue eyes for a long moment, the intensity of his attention and the feel of his hand on my arm tempting me to surrender. "You win, I give up. But let's not assign a time limit to this, forget one week or four. Stay as long as you like, and if I get sick of you, I'll say so."

"Thank you, Calli."

"Don't thank me. None of what you're hoping for is going to happen."

He stroked his fingers over my skin, light and tempting. "At the very least, I'll have gotten to know a sweet lass and gotten to see a new place."

The waitress arrived with our food order, ending the discussion. Aidan moved his chair back to where it belonged. While we ate, we talked about innocuous things like tourist attractions and the weather. But I knew, in a visceral way, something very bad had just happened. We'd gotten...intimate. Discussing our families. Sharing deeply personal things.

Shit. We were dating.

Not that I would ever admit that to him.

Across the table, Aidan smiled that sweetly sexy smile, as if he'd heard my thoughts and knew I'd slipped a little closer to the line I'd sworn never to cross.

I shoved a huge chunk of broccoli into my mouth and chomped on it.

Slippery slope, here I come.

Chapter Nine

The morning after my dinner with Aidan, I sat at my desk in the corner of the living room scouring job sites. I'd had no luck for the past three months, but I kept trying, kept hoping. Somewhere in the middle of scrolling through the listings, my mind had locked up and I'd begun to stare blankly at the screen, the words and images on it blurring.

Misty and Mandy played in front of the sofa, rolling around and barking, but their antics weren't the reason for my mental freeze-up. My thoughts kept wandering back to my second kiss with Aidan, after the wedding, and the way his deft tongue whipped me into a frenzy of need. His heated gaze. His sexy smile. The way he kept touching me in innocent ways that stoked my desire as if he'd cupped my naked breast in his rough palm.

I couldn't concentrate on anything while perpetually aroused.

Slumping back in my chair, I rubbed my hands over my face in an attempt to clear my thoughts. No such luck. Aidan's darkly sexy voice rumbled in my mind. *If I can tempt you to break your first rule, the rest will follow.* Oh, how the idea of surrendering to the lust appealed to me. I might've done it already, if not for his insistence I would fall for him.

Never. Ever. Happen.

But maybe…*Uh-uh-uh. No sex either, dummy, remember?* I sprang forward in my chair, slapping my fingers on the keyboard. If I didn't get back to work, back to hunting for work, I'd soon be penniless and crawling to my brother for help. My savings wouldn't last much longer.

On the screen, a message popped up from my email program, alerting me to a new message. I clicked to open the program, and the list of emails appeared. When I saw the sender's name, I double-clicked to open the email.

Tanner Pierson, the process server I'd hired, had contacted me—but not with the news I'd hoped to hear.

"No dice," he said. "Try again later?"

I threw my hands in the air. "Dammit, Rade. You promised."

Why did I keep believing Rade every time he vowed to be present to accept the papers? I had no choice but to request a second summons and keep trying. If he still evaded Tanner, I'd have to request permission for an alternate delivery method. More delays. I wanted to be free, not hanging in limbo for who knew how long.

The puppies raced around the backside of the sofa, and Misty vaulted over its back to land inches from the coffee table. Little Mandy barked, then zoomed around the furniture to leap on her sister.

I watched them rolling around for a minute, wishing I could bottle up some puppy energy and guzzle it by the gallon. I had to make do with human resources, and mine were running low these days.

Except when I was with Aidan. Something about him reinvigorated me.

Turning back to my computer, I typed out a reply to Tanner. *Afraid I can't afford you anymore. Thank you for all your help, but I'll have to find another way.*

After I hit send, a new email popped up. A message from Rade.

I shouldn't have read the message. I didn't want to read it. Whatever he said would only irritate me further. My finger hovered over the mouse button, wavering side to side as my resolve to delete the email unread wavered too. Morbid curiosity won out, and I clicked to open the message.

"Did I miss your server?" he wrote. "Something came up, and I had to go out for a time."

Bullshit. The man didn't work, didn't need to, so he had no urgent need to leave the house.

I clacked my teeth in a staccato beat as I read the rest of the email.

"Move in with me just for a time. I will sleep on the sofa like before, you have my word." He'd signed it, "Your husband, Rade."

He could keep delaying things because, of course, I had no signed agreement with him. People didn't have lawyers draw up contracts for illegal marriages of convenience. That meant I had nothing but his word, and he'd reneged on it. But why? I didn't understand any of this. After five years of not giving a hoot, five years of living separate lives, he'd suddenly decided he wanted me in his life.

Rade had caught me at my weakest, during the worst time in my life, and talked me into doing him a "small favor" so he could stay in the country. I'd never believed he timed it that way on purpose, to take advantage of my grief over my parents' deaths. He'd kept to our agreement to live separate lives—until I wanted a divorce.

I deleted Rade's email without replying.

Switching back to the jobs website, I took a moment to do some deep breathing exercises and cleanse my mind of the confusion and angst. Rade's voice echoed in my mind, a repetitive loop of all he'd said to me in the past few days. *Hell's bells.* I had to think about something else, or I'd never make any progress on finding work. I needed something to distract me. Something that would wipe away all other thoughts.

A vision of Aidan materialized in my mind. His smile, rife with sensuality. His mouthwatering body, sculpted into firm lines and taut, bulging muscles. I closed my eyes and gave in to the memories, letting my body relive the excitement of almost succumbing to him. I could still taste his mouth, smell his masculine scent, feel his hands on my buttocks. A delicious tingle sparked to life between my thighs, swelling and spreading as I envisioned Aidan's naked chest—a pure fantasy, since I hadn't yet glimpsed it. My mind filled in all the blanks of his physique with exquisite detail, from his abs down to the erection I'd once had pinned to my body.

Wet and aching in all the right places, I let my mind wander through thoughts of all the things Aidan and I could do together. *Mm, yes.* My hand drifted down to the waistband of my sweats, my fingers delved beneath it. I wanted nothing more than to indulge in my every fantasy of Aidan and forget the rest of the world.

My hand slipped inside my sweats. Inside my panties.

Two quick knocks resounded through the front door.

I squeaked like a scared mouse and jumped out of my chair, sending it rolling backward across the wood floor.

The knocker rapped again, three times in rapid succession.

I laid a hand on my chest, my heart pounding beneath it. Gathering the remnants of my wits, and still burning down below from my erotic imaginings, I hurried to the door and squinted through the peephole. The fish-eye lens revealed the rugged, familiar features of Aidan MacTaggart. I rested my forehead on the wood, exhaling the breath I'd held.

"Calli?" Aidan called through the door. "Are you there?"

I took a cleansing breath and swung the door inward.

Aidan smiled. "Glad you're home. I tried to call first, but you didn't answer."

My phone hadn't rung this morning. I slapped my forehead. "Fudge. I forgot to recharge my phone last night. It's probably out of juice."

"Fudge?" he repeated with laughter in his voice. "Never heard anyone say that as a curse before."

"I admit it's not as colorful as the devil's penis, but it works for me." I waved for him to enter as I trotted to the kitchen bar to dig my phone out of my purse and plug it into the wall socket there.

"That's what I love about you," he said, shutting the door. "You're not like anyone else on earth."

"Yep, that's me. A weirdo."

Mandy and Misty erupted from the other side of the sofa, bounding over its back to crash-land on the floor. They rocketed toward Aidan, who knelt to embrace them and babble nonsense to the duo, who had instantly become his two biggest fans.

Second biggest fans. The top spot belonged to me.

I ambled over to the trio, smiling and shaking my head. Could there be anything more adorable than a full-grown man going gaga over silly puppies? Maybe I was enamored of the Scotsman, but that did not mean anything. It didn't.

Uh-huh. That's why I'd thought of myself as his biggest fan.

Which meant nothing. Zippo. Nada.

"Better watch it," I said, folding my arms over my chest. "They'll decide they want to go home with you."

Aidan straightened, but Misty leaped up to slam her big paws onto his stomach. He scratched behind her ears, then gently pushed her away. The puppies hopped back and forth in front of him, panting and wagging their tails. When Aidan turned to me, and they realized the love fest had ended, Misty and Mandy took off out the dog door again.

"Don't be jealous," Aidan said, moving closer, curving a hand over my elbow. "The puppies are sweet, but I came for you."

"When did you do that?" Maybe I'd spent too much of the morning fantasizing about him, but I couldn't stop myself from shamelessly flirting with him. Surprise jolted through me at how much fun this was.

"When did I come for you?" Aidan asked. He glided his hand up my arm, exposed by my short-sleeve T-shirt. "Last night. This morning. More often than I should probably admit to."

My hand floated up to my throat like it had a mind of its own. Had he confessed to getting off to thoughts of me? Yes, he had. Rather than feeling embarrassed or shocked by his revelation, I grew wet and achy again. And my brazen mouth refused to shut up. "Was it good for you?"

His fingers sneaked higher up my arm and beneath my T-shirt's sleeve. "The best I've ever had."

"Guess you don't need the real me." My nipples had gone hard and pebbled, and the fine hairs on my arms shivered erect. "But for the sake of total honesty, I was thinking about you right before you knocked on the door."

"Thinking?" He moved his hands to my waist, tugging me closer. "Please tell me they were salacious thoughts."

"Very." I bent my head back and our gazes collided. He leaned in too, his pupils large and fathomless. I fanned my palms over his chest, swirling them in lazy circles. "If I hadn't been interrupted, I might've come for you."

His chest heaved with each breath, his teeth clamped together. Tugging my hips into him, he said in a husky voice, "*Is iomadh rud a nì dithis dheònach.*"

"What does it mean?"

"Two willing people can do many things together." His hands slid down to my buttocks, his head dipped down until our lips nearly touched. "You *fannadh* for me, I *fannadh* for you. If we're both willing, why donnae ye let me show ye all the things I can do to ye? Ye'll stay a virgin, technically. But I have to touch ye, to feel your slick little *brillean* while I make ye come for me."

I clutched fistfuls of his shirt, all but panting with need. "I only understood half of what you said, but it sounds…good."

He ran his tongue over my bottom lip, his voice becoming more gravelly. "*Fannadh* means masturbate and *brillean* means clitoris. The rest I think you understand. Let me show you."

Chapter Ten

Breathless, my head light and floaty, I clung to him. Desperate to prolong this wonderful sensation, this heady desire, I hesitated for only a second before I said, "Show me."

His shoulders caved in with relief, and he touched his forehead to mine.

So much for resisting him. I could accomplish that only when he wasn't around, and even then, it was dicey. I'd almost given in to my fantasy of him and now he stood before me, offering to do…decadent things.

He moved around behind me and spread his hands over my belly, drawing me snug against him and the raging hard-on barely contained in his jeans. One of his hands stayed on my abdomen, while the other wandered lower, sneaking inside the waistband of my sweats like I'd done moments earlier.

I stalled his progress with one of my hands on his. "Are you sure I'll still be a virgin after this?"

"Positive." He nuzzled my neck, then licked at my earlobe. "Technically. It's no more than what you do to yourself."

My mouth had gone dry, but wetness saturated my sex. No more than what I did? I couldn't believe that, and yet I couldn't muster any guilt over what I was about to let him do. After everything I'd endured, didn't I deserve something pleasurable?

Yes, yes, yes.

"Should I stop?" he asked.

"No. Please don't stop."

As he drew my earlobe into his mouth, suckling softly, he thrust his hand down inside my panties to palm my mound. I sucked in a sharp breath. The weight of his hand, the texture of his calluses, it was the most powerfully erotic thing I'd ever experienced.

Until he dipped a finger between my folds and began circling it around my clitoris.

I crumpled against him, my head falling back onto his chest, exposing my throat.

He rasped his tongue up my neck to the hollow of my throat. His finger toyed with my clit, first whisking round and round it, then rubbing in sure, swift strokes. I arched into his touch, my back bowing and my mouth falling open on a strangled moan. While his finger tormented me, his palm scraped across my mound, the sensation heightening my arousal until my sex throbbed from my clit straight down into my vagina. His free hand glided up under my shirt, cupping my breast through my bra, his thumb and forefinger plucking my nipple.

"Aidan," I gasped. "Yes oh god yes."

I threw my arms above my head to lock my hands around his neck.

While his heavy breaths gusted over my ear, his finger rubbed harder and faster, up and down, then switched to sideways strokes. The tension building inside me, stretching taut, almost snapped. I whimpered, writhing against him, frantic for release.

He shoved his hand deep between my slick folds, plunging his finger inside me. The heel of his hand worked my clit with ruthless fervor as his finger thrust in and out, in and out, joined by a second finger and then a third. He crooked his fingers inside me, pressing on a spot that made electricity fire through my entire body.

"Oh God," I cried, mindless with need. "Please, Aidan, please."

Shifting his hand, he freed his thumb to flick it across my clitoris over and over and over, while his fingers petted that incredible spot inside me.

My orgasm ripped through me.

I clawed at the back of his neck, my heels lifted off the floor, my back arched wildly. Spasm after spasm shot earth-shattering pleasure through me, stealing my breath. My heart thudded so fast and hard my head spun. He kept rubbing until he'd milked every last second of pleasure from my body until the muscles inside me stopped contracting around his fingers and I went boneless in his arms.

He held me against him, his arms wrapped around me, until I regained my equilibrium, in body and mind.

I laid my hands on his forearms. "Wow. I can't think of anything more eloquent to say."

"Mm." He shifted his hips, hissing in a breath, and I felt his erection pulse against my back. "Please excuse me for a moment. I need the bog." He cleared his throat. "The bathroom."

He pulled away from me, robbing me of his body heat.

I spun around to see him hustling toward the hallway in a slightly bow-legged fashion. He veered toward the first door on the right, muttering a curse when he realized it was the laundry room.

"The door on the left," I called out.

He gave a curt nod, his face pinched, and rushed into the open doorway of the bathroom across the hall, slamming it behind him. How could he have missed the bathroom when the door was open? Something had him agitated, for sure.

Tiptoeing to the bathroom door, I raised a hand to knock but hesitated. Odd noises emanated from the other side of the door. Soft grunts. The shuffling of shoes on the vinyl flooring.

"Aidan?" I said, daring to lean a little closer to the door. "You okay in there?"

He muttered a strangled curse. "Aye. Fine."

The strain in his voice belied his words. What on earth was he doing in there?

He let out a sharp grunt, followed by a long, low groan.

Oh. All of a sudden, I had an idea of what he was doing in there. He'd been highly aroused after pleasuring me, so much so his cock had pulsed against my backside. Then he'd excused himself and hurried off with an odd gait, as if his groin pained him. His desperation to get into the bathroom, combined with the noises he'd made, suggested one conclusion.

No, he wouldn't have done that. Not hiding in the bathroom. Aidan MacTaggart was clearly not the kind of guy who'd be ashamed of needing a release of his own. I could imagine him asking me to help him with that or inviting me to watch him do it, but hiding out…

The bathroom door swung inward.

Aidan, his cheeks tinged with red, gusted out breath after breath.

I raised my brows, noting his erection had shrunk. Arms crossed over my chest, I gestured at his groin with one finger. "Did you go in there to, uh…*fannadh?*"

Unsure if I pronounced it right, I did my best to imitate the way he'd said it earlier. I liked that word. It made something down and dirty sound elegant.

Though his breathing had normalized, the spotty redness on his cheeks spread into a full-on blush. He glanced down at the floor and mumbled, "Yes. That's what I did."

He *was* embarrassed. How strange.

I couldn't resist laying a palm on his blush-warmed cheek. "How can a wicked man like you be embarrassed about jerking off?"

"Ahmno embarrassed." His mouth twisted into a warped frown.

"Why did you run away? That implies you're em—"

"I am not embarrassed."

Palms out, I raised both hands. "Okay, okay. No need to get huffy with me."

Aidan rolled his eyes.

"Oh no," I said, locking my arms over my chest again, "don't give me the eye roll either. You're the one who did…what you did to me and then bolted like a kid caught stealing candy."

"I—" He shoved a hand into his hair, grumbling under his breath, probably cursing at me in Gaelic. After a few deep breaths, he seemed to compose himself. Leaning against the doorjamb, he slanted his head down to gaze into my eyes. "I've never had this problem before. The way you reacted when I touched you, the way you came under my hand, you were stunning. And it affected me. So much I thought I'd burst in my pants."

"Burst?" I struggled not to smile. "You can say fuck in front of me, but you can't say you were about to come?"

"I can say it." He angled his body toward me, looping his free arm around my waist. "But I never *caith* in my pants. I never lose control with a woman. This is a new experience for me."

My arms fell away from my chest to dangle at my sides and I found myself leaning toward him just a little. "I'm sure it happens to every guy now and then."

"You don't understand." He skimmed his hand up and down my back. "It's because of you, because I want you more than any other woman I've known."

"Oh." Warmth bloomed under my skin, spreading throughout my body. I rubbed my lips together, not sure why, and stared at his mouth.

An explosive *whack* reverberated through the living room as the puppies tore through the dog door. The magnetic plastic flap snapped back into place behind them.

Misty and Mandy barreled straight toward Aidan.

The duo leaped up onto me on their way to him. I stumbled into the wall. The puppies attacked Aidan with gleeful ardor, totally smitten with the Highlander. I couldn't blame them. He was hard to resist.

After a moment of flinging their little bodies at him and flailing their tongues at any part of him they could reach, the puppies had expended the bulk of their energy. They settled down to lie at his feet and gaze up at him with rapt adoration.

"I have another problem," Aidan said in a casual tone, resting one hand on the doorjamb.

"And is this one also my fault?"

"Not unless you sneaked into my motel last night and ruptured the pipes."

Feigning deep thought, I tapped a finger on my chin. "No, I don't recall doing that. But I might've been sleepwalking."

"Hmm." Aidan danced his fingertip over my lips. "Why would you want me homeless?"

The faint pressure of his finger made me long to suck it into my mouth. "What do you mean homeless?"

"My room was damaged by the burst pipe and there are no other rooms available."

"There are lots of motels around here. I can get the phone book to look up—"

"Please don't." He grunted as Misty hopped up to plant her paws on his stomach. Babbling nonsense to her, he petted her head with one hand and spoke in a hushed tone. "No other rooms available. There's some sort of festival happening and a conference at a nearby university."

"What will you do?"

He shrugged one shoulder. "Donnae know. May have to go back to Chicago."

The thought of him leaving stabbed a pang through my chest. I blurted out a response without bothering to think first. "Stay with me."

He blinked, his eyes widening. "What?"

Now that I'd said it, I couldn't take it back. Didn't want to either, I realized with a start. "I have a spare bedroom. You, um, can stay here with me. As long as you understand this does not mean I'm going to sleep with you."

"Not yet."

I tried to look stern but felt certain I failed. "Not ever."

"You want me and we both know it." He took hold of my right hand, guiding it to his groin until my palm covered his semi-erect penis with only a single layer of denim between my skin and his. "And you know how much I want you."

More than any other woman I've known, he'd told me. The notion of any man lusting for me that much sent a lovely little shiver down my spine. The idea of Aidan lusting for me with such fervor...

That made my sex clench.

I pulled my hand away from his crotch. "You can stay here. But do try to behave yourself."

Aidan grinned. "Why? You don't behave yourself with me."

Before I could issue a smart retort, he trotted out the front door. I peeked through the curtains and watched him retrieving his bags from the rental car.

What on earth had possessed me to invite him to stay with me? Visits from Aidan tested my willpower more than I'd expected. Sharing a house with him—a secluded house in the woods, with no neighbors—this might prove to be the most dangerous decision I'd ever made. My self-control seemed to disintegrate in his presence. With Aidan as my roommate...

I could handle it. I could.

Aidan sauntered back into the house carrying his things. "Where am I, then?"

"Follow me." I led him to the far end of the hall and the open door to my bedroom. I pointed at another door, on the left, kitty-corner to my bedroom. "There's the spare room. Bed's made, and extra pillows are in the closet."

Aidan glanced from the spare room to my bedroom, a mere arm's length away. "You want me close, don't you? Convenient for midnight cravings."

"You are incorrigible."

He smiled brightly. "Thank you."

"I think you're the strangest man I've ever met."

"You like the way I make you feel, though." Setting his bags down, he wrapped one arm around my waist. "One of these nights, maybe you'll show me how you touch yourself."

My mouth opened but my brain couldn't cobble together a single word.

"Think about it," he said, and then picked up his bags.

In that moment, as he lugged his things into the spare room, I understood one fact with glittering clarity. I'd invited him to stay because I wanted him to tempt me. He was right. I liked the way he made me feel.

Appreciated, desired, alive.

But I would not fall for him. No way.

Chapter Eleven

After lunch, I lounged on the sofa waiting for Aidan to return from changing his shirt. Misty had spilled tomato sauce on him in her overly exuberant attempt to smack a doggie kiss on his mouth. Aidan had not only indulged my puppies' obsession with him, and seemed to enjoy it, but he'd also made lunch for me—spaghetti with meatballs and scrumptious blueberry muffins on the side. Then he'd cleaned up the mess he made and washed the dishes, shooing me away when I tried to help.

He really did understand women. After all, what was sexier than a guy who cooked and cleaned? If he scrubbed toilets and vacuumed, he'd be the perfect man.

I glanced out the windows into the backyard. Aidan's furry fans were frolicking among the trees and grass, leaping up on their hind legs to do battle with their front paws on each other's shoulders.

Aidan emerged from the guest room wearing a fresh shirt. Short sleeve, dark blue, and emblazoned with a stylized lion logo above the words "Scotland the Brave."

"Cool shirt," I said. "I can almost hear the bagpipes. Or is that your phone ringing?"

"Not my phone, you cheeky lass." He veered around the sofa and plopped onto the cushion beside mine. "Catriona gave me this shirt. She says American women love this sort of thing." He plucked the shirt with his thumb and forefinger. "I think she might be pulling a Lachlan joke on me. What do you think?"

"I wouldn't say it's on a par with 'every night is kilt night,' but she might be pulling your leg. I like it, though. You look good in blue."

He swiveled his upper body toward me, laying his arm across the sofa behind me. "You look good in anything, but I loved the green dresses you wore at the club and the wedding."

"Tara picked them. She insists green is my signature color, mostly because of my eyes."

"Your beautiful, luminous, emerald eyes." He leaned in closer, gazing into my eyes from a few inches away, the scent of him rushing over me. "They are mesmerizing."

I swallowed, my throat suddenly dry. "You don't talk like any other guys I've met. They said things like 'you look fine' or maybe they'd tell me I had nice eyes. Nobody's ever called me mesmerizing before."

"They were eejits."

"Can't tell if I agree or not, since I have no idea what an eejit is."

"An idiot." Aidan slanted in closer, so near me his breaths slipped between my parted lips. His mouth grazed the corner of mine as he dragged his lips across my cheek to my ear. "Any man who describes your eyes as nice is blind and stupid. You are stunning, Calli."

"Thank y—" My words choked off when he nibbled on my earlobe, then coiled his tongue around it. "Unh."

He shoved his hands under my butt, lifting me up and onto his lap, seating me sideways across his thighs. "I like you speechless. You make the sexiest little noises."

I moaned as he grasped my ass in one hand. "Can't think when your mouth is—mm."

He painted damp kisses along my jaw, down my throat. I turned my head to the side, granting him full access, and he took advantage of the opening to drag his tongue over my throat and nip at my flesh. I flattened my palms on his chest, the cotton of his shirt preventing me from experiencing the sensation of his skin on mine. When he lifted his head, leveling his smoky gaze on me, I ran my hands in circles on his chest.

"Do you know," I said, "I've never seen you shirtless. Fantasized about it, but—"

He picked me up and dropped me back onto the adjacent cushion, my calves draped across his lap. In one smooth motion, he whipped his shirt off over his head, tossing it onto the coffee table. It flumped onto a pile of travel magazines.

Aidan spread his arms over the sofa's back, smiling with masculine satisfaction. "There. Problem solved."

I straightened and soaked in the sight of his fantastic torso. Skin softly bronzed by sun exposure. Hard lines etched by sculpted muscles. Fine, dark hairs sprinkled over his pecs tapered into a trail that vanished beneath the waistband of his jeans. I bit my lower lip, battling against the impulse to unhook the metal button of his jeans, ease the zipper down, and discover where that hair-dusted trail led.

My gaze dropped to the bulge of his penis.

He swept a finger over my lips. "You're drooling."

"Am not." I patted my lips, finding them free of drool, and gave his chest a half-hearted slap. "You're hot, but I can control my lust."

"The way you controlled it this morning? When I had my hand inside your panties and you were screaming my name."

I laid my hands flat on his chest, reveling in the heat of his body and the silkiness of fine hairs teasing my palms. "I didn't have sex with you. That's control."

"But it was a sexual encounter." He settled a hand on my knee, gliding it between my thighs. I couldn't keep from parting them for him, allowing him to skate his hand up to my groin. "I made you come for me."

"I'm aware of that."

"Only one more little step—"

"No stepping. Not even on my tippy toes."

"Hmm." He slid his hand back down to my knee, studying me with a thoughtful expression. "Have you ever seen a man naked?"

"Not in person."

"I can remedy that."

Aidan rose, with me in his arms, and turned around to face the sofa. Setting me on the cushions, he took two steps backward to stand just past the coffee table. While I sat frozen, my gaze glued to him, he unhooked the button of his jeans. Flashing me the kind of smug smile only he could make disarming, he pulled the zipper down, down, down, to unveil the length of his penis inch by tantalizing inch. I ran my tongue over my lips, my mouth suddenly watering. The more of his body he exposed, the more ravenous I grew at the sight of all that delicious male flesh.

His jeans slumped to the floor. He stepped out of them, rolled his shoulders back, and gazed down at me with sultry eyes. "You're drooling again."

"Am not." I was lusting, though, big time. No woman could remain detached when faced with the vision of nude Aidan MacTaggart mere feet away. I let my gaze roam his body, from the lines of his torso muscles—the ones that begged to be traced with a hot, wet tongue—over his narrow-yet-powerful hips and down to…

My focus stalled at his groin. At the sleek length of his cock. The way it had begun to swell and harden. The way a rosy blush now kissed the tip, the color darkening as his erection blossomed before my eyes. I tried to tear my gaze away from it, to admire the thick muscles of his thighs, but my eyes kept snapping back to his cock. I slanted forward without meaning to, my mouth falling open, my tongue slicking my lower lip.

I probably was drooling now. But I didn't give a damn.

Aidan lowered his mouthwatering self onto the coffee table, facing me. His erection had grown stiff enough to bob in the air between us, and I fought the ridiculous and nearly overpowering urge to stretch out a hand, close my fingers around his smooth shaft, pump slowly until he begged me to—

Giving myself a mental slap, I shook off the fantasy. Sort of. My body clung to the imagery, to the sensory details my mind had conjured up.

He tipped toward me, spreading his thighs wide, his cock jutting in my direction. "One little step, that's all it takes."

One little step? I wanted to fling my entire body at him.

"Ah well," he said, unfurling his body, waving his erection in my face. He grabbed his jeans and yanked them on, then snagged his shirt from the table and pulled it on as well. I must've looked disappointed at the way he'd covered up, because he hooked a finger under my chin, encouraging me to gaze up at him. "Donnae worry. You'll get an extended view—one day soon, for as long as you like—when we make love."

"You mean when we have sex."

"No." He ducked down to press his lips to mine in a sweet kiss. "I mean when I make love to you, because we're going to fall in love. Soon."

I marveled at how he could say such outrageously presumptuous things without sounding the least bit arrogant. He spoke with a gentle tone, his thumb rubbing over my chin, his cheeks dimpled with an adorable little smile.

Sweet and wicked. Forward and patient. He was a contradiction, yet the disparities made sense in the context of Aidan.

Or maybe lust had warped my mind.

He flopped onto the sofa beside me, relaxed into the cushions, and linked his hands behind his head. "Your turn."

"My what?"

He propped his feet on the table, ankles crossed. "Your turn to undress."

Speechless, my jaw agape, I managed only a croaking noise.

"I showed you mine," he said, raking his gaze over my clothed body, "so show me yours. I can tell you want to."

The notion of standing nude before Aidan while he devoured me with his gaze made my skin tighten and my pulse accelerate. But I couldn't. I mean, really. Strip for a man I barely knew? A thrill raced through me, awakening every hair on my body. God, but I wanted to do it.

I pulled my knees up and gripped them. "I'm not stripping for you."

Aidan covered one of my hands with his. "It's all right. One day you will. One day very soon. I can wait until you're ready, because once you show me everything, I'll know you're ready for the pleasure I can and will give you." He lifted his hand, brushing the backs of his fingers over my cheek. "And then I'll be inside you, stoking that fire I see burning in you right now, driving you toward an ecstasy that will leave you spent and satisfied beyond your wildest dreams."

I bit down on my tongue to keep from licking my lips. "You're awfully certain you'll rock my world."

"Aye," he said, his expression sober. "Because I will. Because I'll make sure of it. Nothing matters more than ensuring you feel all the pleasure you deserve."

I couldn't look away from his earnest face. He meant it. My pleasure was his top priority. For a man to care this much about satisfying me, to be willing to wait as long as it took for me to be ready, he must feel more than raw lust. He had to...care.

But he lived in another country. Even if he stayed for a month, eventually he'd go home, and I couldn't move to another country even if he asked me. Falling for him was out of the question.

I considered the mound of his erection contained inside his jeans. My pulse picked up speed as I once again wondered what it might be like to lay hands on his engorged penis—or to close my lips around its girth. A blush sizzled on my cheeks.

"You're thinking about it," he said. "About sex. With me."

Shit. How did he know?

"Maybe I am," I said. "Doesn't mean I'll do anything about it."

"Take your time, I'll wait. Unless you're wanting me to go home."

"I don't want that. Having you here is...nice."

He kissed my temple. "Being here is nice."

Yes, and sitting here with him was very, very nice. I shouldn't feel so relaxed and comfortable around him, but I did. He made it easy.

I cleared my throat, straightening my legs to rest my feet on the coffee table. "Would you like to play a board game? The owners left some games behind."

He made a pained face.

"What?" I asked. "If you don't like board games, just say so."

"I like them." He ran a hand over his mouth. "Erica and Lachlan played Monopoly the day after they met. I know you don't like me to repeat things they did together."

"Right. No board games."

Aidan glanced out the windows.

Misty boinged up and flew past the sliding glass doors in midair. She landed and took off across the yard toward Mandy. They collided and rolled, Misty underneath her smaller sister, both baring their teeth in mock combat.

"Let's go outside," Aidan said. "Get fresh air and play with the puppies."

"Sure."

He gave me a sly look. "Maybe you'll roll around on the grass with me. We can take turns being on top."

"Cooking for me is hot, but not quite enough to make me ruin my clothes with grass stains."

"Donnae worry." He stood and offered me his hand, smiling. "My sister Fiona taught me the secret to removing any stain."

I took his hand. He helped me up, then we headed for the sliding doors hand in hand. The way any normal couple might. We weren't normal. We weren't even a couple.

But I was slipping down that slope a little further each day, the one that ended at the feet of Aidan MacTaggart.

Chapter Twelve

Darkness enveloped me as I lay beneath the covers, trying to sleep but too wired to get there. The puppies had stayed in the living room with Aidan, meaning I had nothing to distract me from reliving the day's events. Aidan had given me incredible pleasure. I'd invited him to stay with me. Somehow, having Aidan around made me forget about Rade and the divorce and everything else in the entire world. I had no choice but to resist my lust for Aidan.

Resist hard. Resist like crazy.

I wriggled under the covers, unable to get comfortable, and flopped onto my back.

Aidan had been so sweet today, playing with the puppies, making me lunch and dinner, even washing the dishes. His kindness made me uneasy, because resisting liking him proved harder than resisting his seduction.

Oh, but that orgasm. He'd made me want more—not simply another climax, but more of him. I couldn't stop thinking about him in the bathroom after he'd pleasured me. Unzipping his jeans. Taking his rigid, engorged cock in his hand. Stroking and stroking and stroking. Head thrown back, mouth wide, eyes closed as the ecstasy overtook him.

Hot as that was—and God, was it hot—another fantasy kept tormenting me. Aidan had taken a shower earlier and emerged from the bathroom in jaw-dropping style. Shirtless. Wet. His hair shimmering, droplets of water dripping onto his shoulders and rolling down his sculpted chest. If I hadn't vowed never to sleep with him, I might've lapped up every bead of water and dragged my tongue up the rivulets, laving that smooth skin and tickling each tiny hair with my lips. He would've sucked in a breath, groaned, thrust his hand into my hair. I could've moved lower as I kissed my way down to his waistband, popped the button of his jeans with my teeth, took hold of the fabric and yanked it down to bare his rigid—

Gah. I threw my hands up and let them drop back onto the bed, bouncing a little. I was getting way too turned on thinking about Aidan.

I shoved off the covers and the rush of cooler air on my sensitized skin made my body ache in every naughty way imaginable, plus a few I'd never known before. My satin nightie billowed, and as it settled back down, it teased my taut nipples.

Aidan. Naked. Wet. Groaning while I tasted every inch of his skin.

I shifted position, which only rubbed the slickness drenching my sex onto my thighs.

His hot mouth on my breast. His strong hands on my ass.

My clit pulsed, my nipples shot harder.

I lifted my head to glance around the darkened room. The puppies had stayed in the living room where Aidan was staying up late to chat with his sister Jamie. I'd shut the bedroom door. Alone in my room, I could surrender to the need. It would hardly be the first time I'd done it since Aidan barreled into my life.

Sliding a hand down my body, I brushed the satin fabric of my nightie over my skin, skimmed my fingers over my breast and across my nipple. A little shock of need jolted through me. I envisioned Aidan on all fours above me, lust in his eyes. As I teased my nipple with my thumb and forefinger, I imagined him taking the nipple in his mouth, that agile tongue tormenting my flesh. I stifled a moan.

My hand moved lower as if an outside force commanded it. Across my belly it skated, down over my mound. I dipped one finger inside my folds to find the hard nub of my clit.

One of these nights, maybe you'll show me how you touch yourself.

A husky breath burst out of me. My skin tightened and tingled, every hair erect, every nerve enlivened with anticipation.

I wanted Aidan to watch. I wanted him to see.

And heaven help me, I wanted to come under his molten gaze.

Squirming, I slapped my hands on the mattress and drummed my fingers. I could walk out there and issue my invitation, but the idea of what I was about to do had me so excited I might come just from the sensation of my own thighs rubbing together as I walked, rubbing my swollen sex.

I grabbed my phone from the bedside table, dialing Aidan's number.

He answered on the third ring with a drowsy hello.

"Were you asleep?" I said. "Didn't mean to wake you."

"Not sleeping." He yawned. "Just a wee bit tired after Skyping with Jamie. She's got more energy than your puppies."

One hand on my tummy, I crooked my fingers, anxiety trickling through me. Could I really do this?

"Well," I said, "I should let you get some rest."

Noises indicated he was changing position. "Ahmno sleepy. Why are you calling me when you're down the hall?"

Because I'm a big old chicken. "I, uh...wondered if you'd like to..."

Why couldn't I finish a damn sentence? After our conversation about self-pleasuring, making a lewd invitation shouldn't have tied me up in knots.

"Spit it out," he said. "Unless you want me to come in there and torture it out of you."

My mind spun with visions of all the erotic ways he might torture me with pleasure.

I took a breath, cleared my throat, and said, "Remember that thing you wanted to see?"

"Thing? Are you meaning the quilt on your bed? Or maybe the window drapes."

Was that humor in his voice? Was he teasing me because he knew what I wanted to ask him? I clutched my nightie in one fist. "You said maybe one evening I'd let you watch. How about tonight?"

He choked and sputtered. "Do ye mean—"

"I want you to watch me masturbate."

Silence, interrupted only by the susurrations of his heavy breathing.

My voice low and throaty, I said, "If you're not interested anymore..."

"Ahm interested," he rasped. "When?"

"Now."

Click. The call ended amid the thumping of footfalls in the hallway. The pitter-patter of puppy feet followed in the wake of Aidan's steps.

He flung the door open.

Mandy and Misty careened toward the opening.

Aidan clapped the door shut, muttering, "Sorry, wee lassies."

Breathing hard, hair mussed, he stood near the door, his gaze glued to me. His T-shirt hung loose, the button of his jeans was unhooked.

I crooked a finger. "You can't see anything from way over there."

Puppies whined and pawed at the door.

Aidan's bare feet made hardly a sound on the wood floor as he moseyed to the bed and climbed over my legs to lie down at a diagonal to me with his head near my hip. He braced his head on one palm.

"Should I take my nightie off?" I asked.

"Not this time." He stretched his free arm down to rest one fingertip on my ankle, then glided it up the inside of my leg, past my knee, halfway up my thigh. "I like a bit of mystery."

With that one finger, he pushed the hem of my nightie down to cover me more. His hooded gaze found mine.

Desire wound tight inside me, but a thread of anxiety whipped around it. What the hell was I doing? Letting him touch me had been wild and insane. Inviting him to watch me masturbate, that was a whole new level of crazy. Possibly depraved. A sign of slipping morals, for sure.

I had married a man I didn't love, who now held onto me in spite of his promise to let me go. Didn't I deserve something for myself, something wonderful and wild, something that belonged to me because the choice was mine and mine alone?

"Second thoughts?" Aidan asked, studying my face.

"No." It wasn't cheating, I reminded myself. I'd filed for divorce, and Rade and I had agreed from the start to live separate lives. I reached out to skate my fingers over Aidan's cheek. "I want to do this, but I've never done anything like it before."

"Take your time, I've got all night. And if you change your mind, you can stop anytime. I willnae complain."

His patience and sweetness tugged at my heart but also fired up my libido. I wanted him more than I'd ever dreamed I could want a man. I wouldn't give him what he wanted most—a wife and children—and so I couldn't give him all of me. Not yet. Maybe...I swallowed, knowing that for tonight this was what I could give him.

I spread my hands over my throat, running them down to my collarbone, pausing there to soak in the lust darkening Aidan's eyes and expression. He pressed his lips together, then flicked his tongue out to dampen them. I glided my hands lower until they covered my breasts. The delicate wisp of satin on my skin made me sigh out an uneven breath. His gaze on me, his parted lips, it emboldened me to go on, to go further, cupping my breasts in my hands and flicking my thumbs over the hard nipples while I kneaded my flesh.

Aidan stared at my hands, the way they massaged my breasts. His voice rough and low, he said, "I want to be doing that to you. I want my mouth on you, right where your thumbs are."

His assertion hit me like he'd done exactly that, and I pinched my nipples through the satin, letting out a little moan and rocking my hips. With his gaze pinned to my hands, tracking wherever they moved, I skimmed them down over my belly with deliberate slowness, relishing the feel of smooth, cool fabric on my skin and the sight of him devouring my every movement. My hands breezed over my hips and down onto my thighs. I let one palm stay there, flat on my left thigh, and swept the other up and under the nightie's hem. My fingers grazed my mound. My neck arched, and my head tilted back as my eyes fluttered shut.

"No," he all but growled, "donnae close your eyes. Please, Calli, look at me while you do this."

I opened my eyes and our gazes locked onto each other, bound by an invisible force, a power borne of lust and something deeper, something I couldn't acknowledge even if I'd wanted to, something forbidden—in my world. I didn't care if this was wrong. Didn't care if I should feel guilty. In this moment, connected to him by shared need, I gave in to my deepest, darkest desires.

My fingers slipped between my folds where I was slick and hot and achy. Caught by Aidan's eyes, I couldn't look away from him as I stroked my fingers up and down, two fingers on either side of my cleft, caressing my folds. My clitoris throbbed, begging for attention. As Aidan's mouth fell open and his heavy breaths huffed out of him, I rubbed harder and faster, skirting around my clit, knowing once I touched that nub I'd lose it. Pleasure cascaded through me, intensifying with each stroke of my fingers, heightened by the attention of the wicked Scot lying beside me.

His eyes darted, his gaze switching to my groin, to where my fingers worked my inflamed flesh. My hips gyrated, and my legs moved in restless rhythm with my fingers. He tore his focus away from my loins to fixate on my face again, and his was a look of such desperate longing I couldn't deny him what he clearly wanted more than anything in this moment.

"Watch me touch myself," I said. "Please. I'll keep my eyes open and watch your face."

He exhaled a heavy breath, nodding, and leveled his gaze on my hand moving beneath the nightie.

With my other hand, I eased the fabric higher, revealing a glimpse of my sex, even as I whisked my fingers over my flesh, my breaths shortening into sharp gasps.

Aidan sucked in a long, deep breath. Eyes almost closed, he smiled with intense satisfaction. "You smell like everything I've ever wanted."

Mindless, I scraped my middle finger up my cleft and onto my clit, rubbing the rigid nub with ruthless strength and speed, frantic to achieve release. It roared through me and my back bowed up off the bed, but I kept stroking hard and fast, wringing out wave after wave of pleasure. When I collapsed in a heap, my hands slack on my thighs, Aidan was staring at me with slitted eyes, his mouth tight.

"How was it?" He ground out the words.

"Good," I said, between heavy breaths. "But nowhere near as good as when you touch me."

Ducking his head, he shifted his hips in an uncomfortable movement and exhaled a shaky breath. "Excuse me."

He scrambled off the bed, staggering toward the doorway.

"Wait," I said, and he hesitated with his hand on the knob. From the way he was almost limping, favoring his crotch, I had a suspicion about his need to flee. "Are you running away to relieve your needs in the bathroom? Like you did this morning?"

Body rigid, he growled out a frustrated breath. "Aye."

"You don't have to leave the room." I pushed up into a semi-sitting position, my legs outstretched and my hands on the bed, holding me up. "I want to watch."

"No you don't," he said, tipping his head from one side to the other, shoulders bunching. "Ye donnae want to see my—"

"Come on, I've seen your penis before."

He growled again, letting his head fall back. "Not that. Ye donnae want to see my—to see me—what happens when I—"

"When you come? I can handle seeing you ejaculate."

"Cannae control it." He shoved a hand through his hair, clenching his fingers and mussing his hair. "After watching you…Never been this hard before."

"It's okay." I rose onto my knees, still flushed all over from my orgasm. "Let me see you pleasure yourself, Aidan. It's only fair, since I let you see me."

He twisted his head around to fix his surprised gaze on me. "Are ye sure?"

I nodded, beckoning him with one hand.

With halting steps, he reached the bed.

Smiling, I patted the mattress in front of me.

Aidan settled onto the bed. His erection bulged large and hard inside his jeans, the reddened tip peeking out where the button was undone.

I took hold of the zipper and eased it downward.

Rather than stopping me, he hauled in a deep breath and let it out slowly, his eyes fluttering shut. His rigid cock popped free, bouncing in the air.

"Would you like me to…" I trailed off, uncertain of speaking the words. I burned to enact my fantasies from earlier today, when I'd watched him shuck his clothes and I'd gaped at his erection with a deep, carnal hunger growing inside me. What would it feel like to take his cock in my mouth? What would he taste like? I wanted to give him pleasure so much my chest grew heavy, burdened by the weight of my desires.

"Aye," he said, grinning at me, eyes sparkling, "I'd love you to do that. But not this time. We can save that for after we fuck."

"If we do."

"When," he corrected, eyes crinkling with humor.

"Still arrogantly certain, eh?" I sat back on my heels. A brazen impulse took hold of me and I thrust out a hand to grasp the base of his erection. "Sure you don't want some help?"

His grin broadened for only a second before my firm grip on his shaft made him scrunch up his face.

"Ahhh..." He clenched the sheets as I dragged my hand up his erection. "Calli..."

A drop of liquid oozed out of the head of his penis. I bent over his lap to roll my tongue over his rosy tip. The salty yet earthy flavor of him suffused my mouth.

"You win," he hissed. "Have your bloody way with me. But do it quick, I may not last long."

"If I do something wrong, you can tell me."

"Willnae do it wrong. Follow your instincts and do it quick."

I hopped onto the floor to kneel between his legs and closed my mouth around the head of his cock. Since I'd never done this before, I relied on instinct and the encouragement of his noises to guide me. I drew his thick, sleek shaft into my mouth in one long thrust. He gasped, his entire body as stiff as his erection. With my tongue, I sucked and lapped at his flesh while I withdrew my mouth, only to swallow him once more. One of his hands dived into my hair to cup the back of my head, urging me on with gentle pressure. I consumed him again and again, my mouth ravenous for him, desire surging inside me again with a new kind of need. A need to give him the kind of pleasure he'd given me. To watch him come apart while I milked his cock with my mouth and tongue.

His hips bucked each time I plunged his shaft into my mouth. He gasped, grunted, his face scrunched and tight with a pain that stemmed from the frenzied need to come.

With my hand around the base of his shaft, I pumped in concert with the thrusts of my mouth, licking and suckling as if I'd die without the taste of him on my tongue.

A throaty shout erupted from him as his body convulsed and he exploded in my mouth.

"Mm," I said, sitting back and smiling. "You taste good."

He gaped at me, panting, seeming shocked by my statement. "It's not fair. I haven't tasted you yet."

"Oh, you'll get around to it."

I knew with total certainty he would. My Scotsman was stubborn and committed to toppling each of my rules one by one. I could sleep with him. Breaking my first rule had no effect on my ability to uphold the other two. After what I'd just done for him and to him, I no longer had the luxury of denying how much I wanted him—how much I wanted his body.

Casual sex. Sure, I could do that.

No, I couldn't. Could I?

Chapter Thirteen

A little while later, after Aidan had cleaned up in the bathroom, we lay on the bed together on our sides so we could face each other. I was tucked under the covers in my nightie while he lay on top of the blanket with all his clothes on. I still couldn't believe what I'd done. Letting him watch me masturbate, that was outrageous enough. But pleasuring him…I'd enjoyed it way too much.

I couldn't believe I'd done that. Me. I'd never touched a man's penis before, much less taken one in my mouth. His reactions, the expression on his face, it had all spurred me on and eradicated my inhibitions. I loved making him lose control, the way he made me lose it. Only fair I get my turn.

Still…What we'd done, what I'd done, skirted way too close to a line I'd sworn to him I wouldn't cross. Was I prepared for the consequences if I shattered my first rule? I already liked him. Could I stop this from turning into more than sex?

Anxious to avoid thinking about the ramifications of my actions, I dived into what seemed like a safer subject. Nestling into the covers, I asked, "What are your brothers like?"

"I've told you Lachlan used to be uptight before Erica. He's still overbearing, but a lot more fun than he used to be. Rory's got a caber up his erse, but women seem to like him." Aidan propped his head up on one hand. "Of course, Lachlan and Rory both used to be more like me."

"Caber up his erse?"

"A caber's a bloody great wooden pole. Scotsmen like to chuck them around to show how manly they are. Not me, but others like Lachlan and Rory. And an erse is…" With one hand, he reached behind me to palm one buttock. "An erse."

"More Scottish-isms. I'm learning a new language." I punched my pillow to get it situated better under my head. "You said your brothers used to be like you. What happened?"

"Lachlan married a right bitch." Aidan screwed up his mouth. "Suppose I shouldn't say it, but she wasn't a nice person. Don't know what she did to Lachlan, but he wound up terrified to love anyone else. When he met Erica, he offered her a one-month fling but vowed he'd never love her and couldn't offer anything more substantial. He couldn't help it, though, he fell for her."

"What about Rory?"

Aidan rolled his eyes heavenward, then back to my face. "Ah, Rory. He married three different women who each shoved that caber a bit further up his erse. One left him because he was too boring, being a solicitor and all. The second cheated on him several times. And then there was the third, who left him for another woman."

"Ouch."

"It's no bloody wonder he has no interest in dating anymore." Aidan rubbed his chin thoughtfully. "He does run off on so-called business trips on occasion, though. When he comes back, he's much more cheerful—for a time, at least. Makes me wonder if he's off having one-night stands, to satisfy his needs without risking another disastrous relationship."

"He can't be happy with that lifestyle."

"Clearly not, or he wouldn't have the caber up his erse." Aidan smiled ruefully. "The man needs a good woman to shag some sense into him."

"An American of his own?"

He hooked a finger under my chin and brushed a kiss over my lips. "Couldnae hurt, eh?"

"Don't get any ideas. I'm not your key to happiness."

"How do you know?"

"Take my word for it." I slid a hand over his chest, relishing the solidity of him. "Not sure I'd want to meet Rory if he's that much of a jerk."

"He's not a jerk," Aidan said. "Sometimes he's the old Rory again, smiling and joking, like at Lachlan's wedding. He helps people with their legal problems even if they can't pay him and he donates his money and his time to worthy local causes."

"All right, he sounds like a good guy in spite of the caber." I gave him a teasing smile. "What about your sisters? How do they feel about marriage?"

"Not sure about Fiona and Catriona. They don't talk about it. But Jamie..." He rolled his eyes heavenward once more, shaking his head. "Jamie wants to fall in love at every opportunity until she finally meets her Prince

Charming. Last night, she announced she plans to come to America, stay at Erica's house in Chicago, and look for an American man."

"She's younger than you, right?" When he nodded, I frowned. "Not sure a young woman from another country should be alone in Chicago, especially if she's hunting for a man."

"I agree," he said, "which is why I tried to talk her out of it. She's determined, though, and she'll empty her bank account to pay for the trip. Since she's between jobs, that doesn't seem like a wise choice."

"What will you do about her?" I asked.

"Called Lachlan last night. He's going to give it one more go at convincing her this is a bad idea."

"If he fails?"

Aidan shrugged one shoulder. "Our only idea is I go back to Chicago to keep an eye on her."

The thought of Aidan leaving made me a little queasy. There had to be another way, something that wouldn't require him to leave. For some reason, I couldn't stomach the idea. Not yet.

"What if," I said cautiously, "you didn't have to go away? What if your sister could come here?"

"Here?" His forehead wrinkled. "There are no rooms available in this area."

"I know, but..." I hesitated, feeling a bizarre mixture of excitement and trepidation at what I was about to propose. "Jamie could stay *here* here, in this house. In the guest room."

Aidan watched me for a moment, confusion warring with something like desire on his face. "If she's in the guest room, where would I be?"

"On the sofa."

His lips puckered, he nodded slowly. "Ah, of course. The sofa."

"Were you hoping I'd invite you to sleep in my bedroom?" I nudged him with my knee. "We're not there yet."

He looked dejected, but only for a couple seconds. Then his sly smile returned. "Not yet? You're implying we may get there."

"Don't read too much into everything I say." I rolled onto my back, hands clasped over my belly. Why had I said not yet? I'd meant to say never, but that's not what had come out of my mouth. "I'm trying to keep your sister from getting into trouble."

"And I appreciate it." He sidled closer, his head inches from mine, still braced on one hand. "Tell me, why do you care so much how my family feels about marriage?"

"I suffer from an insatiable and inappropriate curiosity."

"Hmm." He studied me with keen interest, his eyes narrowed. "You say you won't fall in love with me, but you can't marry me. One is a choice, the other implies an impenetrable barrier. Eventually, you will be divorced, which means you could marry me."

"Yes, I suppose I could." I hesitated, unsure how much to say. "But you're better off without me. I'm bad news."

He made an irritated noise. "Stop telling me you're bad. I don't believe it and I never will."

"Stop being so stubborn. Why can't you accept my decision?"

"Because it's clear that's not what you want. I wouldn't be here if it was." He laid a hand on my arm. "Why don't you want to care for me? Am I so frightening?"

"No, of course not. I feel safe with you."

"Donnae understand. Is it your husband who scares you?"

I shut my eyes, covering my face with my hands, letting them slide back down to rest on my chest. My gaze on the ceiling, I said, "Not him. It's way too soon for me to share my deepest fears with you."

Silence. Deep and long and nerve-wracking.

When I could no longer take the silence, I peeked sideways at him.

He watched me, impassive, reminding me of my brother whenever he got fed up with me for not answering a question. I didn't like that look from Aidan. I wanted him to smile or reassure me or…something. My skin crawled from an unsettling realization that I yearned to tell him everything, because he listened and cared and seemed to understand me better than he had a right to, considering how short a time we'd known each other. I shouldn't say more.

Five days. That was the extent of our acquaintance. Five days and counting.

"You're exhausted," he said, caressing my arm with feathery sweeps of his fingers over my skin. "Sleep now, worry later."

Too tired to argue, I curled up against him with my face on his chest. As I drifted off to sleep ensconced in his warmth and his strong but yielding body, I wondered about my actions so far. I vowed to resist him, but at every turn, I surrendered without hesitation. A small but strengthening voice inside me asked why I was fighting my desires. We were consenting adults. I had no reason to avoid enjoying the full benefits of Aidan's company. Maybe…

All thoughts spiraled away from me, banished by the blissful emptiness of sleep.

Chapter Fourteen

The next evening while Aidan was in the shower, I flopped onto the sofa and called Tara. She'd left a message on my phone earlier. I hadn't heard it ringing because I'd forgotten to take it outside with me, too distracted by Aidan and my conflicting desires where he was concerned. Tara's phone rang five times before she answered with a breathless, "Hi, cuz. What's up?"

"You called me earlier." I noted the way she was breathing hard and winced. "Oh God, please tell me I didn't interrupt you and Blake, uh, enjoying wedded bliss."

"What?" After half a second of silence, she laughed. "No, nothing like that. We're on the beach and you interrupted us having a splash fight. This is our last day in Hawaii and we plan on getting totally silly in every way possible."

"Sounds like a plan. How's paradise?"

"Awesome. Love the sun and sand, but it turns out I suck at surfing." Her voice took on the same knowing tone she'd adopted at the wedding reception. "Have you seen Aidan lately?"

"Yes." I couldn't bring myself to lie to her about this. I had enough guilt over keeping other secrets from her. "He's, um…staying with me."

"He moved in?" She almost shouted the words. "Calli Bethany Douglas, are you shacked up with a stranger?"

I held the phone away from my ear until she'd finished. "No, he's staying in the guest room. His motel room got a burst pipe and there wasn't anywhere else for him to go."

"Mm-hm. Naturally, you told him 'hey, sleep naked in the room right next to mine.' Makes perfect sense."

"He—I—"

Tara snickered. "Take it easy. I'm not judging, just surprised. You've been kind of a hermit for a long time."

"Aidan's nice and I like spending time with him."

"Spending time?" Her voice dropped to a conspiratorial whisper. "Is that code for doing the bump and grind?"

"No, you dirty-minded newlywed. I'm not having sex with him." I twirled a lock of hair around my finger, a sliver of guilt piercing me. "Not exactly."

"Oooh," she said, and I could almost hear her rubbing her hands together, "this sounds juicy."

"Let's just say he's a very tempting guy."

"Maybe he's your one guy out of billions."

"If you're implying I'm falling for him, forget it. I don't believe in love at first sight." Or love in six days.

The distinctive rushing of waves created a lulling background to our call. I pictured my little cousin on the beach in a cute little bikini, soaking up the sunshine amid the tropical glory of Hawaii. Down the hallway, the sound of the shower stopped. My image of Tara transformed into a vision of Aidan on a tropical beach, naked, sprawled beside me on the warm sand as he reached out to caress my nude body.

I knew firsthand what he looked like in the buff.

"Are you there?" Tara asked. "Did the hottie Scottie show up or something? I don't think you heard me at all."

"No, sorry, I zoned out for a minute." I craned my neck backward, straining to see down the hallway. No Aidan yet. I couldn't quite glimpse the bathroom door. Giving up on my spying, I told Tara, "Afraid you'll have to repeat whatever you said."

"I said I know you were hot for him at first sight. Maybe it's not love yet, but you must like him. Otherwise, you'd never let him stay in your house."

"Like him? Yeah, I do. It's kind of terrifying."

"When was the last time you had a date?"

I'd tried a few times over the years. But how could I date anyone when I had a husband? Marriage of convenience, sure, but still a marriage. If things got serious with a guy, I'd have to explain my situation. My criminal situation. Unwilling to involve anyone else in my crime, I'd given up on dating.

Until Aidan.

"Well," I said, "I've had quite a few dates this week."

"You and Aidan? Woo-hoo! I'm so happy for you."

"Please don't start planning our wedding." I winced, because only I knew I couldn't marry him or anyone right now. "This may not go anywhere. But yes, I like him and we're—well, I guess we're dating."

The bathroom door opened with a click.

"I have to go," I told Tara. "Have a wonderful rest of your honeymoon and give Blake a hug for me."

"Will do." In a hushed voice, she added, "Give Aidan a kiss for me."

She hung up before I could respond. Give Aidan a kiss? She didn't have to tell me to do that. I lusted for his mouth every second of every day. That and other parts of his anatomy.

Aidan sauntered into the living room, around the sofa, and lowered his gorgeous bod onto the sofa beside me. His hair was wet but loose, the waves curling around his face. Beads of moisture drizzled down his temples.

Why did he have to look so good wet? Or dry. In clothes, out of clothes, in the daytime, at night, anytime and anywhere.

He stretched an arm across the sofa's back. His fingertips grazed my shoulder. "Thought I heard voices."

"Talking to my cousin on the phone."

"How is the wee Tara?"

"Living it up on her Hawaiian honeymoon." For once, I paused to think about what I might say next, instead of blurting out silly things. I decided what the hell. "Tara asked me to give you a kiss for her."

His mouth tightened and curved upward in a half-repressed smile, his eyes sparkled in the low light. "Did she now."

"Mm-hm." I slanted toward him, our mouths almost touching. "Can't let my cousin down, can I?"

He shook his head, those beautiful eyes trained on mine.

I touched my lips to his in a chaste kiss. "That was for Tara. The next one's from me."

Gazing into his slitted eyes, I moistened my lips with two long, slow passes of my tongue. His lips parted, his breathing grew labored. Excitement sizzled over my skin and settled between my thighs, warm and wet and wanting. I laid a hand on his chest and urged him back into the sofa, then I climbed astride him and planted a hand on the sofa's back at either side of his head. He let his head fall back onto the cushions.

Leaning in, I hovered my mouth so close to his our breaths mingled. "I really want to kiss you, but I'm afraid things might get out of hand."

"Then maybe you shouldn't have climbed on top of me."

"Fair point. But I'm already here."

He settled his hands on my hips. "I promise not to take any liberties. Unless you beg me to."

"Beg?" I flicked my tongue out to tease his lower lip. "Not going to happen."

"What if I beg?"

Aidan begging? If he did that, I'd lose all my inhibitions for sure.

Like I hadn't already.

"Please," he said, his voice low and rumbly, "kiss me, ahm begging ye."

Excitement whirled through me in a weightless sensation of floating outside my body and I burned to kiss him, but a cool thread of trepidation wound through me as well, caught up in the head-spinning need. I'd lost my mind with this man too many times. Right here, right now, I'd take back control.

I brushed my lips over his, my skin tightening from the softest taste of him. I nipped and licked at his lips, teasing and tempting us both, hungry for more but unwilling to give in to my desires completely, no matter how much my body craved him. His palms coasted up my back to splay over my shoulder blades. The feel of his hands, gentle and yet strong, weakened my will. But his murmured "please" undid me.

Sinking deeper into his lap, my sex rubbing against his cock through our clothes, I sealed my mouth over his, our parted lips fused as our tongues thrust deep, tangling and questing, hot and silken. The sheer ecstasy of the kiss, of his velvety tongue and the earthy flavor of him, spiked an electric need straight down from my mouth to my clitoris. He explored my mouth with an ardor that stole my breath, yet his tongue moved with surprising languor, as if he took intense pleasure in sampling every inch of me. His hands urged me snugger against him, the hardness of his erection trapped between us. My rigid nipples scraped across his chest as I writhed on his lap, desperate for more, teetering on the edge of succumbing to the need.

His phone rang and vibrated inside his jeans pocket.

We both froze, our lips still pressed to each other. I peeled my eyelids open first, watching as his lids fluttered apart and his gaze met mine. I must've looked as dazed as he did. I felt it, for sure, my mind floating on a warm, feathery cloud.

The phone rang and vibrated again.

Aidan fumbled to get the phone out of his pocket without dumping me off his lap. He kept one hand on my hip while he answered the call with a gruff hello.

"Jamie?" he said, brows dipping low over the bridge of his nose. The tinny sound of an indistinct voice emanated from his phone and his brows rose as his eyes widened the tiniest bit. "She what? Called you?"

Squatting on his lap, I had no choice but to overhear his end of the conversation. I glanced around, shifting my hands here and there, unsure what to do with them. At last, I settled on resting them on my thighs. I hated keeping secrets from him and knowing he kept at least one from me, though I couldn't explain why. He was a stranger I'd known for six days.

Yet he felt like more than that.

"Ignore her," Aidan told Jamie. "I'll speak to Seona myself."

His gaze fell on me and he pulled in a long breath. Those blue eyes darkened and narrowed, focused on my lips.

"Don't worry," he said into the phone. "I will handle it, but I have to go now."

The other voice sounded again, and Aidan bid the caller goodbye.

He dropped the phone on the cushion beside him, reaching for me.

Just as his hands gripped my lower back and his mouth surged toward mine, I held up a hand between our lips. "Was that your sister?"

"Aye."

"Is everything okay? You seemed upset."

His hands raced up my back to pull me closer, my hand the only barrier preventing him from claiming my mouth. "I'll be fine as soon as I'm kissing you again."

I hurled my body to the side, tumbling off his lap and righting myself to sit beside him, my body turned toward him. "I think we need to share a little bit of our secrets. Not knowing and not sharing is probably giving me an ulcer."

He drew his head back, eying me with a strange expression. "You want to tell me your secret?"

"Part of it. The only part I can."

"If you're doing this because you want to know mine, there's no need. I'll tell you anyway."

My head braced with one arm on the sofa, I assured him, "That's not why I'm suggesting this. I want to explain what I can to you, but don't ask me why. I have no answer for that one."

"All right." He turned partway toward me, wriggling a little to get settled. "I'll start. Ask me whatever you like."

"Who is Seona? Is she the one who keeps calling you?"

"Yes." He looked down at his lap. "Seona Ross is a former girlfriend, if you can call it that. We dated for a few months, but it was never serious, nothing more than a pleasant distraction. You might call it a casual sort of arrangement. We got on well." He flattened his lips. "Until the accident."

The tension evidenced on his face tugged at my heart in ways I didn't dare examine. I sneaked a hand out to touch his knee. He aimed a grateful smile at me before turning his gaze down again.

"Six months ago, Seona was seriously injured and spent a long time in the hospital and in rehabilitation. I haven't seen her in about six months. No contact at all. She was angry with me because she bl—" He scrubbed a hand over his face and lifted his gaze to me. "She told me to stay away from her and I did. Had no wish to fash her when she was unwell."

"Makes sense."

"Somehow, she heard I'd come to America and started calling me to ask for money. Ask. No, she's demanding it."

I lighted a hand on his thigh. "Why would she demand money from you?"

"She's very bitter. And maybe she has a point about me owing her, but I donnae have money to give her."

"Why would you owe her?" When he switched his attention to the back-yard view, I slumped into the sofa and said, "You don't have to tell me. I'm not going to tell you my whole story either."

He plowed both hands into his hair. "Seona keeps calling me and now she's called my sister Jamie to enlist her help. Jamie told her no."

"What will you do?"

He sighed, his shoulders flagging. "Donnae know."

"I'm sorry, Aidan." I scooted closer, caressing his cheek. "You don't have to talk about it anymore. I think it's my turn, anyway."

Despite the questions bouncing around in my brain—questions about how Seona was injured, why she would tell Aidan to stay away from her, why he seemed to feel guilty where she was concerned—I kept my curiosity in check. He had no obligation to tell me everything, particularly when I couldn't tell him everything about me.

"You wanted to know why I married a man I never loved."

Aidan nodded. "If you want to tell me. Don't feel you have to because I told you about Seona."

"It's okay. I want to tell you." I gave him a quick kiss. "Though it's very sweet of you to give me an out."

He took both my hands in one of his, holding them to his chest. "What-ever you feel like sharing, I'm listening. You can tell me anything and I will keep your secrets, you have my word."

My heart did a silly flippy-floppy thing. I swallowed against a constriction in my throat. "I met Rade in college. He's from Croatia and came here on a student visa. Though he was two years ahead of me, we became friends and spent a lot of time together—but just as friends. His parents had died when he was eight and he inherited a real fortune. I don't know exactly how much, but it would definitely qualify as stinking rich."

The warmth of Aidan's hand around both of mine anchored me to the present as my thoughts traveled back in time. My stomach hurt at the awareness of what I intended to say next. I'd avoided thinking about it for so long, but somehow, this man made me want to confide.

"Five years ago," I began, "my parents died in a car accident. My brother Gavin didn't handle it well. He'd left the Marines eight months earlier, after a tour in Afghanistan, and he wasn't completely readjusted to civilian life yet. He's the toughest guy I know, but he basically fell apart after our parents died and I had to handle everything. There were bills and debts neither of us had known about because our parents had kept their financial problems a secret. No life insurance, they'd stopped making payments on it. No savings. Almost nothing in their checking account. It was a horrible time, discovering how much they'd kept from us and we couldn't even ask them for an explanation."

Aidan clasped my hands in both of his now, lifting one of mine to place a soft kiss on the back of my hand.

The start of tears burned in my eyes and my throat ached. I forced the words out. "Rade was very kind during those first weeks after the accident. Two months later, he asked me—" How could I explain without mentioning the fraudulent aspect of our marriage? I did the best I could. "He asked me to marry him, for reasons I can't explain. I agreed, not because I wanted to be married to him but because I owed him a lot more than I can tell you."

"You don't have to say any more, if you don't want to."

"Thank you." The tears welled up more, about to spill over onto my cheeks. I sniffled and tried to wrest my hand free of his to swipe at my eyes.

He released my hands to wipe away the tears with his thumbs.

"Rade saved me, in a way," I said. "My life was in shambles, and he stepped in to pay bills I couldn't, helped me stay in school to finish my degree and go on to grad school. He gave me a place to stay too, when I couldn't afford my apartment anymore. When he asked me for a favor, I couldn't say no."

"A favor?" Aidan squinted, studying me. "Marriage isn't a favor."

"Please, Aidan, I can't tell you anything more."

Lips compressed, he watched me for a few seconds. Then he exhaled a long breath and ran the backs of his fingers down my cheek. "I'm sorry. This is not my business, but I don't like the sound of your arrangement with this Rade person."

Arrangement. He couldn't know how accurate that description was.

"Thank you." I kissed his cheek. "You're a very good man, Aidan MacTaggart."

He stood and stretched, his lithe body arching. Offering me his hand, he said, "This has been a tiring evening. To bed with you, Calli."

"You sound like a medieval lord," I said, accepting his aid in getting up off the sofa.

"If I were, you'd have to obey me."

"Lucky for you, I feel like doing what you commanded. Sleep sounds wonderful right about now."

He walked me to my bedroom door, which hung halfway open. Inside, the puppies had already settled in for the night on my bed, Misty at the foot and Mandy half on my pillow.

"Sleep well," Aidan said.

"Good night."

He pressed a kiss to my lips, lingering there for a long moment. When he turned and strode into his room—*the guest room*, I reminded myself, *not his room*—I retreated into my bedroom, acutely aware something had changed between us tonight. Something important. Something irrevocable. I'd opened up to him more than I had to anyone else in a very long time.

As I shut the door, my gaze flitted to the guest room and its closed door. We still had secrets between us, but if I let him stay much longer, we'd wind up revealing all to each other. I knew it, the way I knew the sun would rise in the morning. It was inevitable.

Chapter Fifteen

The next evening, I gazed across the table at Aidan where he lounged in the armchair kitty-corner to the sofa. I sat in the sofa's corner, legs tucked under me, trying very hard not to climb onto Aidan's lap. The remains of our dinner littered the coffee table—two plates scattered with crumbs, two empty water glasses, and two sets of forks and knives. Aidan had insisted on making our meal from scratch, and damn, the man really was a genius in the kitchen.

He hooked one ankle over the opposite knee, his hands on the chair's arms. His feet were bare. Dressed in a gray T-shirt and jeans that hugged his delicious body, he looked at ease and mouthwateringly hot. Of course, he always looked that way. Hot. Nibble-worthy. Tempting beyond belief.

Aidan's gaze swiveled to me and he rubbed his lips together. "What's for dessert?"

The way he spoke those words, he might as well have said *I'm eating you for dessert.*

"Nothing," I said. "Sorry, I didn't have time for baking, what with playing referee between the puppies and every object not nailed down in this house. They're always rambunctious, but they love you so much they're insanely happy."

"The pups are adorable, but not half as adorable as you."

"You're pretty damn adorable yourself."

A devilish smile parted his lips. "I'm wicked, remember? Maybe I need to remind you of it."

How did he do that? Veer the conversation back around to sex, no matter what mundane thing we'd been discussing.

Rising, he stretched his arms into the air and arched his back, tightening muscles and pulling his shirt up just enough to reveal a glimpse of rock-hard abs. "Lachlan sent me another present."

A box had arrived by FedEx overnight delivery, addressed to Aidan care of me. He hadn't shown me its contents, only gave me a secretive smile when I asked about it.

"Thought you hated his presents," I said, failing in my attempt to not gawk at him. Even with his best features masked by jeans and a shirt, I could spy hints of sinuous limbs and all those acres of soft, hair-dusted skin I'd ogled when he'd stripped for me.

"Ah, but this one is for you," he said, ambling toward the kitchen. "I stashed it in a cabinet, behind other things."

I craned my neck to follow his movements. "Do I want to know what this gift is?"

"Something I want to share with you." Giving me a mysterious smile, he bent down to retrieve the item in question, disappearing behind the bar. When he popped up again, he held something behind his back. "Close your eyes."

"Why?"

"So suspicious," he chided with humor in his tone and in his eyes. "Trust me."

I settled back into the sofa cushions and shut my eyes.

Aidan's footsteps padded on the carpet, and within a moment, his weight settled onto the cushion beside me. "Open your eyes."

Blinking slowly, I turned my attention to the object in his hand. His fingers wrapped around a bottle of liquor filled with a golden liquid that almost glowed in the lamplight. He rotated the bottle so I could see the label. Reading it aloud, pronouncing the name carefully, I said, "Talisker single-malt Scotch whisky."

He nodded, proud of himself for this offering.

"Whisky?" I said. Scots apparently spelled it without the E before the Y. Interesting. "You know I don't drink."

"Because you've never tasted a drink you like, that's what you said." He wagged the bottle. "You'll like this. It's made on the Isle of Skye, off the western coast of the Highlands."

"I've heard of Skye, but I seriously doubt I'm going to like its whisky."

"Not just any whisky." He lifted his chin. "Scottish whisky. A single malt distilled on a mystical island where the ancients held their mysterious rituals to commune with the gods."

"How will a history lesson make me like the booze?"

He huffed. "Will you not let me tell you about the whisky? I'm trying to paint a picture for you."

"I'm sorry, really. You're creating a wonderful picture for me, but I doubt anything you say could alter my taste buds." I eyed the bottle with faux suspicion. "Are you trying to get me drunk, Mr. MacTaggart?"

"Don't need to get you drunk to have my way with you." He tipped the bottle to one side. "Will you try it once?"

I considered the bottle for a moment, absorbing the warm and smoky color of the whisky. It did look good, and this seemed oddly important to him. "Okay. One sip."

With a grateful smile, he plucked up the small glass he must've hidden with the bottle. A whisky glass, I guessed. He opened the bottle, his arm muscles tautening with the effort, and decanted the liquor into the glass, filling it with one inch of amber liquid.

He offered me the glass. "Taste the legend of Skye."

I gave him a playful smile. "You're starting to sound like a Scottish tourism brochure."

"Taste the bloody whisky."

"Yes, sir." I lifted the glass, sniffing the amber liquid. A strong, acrid scent filled my nostrils. I wrinkled my nose. "Smells like bad vinegar."

His lips tightened, his eyes went squinty. But he regained his composure in a heartbeat, his lips curling into a sensual expression. "Take a sip, let it slide down your throat, and feel the whisky penetrate your body."

I dipped my nose to sniff again.

Aidan slapped a hand over the glass, blocking my olfactory attempt. "Drink, don't smell."

"Okay, okay." I waited for him to remove his hand, then lifted the glass to my mouth. It felt cool against my lips. "Here goes."

I took a sip—and gagged.

Before I could even swallow, the whisky seared my mouth and its acrid taste invaded my senses. I gulped it down, desperate to get it out of my mouth, but the bluckiness seemed trapped on my tongue. I shoved the glass at Aidan and used my shirt to scrub my tongue as a coughing fit overtook me.

Aidan stared at me, face slack, the glass in one hand and the bottle in the other.

Recovering from the coughing, I cleared my throat several times in quick succession. My voice hoarse, I declared, "That's the most awful thing I've ever put in my mouth."

He collapsed against the sofa, facing forward. The bottle rested between his thighs, but he held the glass on his lap. His expression resembled total defeat.

"Cannae believe it," he mumbled. "This worked for Lachlan."

The words sifted into my brain, their meaning hitting me like a splash of cold water. I sat up and looked straight at him. "Was this another thing

Lachlan did with Erica?"

"Aye," he admitted miserably, rubbing his forehead. "It's how he started his seduction. She loved the whisky."

I cringed a little, experiencing a twinge of guilt for my reaction. Maybe I should've pretended to like it, or at least hidden my disgust, but I wasn't that good a liar. "Two days ago, you wouldn't play a board game with me because Lachlan and Erica did that. Why are you back to reenacting their affair?"

"Wanted to do something special, but I couldn't think of anything. Seemed like a good idea until you drank the whisky."

I laid a hand on his arm. "I was kind of obnoxious about that. Can you forgive me?"

"Aye, it's not your fault." He let his head fall back. "I'm the eejit who keeps trying to recreate my brother's affair. I figured if it worked for uptight Lachie, then it has to work for me."

"I'm not Erica and you're not Lachlan. How about we try being ourselves? You don't need to win me over with liquor and flowery descriptions of an island. I like you, Aidan. I'm here with you, not your brother."

He grumbled. "If you met Lachlan, you'd probably like him better."

"Bullshit." I rested my chin on his shoulder, sliding my hand over his abdomen, relishing the texture of hard muscle beneath the smooth cloth of his shirt. "You don't need props to impress me."

He swigged a mouthful of whisky, a bit of it spilling onto his lips.

I took his face in my hands, sat up, and dragged my tongue across first his bottom lip, then his upper lip. "Mm, it tastes better on you."

His breath hitched, his eyes locked onto mine.

My hands still bracketing his face, I tugged him closer. Our gazes never separated, as if a rope bound us to each other. I captured his lower lip between mine and suckled, gently at first, then with more hunger as the familiar, heady desire flared inside me. Though he held onto the whisky bottle with one hand, the other settled onto my hip, his fingers curling around it.

I released his lip.

Our labored breaths reflected off each other amid the whispers of our exhalations. I scented the whisky on his breath, and suddenly, an overpowering need to taste it on his tongue seized me.

I crushed my mouth to his.

He made a soft noise—part groan, part gasp—and opened his mouth to me.

Need pulsed through me, from my nipples mashed to his hard chest straight down to my tightening clitoris. I held fast to his face as I thrust my tongue inside his soft, hot mouth. He coiled his tongue around mine in a slow and seductive movement that drove me to quest deeper, to lap up the flavor of whisky and Aidan, to draw a piece of him into myself. The texture of his mouth, a juxtaposition of satiny softness and unyielding teeth, had me virtually panting into his mouth, my breasts heaving against his torso, rubbing my rigid nipples.

He surged up off the sofa, leaving me in a daze on the cushions.

I blinked up at him, struggling to clear the haze of desire and catch my breath.

Aidan gulped down a mouthful of whisky, then clapped the bottle down on the coffee table. Swiping at his mouth with the back of his hand, he glanced down at me with parted lips and ruddy cheeks.

"Best stop," he said, and stalked around the sofa to the bar where he planted both palms on the surface, leaning into it with his head bowed.

I sat there for a moment, confused. He couldn't have been offended I kissed him. What, then, had made him stop?

Pushing up off the sofa, I marched over to the bar and halted beside Aidan. He didn't move, his head still down and his eyes closed. I placed one hand on his and he tensed the tiniest bit.

"What is it?" I asked. "Thought you liked kissing me."

"I love it," he said in a hushed voice. "But I want more than kissing."

Keeping my hand on his, I bent one finger to stroke the back of his hand. "I know. You want sex. I want—"

"No." He pulled his hand away, turned, and walked halfway across the living room. Scrubbing his face with one hand, he sighed. "I want more than sex. You know that."

I leaned against the bar, my elbow braced on it. "Okay, but you said sex would come first."

He faced me, standing straight and certain. "Marry me."

"What?" I almost shouted the word, shocked by his declaration. "Where is this coming from? You know I can't marry you. Even if I wanted to, we barely know each other."

"Aye, but I know what I want."

My stomach fluttered, and my pulse began to race. Seven days, that's how long I'd known this man. Seven days, and I already got excited at the prospect of marrying him. He wasn't Rade, he wasn't Tara's first husband, he wasn't anything like Gavin's ex-wife. I knew this, and yet I feared I'd make another mistake that would trap me.

Aidan took two steps toward me, hesitating five feet away. "Please, Calli, marry me. I swear I'll make you happy and you'll never regret this. One day, maybe you'll even love me."

"Do you love me?"

He lowered his gaze and scratched the back of his head. "Not yet."

"Then why would you want to marry me? What's the rush?"

One of his shoulders hiked up. He stared at the floor, his mouth tight, as seconds ticked by on the clock in my head. After a couple minutes, he shuffled to the padded chair on the other side of the living room, the one situated against the wall under a topographic map of the Upper Peninsula. He fell into the chair with a groaning sigh, his shoulders deflating, his entire body slumping. Hands on the chair's arms, he refused to look up at me, even as I crossed the room to kneel before him.

"Aidan." I placed my hands on his knees. "Please tell me what's going on with you."

"Ye donnae want to hear."

I shifted my hands to his thighs. "Yes, I do."

He made a pitiful noise, his mouth twisted. "Lachlan didn't want a wife, but he found one. Thought if I did what he'd done, I could change your mind about me. But ye still donnae want me, not the way I want you."

"Did Lachlan propose to Erica after one week?"

"No." Aidan fidgeted in his seat. "First, he broke her heart and left her for two months. Then, he begged her to marry him."

"Uh-huh." I tapped a finger on his chest. "Why would you want to re-enact that? Sounds like the Amazing Lachlan fucked it up with Erica and then got lucky when she generously took him back. Is that really how you want things to go with me?"

His eyes rolled up to meet mine. His lips curled up at the corners. "You said fuck."

"That's what you took away from what I said?"

"No, I understood the rest." He bent one arm to prop his chin on his knuckles. "But I've never heard you say fuck before. Kind of like it, though I'd rather hear it from you when we're both naked."

I sat back on my heels, giving him a sardonic smile. "Getting back to Lachlan…"

Aidan puckered his lips. "I do see your point. Lachlan made a mess of things, but I was hoping some of his methods might work for me. This is the first time I've tried to win a wife. No bloody idea what I'm doing."

"Oh, I'd say you're doing fine all on your own."

"You still don't want to love me."

"Sure, but you don't love me either."

He studied me for a moment, his expression thoughtful. "I want to. That's the difference. Deep down, though, I think you want to love me too."

"Give it up, Kilt Boy. I am not falling for you." So why did I care about making him feel better? Why did his emotional turmoil make my heart clench?

Dropping his hand, letting it dangle over the chair's arm onto his lap, he frowned. "Then you won't be sleeping with me."

I flattened my palms on his thighs and leaned in, pushing between his legs to get closer. With our faces so near I could've flicked my tongue out to sample his lips, I met his gaze head-on. "I've already decided to have sex with you."

His eyes flared wide. "You what? Why?"

Laughing softly, I squeezed further between his thighs until I could feel his penis hardening inside his jeans. "I like you, Aidan. You're sweet and funny and smart and you make me feel good." I moved my hands to his chest, toying with the neckline of his T-shirt. "And you're the sexiest man on earth."

"Sexiest? Do I get a trophy for that?"

"No, but you do get a prize." I slid my hands down his torso. "Me."

"But—ah." He flinched as I cupped his erection. "You know I want you. Badly. But not like this, I need to prepare."

I plastered my body to his, running my hands up his massive biceps, loving the sensation of taut muscles bunching under my touch and his breaths whispering over my cheek. "Prepare? I have condoms. Bought them at the store today when you were contemplating the avocados."

"Not that." His face pinched, he gripped the arms of the chair. "Need to set the scene, make it special."

"How long will that take?" I nipped at the tender flesh at the juncture of his jaw, rewarded by his sharp intake of breath.

"Might need a day, maybe two."

"A day or two?" I drew my head back. "You're kidding, right? I offer myself to you and all you can say is let's wait two days."

"Donnae want to."

I scrutinized him for a moment, and with a mental bolt of lightning, the truth struck me. "Is this what Lachlan did with Erica?"

He scratched his cheek. "Aye."

"For heaven's sake." I grasped his head in both hands and told him in my sternest voice, "Stop with the Lachlan and Erica reenactment. I told you I don't want that. I want you. Can you get that through your thick, Scottish head? I want you. Tonight. Forget about your brother, forget about everyone else. Do this your way."

"My way would be I carry you into the bedroom and strip you naked right this minute."

"Yes. Please do."

He grinned. "You are wonderful."

I rubbed my body against his straining erection. "You gonna fuck me or what?"

"Aye." He scooped me up in his arms at the same instant he surged up from the chair. His muscles flexed and tautened around me as he carried me down the hallway and into the bedroom. When he spotted the puppies asleep on the quilt, he called out, "Time to go, furry lassies."

Misty and Mandy flew off the bed and out of the room. The doggie door whapped closed behind them as Aidan kicked the bedroom door shut.

"Need privacy," he said, setting me on my feet, "for what I'm going to do to you."

A shiver of anticipation rippled through me.

He took hold of my waist, tugging me into him. "I'm about to show you how wicked I really am."

Chapter Sixteen

is fingers slipped under my shirt, gliding upward, taking the fabric with them. Cool air whispered over my skin as he exposed my belly in leisurely increments. The hairs all over my body went erect and a breathtaking tingle swept over my skin. Eyes half closed, I let my hands rest on his chest, awaiting the moment when I would be bared to him.

Aidan froze, his fingertips a hair's breadth below my bra.

"No," he said, "not like this."

Irrational annoyance blustered through me and I threw my hands up. "What now? If you say we have to wait so you can do whatever Lachlan did—"

His soft, throaty chuckle caressed my senses. "I meant not with me undressing you. I want you to strip for me."

"Oh." My cheeks grew warm with a rising blush. "Sorry."

"Don't be." He tipped my chin up with one finger. "I like your passion."

"Apparently, I get a little irrational when I'm sexually frustrated."

He kissed me—a quick, light touch. "I'll take care of that soon enough. First, I want to watch you."

With a suggestive smirk on his lips, he sauntered to the bed and lowered his big body onto the mattress. It creaked under his weight. His hands lay on the quilt, but his eyes stayed glued to me.

I stood there, immobilized by uncertainty. How did a woman strip for a man? Was I supposed to do some kind of sexy dance? *Ugh*. I had no clue how to do that.

"Relax," he said, canting his head as he swept his gaze down the length of my body and back up to my face. "Just take your clothes off. I'm easy to please, trust me."

Okay. I could do this. Strip. How hard could it be?

I chewed the inside of my lip, fingering the hem of my shirt, my gaze averted to the dresser.

"Look at me," he murmured. "Keep your eyes on me and try to relax. Look like you've got a caber up your erse."

"You have a caber fetish, don't you?"

"I've got a fetish for watching you undress."

The smoldering fire in his gaze heated me up, softening the tension from my muscles, melting me from the inside out. I took hold of my shirt and drew it up over my head, then tossed it to the floor.

"Oops," I said, my hand flying to my mouth. "Was that too fast? Should I do it slower?"

"It was fine." He moved his hands behind his butt and leaned back on them. The pink tip of his tongue poked out between his lips, tracing the seam. "Keep going."

The husky tone of his voice electrified my body. My breasts grew tight and my nipples ached, desperate to escape the confines of my bra. I unzipped my pants, shimmying out of them under Aidan's attentive gaze. His lips parted as he tracked my every movement, and when I kicked my jeans away, he swallowed visibly. I turned my back to him and looked at him over my shoulder with my best attempt at a saucy smile.

"More," he growled, his breaths labored.

Emboldened, I unhooked my bra and let it tumble off my shoulders, fluttering down to the floor. I slid my thumbs inside the waistband of my panties, and little by little, I eased them down while swaying my hips, dragging the fabric over my buttocks. The slow slide of cotton on my skin amped up my own arousal—but it was the hungry, almost crazed, look on Aidan's face that triggered a deep, wet ache in my sex.

Nude at last, I folded my arms around me, still gazing at him over my shoulder.

He twirled one finger in the air. "Turn, please. Slowly."

His erotic command burned through my inhibitions, incinerating every last shred of self-consciousness. I brushed my hands up and down my arms, swiveling my hips, then spread my palms over my hips, undulating my whole body as I rotated to face him.

His mouth had fallen open. Really, truly fallen open. His half-closed eyes drank me in from head to toe, his gaze searing my skin like a physical touch as he absorbed the sight of my breasts and rigid nipples, the planes of my stomach, the curly hairs at the apex of my thighs. His attention stalled there, and he licked his lips.

A wild, heady freedom rushed through me.

I walked up to him, lifted one leg, and set my foot on the bed next to him. Exposed to him in the most intimate way, I draped my hands on his shoulders. His focus snapped to my groin. His chest heaved, and I swore he growled low in his throat, a possessive and feral sound that set off a wave of liquid fire in my sex. I followed his gaze to my body, to the glistening flesh revealed to him, to the drops of my own juices clinging to the fine hairs on my mound.

"So bonnie," he said breathlessly. "So bloody perfect. Pink and slick and begging to be tasted."

He lifted one hand, as if in slow motion, and held it near my throbbing sex without contacting my flesh. His palm would've cupped me if he'd moved a touch closer, but instead, he wiggled his fingers to tease the hairs.

My fingers dug into his shoulders.

"Cannae wait," he hissed, and grasped my hips in both his strong hands. He slanted toward me at the same time he tipped my hips toward him. His mouth closed around my clitoris. I gasped, clutching him so hard it must've hurt him, but he gave no sign of noticing. My head fell back as he licked and nipped at my nub, swirling his tongue, suckling gently and then so hard I cried out.

His hands shifted to my ass. He held me in place with my foot still on the bed, while he lavished my clit with rough swipes of his tongue, increasing the pace with every pass. His tongue raked my flesh up and down, up and down, side to side, up and down. He paused for a heart-stopping second, then devoured my flesh again and worked my hard nub until I was moaning and thrashing my head, clinging to him like I'd fly away into the heavens if I let go.

My climax slammed through me. Scorching, wrenching, mind-altering pleasure that had me writhing in his grasp and letting out a strangled scream.

Aidan tilted his head back to gaze up at me over my mound. His lips glistened with the moisture from…me. "Ah, Calli, you taste like everything wonderful. I could feast on you all night, but I've got other plans."

Still stunned by the exquisite orgasm he'd gifted me with, I dropped my foot to the floor and steadied myself with his solid body. My mind gradually came back to reality and I noted one salient fact.

Flicking a finger on the neck of his T-shirt, I said, "You're not naked."

"Noticed, did ye?" His lips quirked, his eyes sparkled. "Nothing gets by you."

I slapped his shoulder. "Well, get rid of your damn clothes."

"If you insist." He pressed his mouth to the sensitive skin just above my mound, eliciting a small shiver from me. "Wanted to taste you since the night we met. Now, I want to make you mine."

"Get naked already."

He laughed but did not move.

Despite my orgasm, I endured a deep, pulsating tingle that would not be satisfied until he drove into me. I knew this, though I couldn't explain how. My body knew it.

And I couldn't wait one more second.

With a sharp huff, I grabbed the hem of his shirt and yanked it up. He arched one brow but raised his arms so I could haul the garment off of him and fling it aside. The shirt landed on the dresser with a *whuft* sound. I knelt between his thighs, fumbling to undo the button of his jeans, but my fingers had begun to tremble and I couldn't quite grasp the damn thing.

He caught my hands. "Easy, love."

In one fluid movement, he wrapped an arm around me to crush me to his body, rose off the bed, and with his free hand hurled the covers aside. A puff of air rustled my hair from the sudden motion of the quilt and blanket. The top sheet billowed, then settled onto the bed.

Aidan tossed me onto the mattress.

I landed with a bounce and a little yelp. "Hey! What are you doing?"

"Speeding things up." He stripped off his jeans and kicked them out of the way. Since he didn't bother with underwear, I now gazed with rapt attention at the buck-naked Highlander before me.

I'd seen him naked before. This time was different. Helpless to tear my gaze away from his body, I let my focus wander over acres of burnished, firm flesh and the sharp lines of defined muscles. The delicious planes of his torso, sprinkled with fine hairs, inexorably lured my gaze lower and lower, tracking the path of hairs as they tapered down to a point, an arrow pointing straight to the glorious, thick, veined cock I craved.

"But you wanted me to go slow," I said, feigning a pout.

"I'm fickle." His grin was salacious and teasing. "Should I leave?"

"Don't you dare."

He planted one knee on the bed alongside my hip, preparing to straddle me, but stopped. His lips compressed, he scrunched his eyebrows.

"What is it?" I asked, pushing up onto my elbows.

Lips working, he stared at me for several seconds. "Are you certain you want to do this? If I'm your first, you'll always remember me."

"Hate to break it to you," I said, nudging him with my knee, "but even if we don't have sex, there's no way I'd ever forget you. Even if you'd never touched me. Or kissed me. You are unforgettable."

"So are you." He swung his other leg over my body to straddle my hips, landing on his knees, poised above me like a medieval warrior about to claim his mate. His hair curled wild around his face and ears. Lips parted, his gaze searing into me, he slanted forward to plant his hands at either side of my head. "Guess you're stuck with me, then, even after you tell me to bugger off."

A pang lanced my heart at the thought of him leaving. I had no time to ponder the reason for it, though, because he dipped his head to mine and his warm, inviting mouth teased my lips with swift brushes.

I dissolved for him in an instant, my body lax and limp beneath him despite the desire swirling through me, coiling ever tighter in my belly.

"Tell me," he said, "what would ye like me to do first?"

"Anything. Everything."

His chuckle resonated through his chest. "Hard to do everything at once."

"You pick. I—"

He caught my lower lip with his teeth and released it with maddening slowness while his shaft rubbed across my abdomen, spreading a drop of moisture onto my skin. I glanced down at that impressive cock and flashed back to another night, when I'd taken him into my mouth. The flavor and feel of him rushed through my senses anew, drawing a faint moan from me.

"What are ye thinking?" he asked, his lips barely touching mine, his eyes blazing into me.

Unable to form words, enveloped in the aura of all that manly flesh, I snaked a hand down to fold my fingers around his erection. His eyelids fluttered as if he fought to keep them open. I glided my hand up and down his firm, velvety flesh.

"Ah," he hissed, and seized my hand to pull it free of his cock. "Not this time, *mo chridhe.*"

I reached down with my free hand, intent on capturing him again.

His lips twitched with wry amusement as he collared that hand too, pinning both above my head. "Behave."

I lifted my brows as I arched my hips into his hard-on. "Since when do you want me to behave? You've spent over a week trying to convince me to do the exact opposite."

"Did the job a wee bit too well, eh?" His body descended onto mine, slowly, delicately, the weight of him pressing me into the mattress. He threaded his fingers through mine, our hands linked above my pillow, and nibbled at my lower lip.

I wrapped my arms around his back, splayed my fingers, and reveled in the sensation of all that muscle, all that power, concentrated on pleasure—my pleasure. And suddenly, I couldn't wait. "What happened to speeding things up?"

"Easy, lass." He savored my mouth with flicks of his tongue, the touch light and sweet yet decadently arousing. "We have all night."

Desperate for more of him, I lunged my head forward to kiss him. He pulled back, grinning with that naughty gleam in his eyes.

"Uh-uh-uh," he said, shaking his head.

I huffed. "Well, dammit, do something."

"Maybe I should take pity on you since this is your first time." He muffled my complaint with his mouth, crushing it to mine with brutal passion, thrusting his tongue between my lips to forge deep inside. With strong, punishing strokes, he ignited my simmering desire into a roaring, all-consuming conflagration. I plundered his mouth while he plundered mine, our teeth clashing, our tongues tangling, our lips fused like nothing short of a chainsaw could separate us. I clutched him tighter, my nails sinking into his back, and hoisted my knees up to spread my legs for him.

He drew his head back, panting, lips slick and swollen from our kiss. "Guess ye cannae wait, can ye?"

I shook my head furiously, breathing hard, my hair flapping around my face.

"Well then." He rose onto all fours, his engorged penis dangling between our bodies, curving up toward his taut belly. "Hell with taking it slow."

I sucked in a sharp breath, anticipation a palpable sensation on my skin, sizzling and snapping through my body. "Oh yes, please, Aidan."

"Condom?" he asked.

Jerking my head, I indicated the bedside table. "Drawer."

He yanked open the drawer, snagged a condom packet from inside it, and shut it with a *thwack*. He almost wheezed with the effort to catch his breath and his cock twitched as he fumbled to open the condom packet with one hand and his teeth.

I snatched the packet from him. With a rough ripping noise, I tore it open with my teeth and handed the packet back to him.

He gazed at me open-mouthed. "Ahm getting the impression ye willnae be passive when I take ye."

"You wouldn't want me to be." I scraped my nails down his chest in one long, slow sweep. "Take too long and I might fuck you instead."

Laughing, he sat back on his heels to sheath his thick shaft with the condom. "Ye willnae get the chance. Not this time."

He bent over me again, dropping his head to take one nipple in his mouth. He swirled his tongue around the swollen peak, just as his hand closed around the other breast, his thumb and forefinger plucking at the nipple. His mouth devoured my other breast, consuming the whole areola along with the tip. He suckled hard enough to squeeze a gasp from me while his hand kneaded my other breast.

Frantic for more, I lodged my heels on the mattress and hoisted my hips up, struggling to catch his cock but missing. As my butt flopped back onto the bed, Aidan withdrew his mouth from my nipple. The air cooled my damp, pebbled skin.

He beheld me with keen interest and deep lust. "Not one for foreplay, are ye?"

"Maybe next time."

"All right. Have it your way."

He grasped my knees and pushed them toward my chest, forcing my legs to bend. With my knees drawn up and his weight penning me, I could do nothing except gaze at him, almost panting from the need to have him inside me.

"Please," I moaned. "Please, now."

"Cannae let my woman suffer." He grasped my ankles and lifted them, settling my knees on his shoulders. "Donnae want to hurt ye, so tell me if—"

"Now, Aidan. Take me *now*."

He drove into me with one long, smooth stroke, his cock penetrating deep until it felt as if he filled every space within me. I let out a sharp cry, part gasp, part yelp.

Aidan froze, buried within my body. "Did I hurt you?"

"No," I said, breathless. "Don't stop."

Motionless, unblinking, he looked at me as if he were seeing me for the first time. As if I'd transformed into a glowing, ethereal angel right before his eyes. As if he might change his mind and leave me aching for him.

"Please," I whispered, clasping his wrists. "Please don't stop."

"Won't." He slipped free of my hands and shifted my legs off his shoulders. My soles fell to the mattress, though my knees stayed bent at either side of him. Still buried inside me to the hilt, he settled his big body on top of mine, braced on his elbows with his hands at either side of my head so he could stroke my face with his fingers. "I would never leave you wanting."

It was almost like he'd read my thoughts, knew I'd worried he might give up on this. My throat constricted at the fondness in his expression as he lowered his mouth to mine and kissed me with all the sweetness of a man worshiping his true love.

He couldn't love me, not yet. He'd said he didn't. But the way he gazed at me, I could only describe it as…adoring.

The brush of his lips on mine became a sweet, exquisitely tender kiss, with our lips caressing each other in a questing exploration. Then he began to move inside me, easing out of me until only the tip of his penis touched my opening and plunging back in with a long, lazy glide that awakened every inch of sensitized flesh within my body. I arched my hips up to meet his thrusts, my hands gripping his upper arms. With his full weight on me, I felt connected with him in a way I had no words to describe. The whole time—while his cock glided in and out, consuming me with lush strokes only to abandon me once again—he kept kissing me, savoring my lips with tiny licks but never delving inside. The sweet torment of it intensified my arousal, even as his gentle mouth eased the knife-sharp need just enough to keep me from tipping over the edge.

This man was driving me out of my mind with tenderness.

I hadn't known it was possible for him to ease me toward climax with such deliciously sweet seduction. My sex grew wetter, hotter, pulsating from my clit down to my opening and straight into my core, where he teased my swollen flesh into ever-increasing passion.

"Oh God, Aidan," I moaned against his lips. "Please."

"Tell me what you want." His words groaned out of him, as he dived into me with another sure, measured thrust. "Tell me."

"More. I want more."

He seemed to know what I meant, though I wasn't sure what I needed. This hunger simmering inside me, rising toward a full-on boil, scattered my wits. But he understood what I couldn't voice. Mashing his mouth to mine, he withdrew his cock and plunged his tongue deep at the same instant he plowed into me with one swift, powerful thrust.

Everything inside me exploded.

Not an orgasm, not yet. My nerves erupted in a torrid cascade that crashed through me from the inside out.

He tore his mouth from mine to growl, "More?"

"Oh yes, Aidan, more." I lunged my hips up as he drove into me again. "Yes-yes, oh God, yes."

Pushing up onto his straight arms, hands braced at either side of my shoulders, he pistoned his cock into me again and again, hips undulating, muscles rippling all over his body with the effort of pleasuring me. I clutched at his arms while little cries of joy burst out of me one after another and my body tightened with an oncoming climax. He grunted with every devouring thrust, bouncing me on the bed, and I clamped my legs around him, my heels digging into his ass. I had no idea what I was doing, only that I craved more of him, all of him, every ounce of pleasure he could feed into me.

My sex clenched around his shaft.

The orgasm seized my body, shocking in its intensity, wrenching a hoarse scream from me. My sex clenched around his shaft again and again, milking every last ounce of pleasure from the climax. I screamed again as the last burst of mind-altering ecstasy roared through me and faded into a lovely afterglow.

Aidan's entire body went rigid, his features contorted with a desperate need.

I felt his release pulse inside me as he drove into me once, twice more.

With a long, deep groan, he collapsed to the bed beside me. He shed the condom and shucked it into the little trash can beside the bed. Breathing hard, he pulled me against him and held me gently in his arms. I nestled my cheek against his chest and listened to the thudding of his heartbeats. Gradually, they slowed along with mine.

He ran his hand up and down my arm. "Sorry about that."

I raised my head to squint at him. "You better not be apologizing for having sex with me."

"No." He sighed, shutting his eyes for a moment. "I meant to take it slow, make it special. This was your first time."

"It was special." I wriggled until I could get in a position to press a kiss to his lips. "What you gave me tonight, it was perfect."

One chestnut brow hiked up. "Perfect? I'm good, but I'm not that good."

"Not actually perfect," I said with a laugh. "But for me, that was the perfect first time. I should be thanking you."

"Are you sure you don't mind having me as your first?"

"Why would I mind?" I studied his face but couldn't puzzle out his mood. "You are sweet, funny, gorgeous, and incredibly sexy. You make me feel...treasured."

"Because you are." A slight smile kinked his mouth as he slid a hand into my hair, massaging my scalp. "I want you for more than sex. I know you think you don't want me for more. You don't love me yet, but you will."

"You can't make me love you by repeatedly telling me I will."

"Can't hurt." He placed a finger on my sealed lips. "You did vow you'd never have sex with me. And look how that worked out."

"Uh-huh." No idea what to say to that, since he was right. I'd broken my first rule.

If I can tempt you to break your first rule, the rest will follow, he'd said a few days ago on the beach. No sex, no love, no marriage. Scratch number one. The rest would not follow, no way, I couldn't risk it. I wasn't falling for him.

I could stop it from happening. I had to.

Aidan pulled me tighter against him.

Without thinking, I snuggled into him with my head in the crook of his neck. He smelled of sweat and sex and pure man. With his arms around me, his warm body beneath mine, I felt safer than I had in years.

Not falling for him.

The pain in my chest disagreed.

Chapter Seventeen

I woke to the steady whisper of breaths from one hunky man and two furry females. Sometime after midnight, the puppies had whined and pawed at the bedroom door and Aidan had gotten up to let them in. This morning, he lay sleeping beside me with one arm holding me against his body. Misty lay stretched across him with her back end between his legs and her head on his tummy. Mandy was curled up by his feet.

The little traitors had abandoned me.

Not that I could blame them. Cuddling with Aidan would make even the toughest woman melt. And my puppies weren't exactly struggling to resist his charms.

Unwilling to move my head from the hollow of his shoulder, I luxuriated in the feel of him pressed against me. I wasn't resisting him anymore either.

Aidan stirred.

I tried to roll onto my back, away from him.

His arm pinned me in place, and when I pushed against it, he tugged me into his hard body in a firmer hold.

"Morning," he murmured in a sleepy voice.

"Good morning." Having never woken up nude with a man—or anyone—before, I endured a twinge of embarrassment and uncertainty. The discomfort spurred me to say the dumbest thing. "How are you?"

He chuckled. "In rude health. And you?"

Mocking me, he was. But with affection.

I nudged him with my elbow. "Being held prisoner by a presumptuous Scotsman."

"Hm." Aidan clamped both arms around me. "Never had a captive woman before. It has interesting possibilities."

The movement had roused Misty, who gave a loud, high-pitched yawn and rolled onto her belly, her front paws on Aidan's chest. Her tail thumped on the bed, which awakened her sister. Mandy sat up and wagged her tail. Aidan held onto me as both puppies sprang up and hopped around on the bed making excited little growling and snuffing noises, storming over me and Aidan to slaver all over any exposed body part they could reach.

I squealed when Misty jammed her wet doggie nose into my ear and Mandy laid a sloppy kiss smack on my lips. Spluttering, I tried to push the puppies away.

Aidan surged out of bed and hooked an arm around first one puppy, then the other. With one under each arm, he marched out of the room. I heard the dog door flap-flap-flap. A moment later, as I swung my legs over the bed's edge, Aidan strode back into the room and shut the door.

His erection waved in front of his belly.

The memory of last night, of his body covering mine and his swollen shaft buried deep inside me, had me growing more aroused by the second.

Instead of pouncing on me for another bout of ravishing sex, he strolled to where his clothes lay heaped on the floor and picked up his jeans.

"Hey!" I complained. "You can't get dressed yet."

Fighting to repress a smile, he paused with the jeans dangling from his hand. "Can't I?"

"No." I crossed my arms over my breasts, my own skin raking across my hardening nipples. But I had feigned indignation to uphold. "I was expecting a night of hot, sweaty sex."

He swung the jeans from one strong finger. "We had hot, sweaty sex."

"Only once. You were supposed to have your way with me all night like a proper, wicked sex fiend. I got cheated."

Aidan tossed the jeans aside and lunged to his knees before me, one large hand on each of my knees. With a look of mock shame, he said, "Please forgive me, my darling Calli. How could I have been so remiss in my seducer duties?"

I couldn't help it. Laughter bubbled out of me and I let my arms fall, my hands coming to rest on my thighs. "All joking aside, I was hoping for more than once."

"Didn't want to hurt you." The humor vacated his face and he studied me with real concern. "This was your first time. Are you sore?"

"I'm fine."

He gave me a dubious look. "I, ah...took you rather hard."

"Think I'm lying?"

"No…"

I clasped one of his hands in each of mine and guided them up the insides of my thighs. "Why don't you test me?"

Spreading my legs, I moved his hands to my hips and scooted forward until my behind rested on the edge of the bed. Might as well have worn a flashing neon sign that said, "Do me now, you big, stubborn Scot."

Aidan's gaze dropped to my sex. He sucked in a breath through his nostrils. His eyes drifted partway closed, his lips forming a smile of pure pleasure.

"*Bod an Donais*," he hissed, nailing his gaze to mine. "You smell like sin, and I want to feast on you."

"Go right ahead."

His focus wandered back down to the hairs between my legs and the slick flesh beneath. His tongue poked out between his lips as his famished gaze devoured me. "Love to, but Lachlan's ringing me in half an hour to talk about Jamie."

"We have time," I said, doing my damnedest to sound sultry and irresistible. "Aidan, I need you inside me. Fucking me like a demon."

He stared at me, wide-eyed. Not shock, I could tell that much. More lustful, delighted surprise.

"Ahmno a demon," he said, as he rose up before me, his erection in my face. "But I can fuck ye like a man who hasnae had a woman in centuries. Will that do?"

"Yes-yes-yes."

He crawled onto the bed, moving behind me on all fours. Sliding his legs around me on either side, he nestled his groin against my behind and his hard cock against my back. When his hands lighted on my thighs, I leaned back into him. He planted his feet on the floor and eased one hand between my thighs. The second his fingers delved between my wet folds, I moaned.

"Thought you wanted to feast on me," I said, as my head lolled against his shoulder.

"Another time." He petted my folds, his touch delicate and maddeningly arousing. "Do ye trust me?"

"Completely." And I did, bizarre as it sounded given how short a time we'd known each other. Maybe I should've worried about what that implied about my feelings toward him, but his touch stripped away all my capacity for thought.

His fingers toyed with my flesh, sliding around my outer folds and into the inner lips of my sex. He stroked slowly up and down, denying me the bliss of his fingers on my clit, where I needed him the most. He sank one finger inside me, then another, pushing them as deep as possible. The heel of his hand covered my mound, but he wriggled it until his rough, bare palm pressed into my clitoris.

"Aidan," I moaned.

"Shh," he whispered into my ear. "Let me take care of everything."

In the most merciless, languid motions, he rubbed his hand into my hardened nub while his fingers withdrew and plunged inside again and again. I grasped his thighs, writhing mindlessly against him, rolling my hips into his palm and his thrusting fingers. The climax swept over me in sweet, lazy waves, scorching and overwhelming but with an underlying tenderness. I whimpered with each pulse of delicious pleasure, still thrusting against his palm even when he slid his fingers out.

Aidan leaned around me to retrieve a condom from the drawer. He pulled away from my backside a little and I heard the ripping of foil. A few seconds later, he grasped my hips and hoisted me up and onto his lap, impaling me on his shaft.

"Oh," I gasped, surprised by the sudden fullness of his cock buried to the hilt.

He barred one arm over my belly and pitched backward, supported on his other arm. Before I could question his plans, he started thrusting in easy strokes that escalated into a pounding rhythm as he punched into me, inflaming every nerve inside my sex, inside my entire body. My nipples ached, harder than they'd ever been before, and I sensed an orgasm building with fiery intensity. He pounded with so much force my ass bounced up off his cock, and when I slammed back down, his balls slapped into my ass. Each punishing thrust set off another round of wet slapping as our bodies converged, separated, converged again. Our fevered cries echoed around us and the musky scent of sex engulfed us.

I came with an erratic scream, my body still bouncing up and down his cock.

Aidan thrust once more, letting out a hoarse bellow as his own release overtook him. Then he fell backward onto the bed, taking me with him, his softening shaft wedged inside me.

The sound of puppies barking at last penetrated the fog of our sexual fervor.

"Better see what's going on out there," I said between heaving breaths as I climbed off Aidan.

He groaned, sprawled on the bed.

I grinned at him. "That's okay, you stay there."

"Thanks." He gave me a lopsided smile. "Still feeling cheated?"

"Not in the least."

Chapter Eighteen

I emerged from the bathroom after taking a shower and noted the sound of puppies barking outside and human voices in the living room. Voices, plural. Yawning and stretching, I sat up and listened to the two distinct voices, but I couldn't make out the words. Sounded like two men talking. Had Aidan invited someone into the house without asking me?

Hurrying down the hallway in my socked feet, I stopped at the edge of the living room. Aidan slouched into the sofa, his mouth twisted into a half frown, his gaze aimed at the empty space in the general direction of the windows overlooking the backyard. I spotted puppy-shaped blurs racing back and forth across the lawn, slaloming around the cedar trees.

"Don't be stubborn, Aidan," said a slightly tinny voice originating from nowhere, as far as I could tell. The stranger had the same sexy brogue as Aidan and their voices sounded somewhat alike, but I would never have confused the two. One of his brothers, maybe?

Aidan pinched the bridge of his nose with his thumb and forefinger, glancing down at his lap. "I do not want your money."

Tiptoeing forward, I crept up behind the sofa but halted six feet from Aidan's head when the other voice piped up again.

"You're skint," the other man said, "and we can help. There's no shame in letting your family lend a hand."

"It's not a hand," Aidan groused. "It's charity."

Skulking a teensy bit closer, I raised onto my toes and peeked over Aidan's shoulder. He sat with one ankle lodged on the opposite knee, his phone balanced on the tilted knee. The voice of the other man emerged from the phone's speaker.

"Erica worries about you," the other man said, "and she won't give up until I convince you to take the bloody money."

"Cannae say no to your wife, Lachie?" Aidan shook his head, a teasing lilt in his voice.

"I know what you're doing, Aidan. Calling me Lachie to fash me, hoping I'll give up. But you know how Erica is when she sets her mind to something."

"Aye, I know," Aidan sighed. "But I've got my pride. No money, Lachlan."

Some kind of noise in the background of the call made Lachlan MacTaggart grunt. "Erica says to tell you you're a pigheaded goof and when you're home she's going to—I'm not saying that, love."

The last bit had clearly been aimed at his wife.

"What are you not going to do, Lachie?" Aidan asked, sounding immensely amused.

Lachlan groaned out a sigh. "She says she'll whoop your stubborn erse until it shines bright red like Rudolph's reindeer nose."

"Och," Aidan said, chuckling, "I'm terrified. Never coming home now."

He turned his head the tiniest bit, arching one brow—at me.

Busted.

I moved forward, bending down to rest my forearms on the sofa's back at either side of Aidan's head. He slipped a hand over one of mine, caressing my palm with his fingertips.

"You have to help me," Lachlan said, "to keep my wife satisfied. At least let us arrange a better car and hotel for you, and just a wee bit of cash to—"

"No." Aidan slapped his free hand on his thigh, but the irritation left his face swiftly, replaced by a faint smirk. "It's not my fault you can't satisfy your wife."

"Aidan." The elder MacTaggart adopted a stern tone that wasn't quite convincing.

"Do I need to spell the word for you? N-O."

The conversation was clearly spinning in circles, with neither brother willing to concede an iota. Lachlan sounded tense and frustrated, but Aidan looked it. His shoulders had hunched a little, his mouth flattened into a line, and the fingers of the hand on his thigh crooked, clawing at the denim of his jeans.

I experienced a powerful urge to ease his tension, and I had an idea of how to accomplish it.

Leaning in, I trailed my fingers down his throat and whispered in his ear. "Let's make out."

He fidgeted, casting me a sideways glance.

The other MacTaggart kept talking. "Say yes, Aidan, or I'll tell our mother to call you."

I took Aidan's earlobe in my mouth, flicking my tongue over it. He hissed in a breath. I laid my palms over his collarbone and slid them down his chest toward his waistband. "Want to kiss me?"

He swiveled his head toward me, our lips grazing each other. "Aye."

"Thank heavens," Lachlan said, with great relief in his voice. "I'll take care of everything right away."

"What?" Aidan's head snapped to the front again, his eyes went wide. He snatched the phone from his knee. "No-no-no, I wasnae talking to you, Lachlan."

"Who were you talking to?"

Aidan's gaze darted to me and he shook his head with mock chastisement. "I'm with a saucy wench who's trying to seduce me."

"Wench?" Lachlan said with amusement. "Have you become a pirate?"

"Go ravish your wife, Lachlan." Aidan disconnected the call and tossed his phone on the table. He twisted around to grab me by the waist and haul me onto his lap, where I landed sideways. Cupping my face in one hand, he drew me closer. "Now, about your offer to make out."

"Still open."

"Good." He moved his hand to my nape, tipping my head back. "You tricked me into taking my brother's handout, which means you owe me."

"I wasn't trying to trick you. Just wanted a kiss."

"Mm." He brushed his mouth over mine and his lips vibrated my flesh when he spoke again. "You're wanting more than a kiss, aren't you?"

"Yes." Before I could close my mouth, he possessed it with his own, thrusting his tongue inside for a deep, wet, ravenous kiss. "Thought you were talking to Lachlan about your sister."

"We talked about her." He dragged his tongue up my throat while his hand closed around my breast, my shirt no protection from his touch. "Are you sure you want my sister staying here?"

"If the alternative is you going back to Chicago, yes." I worked a hand down between our bodies to rub his hardening penis through his jeans. "I want you here. Both in the sense of you staying in this house and in the sense of you taking me right here, right now."

"Let's wait a bit for that. I'll feel better when I'm sure you're not too sore."

"If that's what you really want." I clambered off his lap to sit beside him. "Sorry I inadvertently helped your brother get his way."

"Doesn't matter." Aidan let his head fall back on the sofa, his hands loose at his sides. "Lachlan would've gotten his way eventually."

"I can relate. Gavin is always positive he knows best when it comes to my life."

"Lachlan's the same." Aidan laid an arm across my shoulders and I cuddled into him. "My family thinks I'm incapable of taking care of myself."

"Your brother said you're skint. Are you unemployed?"

"I like to say I'm between opportunities." He almost smiled, but it faded away. "Told you I had a construction company, but the business dried up and now it's gone. I'm bankrupt. My bank accounts are almost empty."

Twisting my head around to look at him, I said, "Aidan, I'm so sorry."

"Doesnae matter."

I rested a hand on his chest, over his heart. "Um, I hope you won't take this the wrong way…"

"Just say it." He let his hand fall over my shoulder. "Ahmno sensitive."

"Yes, I've noticed that." I hesitated, but then plowed ahead. "I'm wondering why you're on the hunt for a wife, with the intention of starting a family, when you're bankrupt and unemployed. If you're looking for a rich woman who'll support you, I have to tell you I'm as poor as you are."

He stiffened but kept his hand on my shoulder. "I am not looking for a rich woman. And I didnae plan anything. Acted on impulse is what I did." He clenched his jaw, averting his eyes. "Begged Lachlan for a loan to finance my trip to America, but I wouldnae take more than I needed, and I insisted on staying at Erica's house in Chicago instead of a posh hotel. Had to give in a little, since Lachlan refused to help me at all unless I flew here in his jet. But I will pay him back for every penny I owe him."

I cringed inwardly. "And I made sure you owe him even more, thanks to you accidentally agreeing to let him do more for you."

Aidan pulled me in closer, sheltered under his arm. "I told you, Lachlan usually gets his way in the end. Being the oldest, he thinks it's his right and duty to stick his nose in the lives of every one of his brothers and sisters. And he's right, more often than not."

"He's not one of those greedy people who won't help out their relatives."

"Definitely not. He loves spending money on us. You should've seen how much he spent getting Erica cleared of embezzling charges after her former lover set her up. Lachlan is the most generous person you'll ever meet—except for Rory. They're tied for the title."

I rested my chin on his shoulder. "You love your brothers, don't you?"

"Of course I do. Love all my brothers and sisters." He kissed my forehead and tucked a lock of hair behind my ear. "I hope one day you'll tell me what's going on with you, why you're hiding in the woods."

"It's a very long, very tedious story."

"Doubt that." He whisked his hand up and down my arm in a comforting gesture, and I laid my head on his chest. He murmured, "Nothing about you is tedious."

"You either. But you have to take my word for it that you probably wouldn't like it if you knew everything about me."

He rested his head against mine, his breaths ruffling my hair. "No judgment from me. Made plenty of mistakes, some worse than others."

Wouldn't ask him for details, though my curiosity prodded me to do exactly that. As long as I refused to confide in him, my curiosity would have to shut up. Changing the subject seemed the most prudent action.

An idea occurred to me and I said, "Should we take a drive today? I can show you my favorite parts of the scenery."

"I'll go anywhere with you. Anywhere at all." He placed his palm over my hand, on my lap, and threaded his fingers through mine. "I'm easy to please."

Right. All he wanted was me—body, heart, and soul.

My first rule was shattered. Maintaining the other two suddenly became of the utmost importance as if the safety of my very soul depended on it. I'd given away a sliver of myself when I agreed to marry Rade and participate in a fraud, violating the law out of guilt over everything he'd done for me. Had he planned it that way? Taking advantage of my grief and desperation to trick me into helping him.

I couldn't believe that. If I did, then everything I'd thought I knew about the man I'd married was wrong. And if I could be wrong about a man I'd known for seven years, two of those years before we married, then I couldn't trust my instincts about anyone.

As I sat there, enveloped by Aidan, I remembered how I'd told him I trusted him. And I began to wonder if I should.

Chapter Nineteen

An hour later, we were preparing to climb into my old car when the crunching of tires on gravel drew our attention to the long driveway, where it wound through the deep woods toward the house. The vehicle became visible gradually as it passed through the shadows into the dappled sunlight and, finally, into the full sun. A blond-haired man sat behind the wheel of the red sports car, which he parked alongside my old beater. Aidan's rental was stashed on the opposite side of my car.

The blond man shut off the car's engine, swung open the door, and hopped out with a big smile on his face. He turned to Aidan, offering his hand. "Mr. MacTaggart?"

Aidan, appearing wary and somewhat confused, took the man's hand. "Aye, I'm Aidan MacTaggart. Who are you?"

"Billy, from the rental agency."

My Scot's eyebrows knit together. "From the what?"

"The car rental agency. Your brother called about getting you an upgrade."

"Upgrade?" Aidan's confusion crumbled away, replaced by the light of understanding. "Ah, Lachlan said he was going to get me a better car. I almost forgot."

He sounded like he wished Lachlan had forgotten.

Billy the Car Guy handed Aidan the keys to the cherry-red vehicle. "It's a convertible, by the way, perfect for beautiful summer days."

Aidan accepted the keys, but his gaze swiveled to me and he smiled in his secret way that made my body hum. "Mm, perfect for enjoying a beautiful lass on a beautiful summer day."

"Exactly," Billy said, seeming oblivious of the innuendo in Aidan's words.

I understood what he meant by enjoying me—and he wasn't talking about making me laugh. The sparkle in his eyes confirmed my analysis.

Aidan hooked the key ring over his middle finger and flipped the keys around it once, with a bright jangling sound. "Billy, how are you to get back to wherever you came from?"

"I'll take the other car. The one you rented yourself."

"Of course." Aidan extracted the keys to that vehicle and tossed them to Billy. "Do I tip you? I'm new to this country, and I don't know all the etiquette."

"No tip required, sir. Your brother took care of everything."

Aidan's mouth warped downward at one corner, half annoyance, half humor. "Naturally, he did. Lachlan takes care of everything for everyone, whether you want him to or not."

I slipped my arm through his, leaning into him. "Brothers. They can be presumptuous, but they do it out of love."

Billy glanced back and forth between us, his brows furrowed. "Sure, I guess they do. I should get back to work. Have fun with the car."

The youthful blond all but ran to the other rental car, apparently put off by our conversation. The poor boy must've been confused by our interactions. As the rejected rental roared off down the gravel drive, spewing dust and gravel in its wake, I rested my cheek on Aidan's upper arm and gazed up at him.

"So," I said, "shall we take your gift for a drive?"

"Yes." He straightened, determination on his face. "I planned to take you for a drive and I intend to keep my word."

"Actually, it was my idea." I stepped away from him to circle around the front of the sports car, approaching the driver's side. "Cool, it's a Mustang."

"If Lachlan could've hired an Aston Martin, I'm sure he would have."

"Here in the U.P., you aren't likely to find a rentable luxury car, especially not one as expensive as an Aston Martin."

"Lachlan owns two of them." Aidan puckered his mouth. "He keeps trying to give me one."

"Oh, don't be so petulant about it. Your brother's only trying to help." I walked back to him and looped my arms around his neck. "I think it's nice your rich brother wants to help out his family. In my experience, a lot of people who have money don't like to share it with anyone. Or if they do share, it comes with chains attached."

"Chains?" He crooked a finger under my chin, tipping my head up until our gazes met. "You say the oddest things at times. Have you known someone who—"

"Let's not talk about serious things." I tightened my arms around his neck, pulling my body snug against his, loving the feel of his hard muscles pressed into my breasts. "Let's take advantage of this wonderful summer's day."

"We will." He peeled my hands away from his neck, taking one in his big hand and leading me toward the Mustang's passenger door. Like a perfect gentleman, he held the door open while I climbed inside and settled onto the lush leather seat. I ran my hands over the upholstery. "Oooh, this is nice. I could get used to the high life."

He frowned. "Guess Lachlan should be dating you."

Before I could respond, he slammed the door shut. I watched him stalk around the front of the vehicle, tear open the driver's door, and throw his big body into the seat. He yanked the door shut with a huff.

"Oh come on," I said. "You have to get over this aversion to being pampered. Are you jealous of Lachlan? Because I'm here with you. I invited you to stay with me, not your brother. I'm sleeping with you, not your brother."

"If you met Lachlan, you'd probably prefer him. Or maybe Rory." Aidan jammed the key in the ignition, jerking it to stir the engine to grumbling life.

I let that go for the moment, more concerned with the nature of Aidan's statement. "Is Rory well off too? Because if he is, I'm starting to see a definite pattern."

"He's got money. Not as much as Lachlan, but at least fifty-fold more than I've got." He shifted the car into reverse, flung an arm over the back of my seat, and craned his neck to glance behind. "And of course there's a pattern. They're successful and I'm a failure."

"That is not true."

He swerved the car backward in a semicircle, so fast I was thrown forward. Since I hadn't done up my seatbelt yet, I had to thrust my hands out to stop from careening into the dashboard. I yelped.

Aidan hit the brakes hard, which flung me backward into my seat.

"Jesus Christ," I hissed, "if this is how you drive, you can forget me going anywhere with you."

He dropped his face into his hands briefly, then looked at me with regret in his eyes. "I'm sorry. That was childish and stupid, and I could've hurt you. It will never happen again."

"Damn straight it won't. If it does, I'm out of here and you can sleep in this car."

"I'll be more careful, I swear it." He pointed at my lap. "But you should still do up your seatbelt."

"Oh yeah." I secured the belt and rested my arm on the center console. "By the way, you are not a failure. Everybody has bad times, and that does not make you a failure in life in general."

He grunted, then shifted the car into drive and eased it down the gravel road.

Okay, I guessed we weren't going to talk about this anymore for the moment. Probably for the best, since I had no desire to become roadkill. Men could be sensitive about money and perceived status, even men who were otherwise self-assured. When it came to seduction, Aidan had no doubts about himself. But clearly, his brothers and their monetary success made him feel inferior. In a way, I could understand. As someone who'd suffered my own financial woes, I knew how easy it was to define yourself by the lack of zeroes at the end of your bank balance. I'd also learned to avoid that particular trap.

Aidan would have to figure that out on his own, though. I couldn't make him believe it.

Just like he couldn't make me believe we belonged together.

Sighing, Aidan relaxed into his driving with a satisfied smile on his lips. "Where should we go?"

"What are you in the mood for? Secluded or crowded?"

"Secluded." He glanced at me sideways, his smile heating up to a steamy simmer. "I have plans for you that might be illegal in public."

I sank into my seat, warm and soft and tingling with anticipation. "Take a left at the end of the driveway. We're heading north, into the wilds."

Chapter Twenty

The Mustang hugged the asphalt as it flew up the winding, two-lane highway through the woods toward the summit of Brockway Mountain. Aidan had rolled the top down. I luxuriated in the wind whipping through my hair, the sensuousness of the cushy leather seat enveloping me, and the warmth of Aidan's hand wrapped around mine. He drove with one hand draped over the wheel, his muscular body cradled in his seat. Our joined hands lay on the center console, our fingers intertwined.

I hadn't felt this relaxed in years. Relaxed and…content.

"There," Aidan said with great conviction, pointing at a turnout along the side of the highway. "We'll stop for a bit."

"Okay, but it's just a view of trees."

"It's secluded." He glanced in the rearview mirror. "And we have no company at the moment."

The side mirror showed me no cars behind us and I noted the lack of oncoming traffic he'd mentioned. No big surprise. Even at the height of tourist season, this road wasn't packed.

Aidan slowed the Mustang, pulling off into the turnout. It was a dirt patch situated at the edge of the mountainside, hemmed in by a wooden railing. Aidan stood up and stepped out of the car over the top of the door.

I watched in awe as he strode around the front of the car to swing my door open for me. "You have something against using the driver's door?"

"With the top down, I don't need the door."

"Uh-huh." I took the hand he offered me and let him help me out of the vehicle. "I've never seen anyone get out of a car that way. Got to admit, it's kind of sexy."

"Kind of? Is that all?" He feigned a scoff. "Must've done it wrong. You should've been weak with desire after witnessing my stunning display of masculine prowess."

I laughed and leaned in, lifting onto my tiptoes to peck a kiss on his lips. "I was very impressed. Does that count?"

He pretended to consider my question. "I suppose I'll accept it."

Couldn't help it, I laughed again.

Aidan folded his hand around mine, shut the car door, and guided me toward the railing. We admired the view for about a minute before he said, "Back in the car."

"Don't you want to absorb the scenery a little longer?"

"Ahmno interested in trees or water at the moment." He threw an arm around my waist, pulling me tight against him. His blue eyes blazed with a need I recognized. My body responded of its own volition, softening and warming. He dipped his head close to mine. "I have other ideas."

His hands slid down to cover my behind. Long, powerful fingers massaged my flesh through my jeans, arousing a fire deep inside me. He tugged me forward and upward, pressing the rigid line of his erection into my groin. My breaths quickened, and my head grew light, as if the oxygen content of the air had dropped and the only thing that could fill my lungs was his kiss. My gaze flew to his mouth and those luscious, parted lips.

My tongue sneaked out to glide across my lower lip.

Aidan growled low in his throat, so animalistic, so masculine and possessive. His hands gripped my ass more firmly and his fingers dug into my flesh. Not painful, the pressure whetted my appetite for more. Possessed by a compulsion to ravage his mouth, I moved to kiss him.

Clucking his tongue, he pulled his head back. "Not yet, my impatient angel. Ye cannae have me until I've had your pleasure."

An irritated little noise squeaked out of me. I flung my hands up to grasp his face, intent on dragging him in for a bone-melting kiss.

He captured my wrists in his hands, brought them behind my back, and secured them there with one hand. His free hand shifted in front of me, rushing down between our bodies, cupping my groin through my clothes, sliding lower until the heel of his hand rested on my mound and his long fingers stretched between my thighs, hot and strong against my throbbing core. I sucked in a sharp breath, desperate to rip my clothes off right here and now—or to let him do the ripping for me.

As he rubbed his fingers up and down my cleft, the friction of my panties on my bare, swollen flesh somehow intensified the glorious sensation. *Oh God, yes. More of this, more of it now.* I rocked my hips, urging him to rub harder, faster.

Chuckling, he stilled his fingers. "Easy. No need to rush."

"Why the hell not?"

He grazed his lips across mine, flicking his tongue out to tease the seam. Against my mouth, he murmured, "I want to drive you wild until you beg me to take you. And you will, that's a promise."

As if punctuating his vow, he scraped his fingers up and down my cleft three times in rapid succession. I whimpered, my knees threatening to buckle. He released my wrists to clamp his arm around my back, pinning me to his hard body and pinning his hand to my crotch. He rubbed and rubbed, fast and then slow, faster again until I clutched at his shoulders and threw my head back, lost to the bliss of his touch. The pleasure pulsated through me, stronger every second, driving me toward climax.

Just as I teetered on the brink, he removed his hand and stepped back. He took hold of my hips to keep me from tumbling to the ground.

I gaped at him, panting too hard to speak, on fire in the most intimate ways.

He turned me toward the view, his hands still on my hips, and backed me up toward the car. When my behind bumped the passenger door, he set my hands on the top of the door. "Hold on."

Before I could ask why, he knelt before me and ripped the zipper of my pants down. His fingers dived inside the waistband of my panties. He yanked both pants and panties down over my hips, all the way to my ankles. Exposed to the world, I beheld the man crouched at my feet.

Maybe I should've been nervous about his intentions. Maybe I should've worried about doing this outdoors, where anyone might stumble onto us in flagrante. He'd made sure no other cars were around, and this was a remote area. With Aidan, I never worried about my safety. He gave me a sense of security unlike any I'd known in my life, a sense that nothing bad could come of anything we did together. He would take care of me, no matter what.

A chill tingled over my scalp and down my spine. I trusted this man. Though I'd told him as much this morning, the import of my declaration hadn't hit me until this moment, with my backside squashed against the car and his head between my legs. I trusted him, really trusted him. After seven days together. Seven freaking days.

He picked up one of my feet, moving it to the side, spreading my legs.

The chill dissolved into the sparkling fire of my passion for him, erasing my worries, erasing every thought except my awareness of his hands on my skin and his sizzling appraisal of my body. I still pulsated with a thwarted release. Catching my breath had become impossible, and as I watched him part my folds with his fingers, I lost my breath.

How did he do this to me? How—

Aidan blew on my overheated flesh.

I whimpered, slumping against the car.

He thrust his tongue deep between my folds and dragged it up toward my clitoris. The instant before he would've contacted my rigid, aching nub, he withdrew his tongue.

My head fell back. "Please, Aidan."

That devious tongue of his skimmed along my outer folds—up one side, down the other—over and over until my knees went weak. He grasped my hips to hold me up, then rolled his gaze up to me. "Please what, *mo chridhe*?"

"Take me, Aidan, please."

He sealed his mouth over my clit and sucked hard.

The orgasm rocketed through me with an intensity that had my heart thudding and my knees buckling, my body held up solely by the car and Aidan.

He flipped me around and laid my hands on the top of the door again. "Are ye ready?"

Speechless, breathless, I nodded.

The *zzzt* of a zipper. A grunt. The crinkle of foil ripping. A heavy, relieved exhalation.

With both hands, he took hold of my hips once more. Tilted them up and back. Kissed my neck. And plowed into me in one long, powerful stroke. He froze there, clutching me to him.

"Okay?" he asked, his voice rough, almost hoarse.

"Uh-huh."

He drove into me again and again, flesh slapping against flesh, his balls slapping on my ass with each withdrawal and thrust of his velvety shaft. I threw my head back, my fingers clenched over the doorframe. He grunted every time he plunged inside me, driving harder and faster, lifting my hips into his thrusts with his fingers digging into me. My body tightened around his cock, gripping him like a vise as I came again, helpless to resist the onslaught of sensations. My fingers gripped the car so hard it hurt, but I could do nothing except ride the storm of pleasure, my sex clutching him with the same desperate need that pushed me to scream his name and buck my hips up to take him deeper inside me.

My cries echoed off the trees.

Aidan punched into me twice more until his own release had him shouting to the heavens, his entire body stiff as steel. He relaxed gradually, loosening his fingers on my hips, and leaned forward to seal his mouth over my ear. "Now that's how to enjoy the scenery."

"The scenery?" I said, breathless. "All you saw was my ass."

"And your sweet, pink flesh."

He tugged my underwear and pants back into place, zipping them up for me. I heard him doing the same, and I staggered in my attempt to turn toward him.

Aidan picked me up and deposited me in the passenger seat without bothering to open the door. He hooked my seatbelt in position, then strode around to the driver's side and vaulted over the door to land in his seat. With a flick of his wrist, he turned the key in the ignition.

My body thrummed like a guitar string, alive and satisfied from our surprise encounter.

Aidan navigated the car back onto the road.

"You really are sex incarnate," I said.

"I'm what?" he asked, with a hitch of laughter in his voice.

"When we first met, I decided you were sex incarnate. You radiate sensuality like it's a part of your essence."

He cast me a sidelong look, brows raised. "I've never been called sex incarnate before."

"Never? Haven't you done this sort of thing before? To other women, I mean."

"No. Only you."

The afterglow of total satiation seemed to heighten my senses, making me hyperaware of the wind buffeting my face, my hair whipping around my head, the scent of flowers and grass and leather. I glanced at Aidan, but his gaze never wavered from the road ahead. Even when I sneaked a hand out to squeeze his thigh, he smiled but maintained impeccable control as he steered the Mustang around a sharp curve.

I raked my nails up and down his thigh until he laid his hand over mine to still it. "Which part have you done only with me?"

"Most everything I've done with you is new for me."

"Why are you different with me than with those seven other women?"

"Because you are different. It was always casual before, but this time I want it to be more." He curled his fingers around mine on his thigh. "I want everything with you."

My mouth opened, but for the longest moment, I couldn't make any sound come out. "You know I can't give you what you want."

"I know you think you can't—or think you don't want to." He lifted my hand to his lips and peppered kisses over my knuckles, his expression going soft and...affectionate. "We could be happy together, I know we can. Please let yourself think about the possibility, instead of dismissing it out of hand."

Pulling in a deep breath, I exhaled it slowly. "I'll consider your request."

"That's all I ask."

He set my hand on my leg and withdrew his hand, leaving me bereft at the sudden loss of contact. I'd grown dangerously addicted to his touch, his kiss, his unbelievable talent for tempting into me doing things I shouldn't do. Worst of all, he was tempting me to break rule number two.

No love.

I let my gaze wander to his face. The sweet little smile on his lips. The faint lines around his eyes, lines of happiness. I relaxed into the soft leather of the seat, my head lolling to the side so I could gaze at him a little longer. His profile entranced me, and when he turned his head to smile at me, I smiled back. Feeling girlish. Frivolous. Ridiculously happy.

I swung my head to the front, fixated on the road ahead and the yellow line speeding past us.

Dear God. I was falling for him.

Chapter Twenty-One

On this morning, I sat at my desk in the corner of the living room, swiveling my chair side to side, struggling to concentrate on my job search as I scoured websites for any kind of openings. For the past three days, Aidan and I had explored the western U.P. during day trips in his rented Mustang. We visited waterfalls and inland lakes, Lake Superior beaches and state parks, historic copper mines and little museums in between finding remote places to drive each other mad with our shared ardor and fantastic orgasms. He made me come hard, yes. But he also made me laugh, made me feel appreciated and understood, and not once did he pester me to tell him why I wouldn't marry him.

Twice during our day trips, he received calls from Seona that left him agitated. I wouldn't tell him everything about me yet, so I couldn't ask for details about what hold she had on him. Why she was demanding money. Why he might give it to her, if he had the money.

When we'd reached the top of Brockway Mountain on the first day of our sojourns, Aidan had marveled at the panoramic view of the tip of the Keweenaw. Lake Superior stretched along one side of our view and the woods sloped down in front of us. Behind us, the shuttered gift shop stood silent and rather melancholy, but I couldn't stop smiling as I pointed out an ore boat on the lake and an eagle soaring above our heads.

Leaning against the concrete wall at the cliff's edge, Aidan had informed me that "this view is nice, but it can't compare to seeing Loch Leven from the top of Beinn a' Bheithir."

"You're not speaking American, are you?"

He winked and grinned. "Gaelic. It's the name of a mountain near Ballachulish."

"Do you climb mountains?"

"No, I—" He turned his face away from me, swallowing visibly. "Not anymore."

I took his hand to settle his arm over my shoulders. Tucked against his body, I slipped my arms around him. "I didn't mean to bring up bad memories."

"Not your fault." He wrapped his arms around me, burrowing his face into my hair, drawing in a long breath as if the scent of my shampoo could sustain him. "Why marry a man you didn't love?"

"Why does Seona expect you to pay her off?" When he said nothing, I tilted my head up to look at him. "See, we both have secrets. I don't expect you to tell me all of yours."

"And I'd be a hypocrite if I expected you to answer my question. You're right. No more questions about your marriage." He kissed the top of my head and smiled. "Why don't we get back to our drive?"

Just like that, he'd morphed back into happy Aidan. Seeing him in pain, even for a few minutes, had set off a twinge in my chest that reminded me of my revelation in the car. I had to be wrong. I wasn't falling for this man I'd known for a week. Still, our acquaintance seemed to be turning into a whirlwind…romance.

Back in the present, my arms began to ache. I suddenly realized I'd been hovering my hands over the keyboard for so long my muscles had started to complain about it. Lowering my hands onto my lap, I stared at the computer screen. Since getting up at six thirty this morning, I'd found exactly zero postings for which I was qualified. Partly because my eyes kept swimming out of focus and my thoughts kept wandering.

Hard to focus when I kept thinking about Aidan.

We'd indulged in quite a few erotic encounters, in various spots along our journey. I'd learned I was as insatiable as he was—and that I loved trying new things with him. Nothing kinky, just scorching sex in every position imaginable, and in the upcoming days, maybe a few neither of us had thought of yet.

Rubbing my eyes, I groaned in frustration. Letting a hot guy drive me to distraction was idiotic. Time to suck it up, banish thoughts of *him* and especially thoughts of my confused feelings for him, and concentrate on the task at hand. Find a goddamn job. I'd neglected my job search for three days, too caught up in Aidan to think about anything else. I set my fingers on the keyboard and typed salient phrases into a job search site. Ten minutes later, I'd found one listing for a part-time, seasonal secretary—in remote Alaska. And it paid minimum wage. No stipend for moving expenses either.

My mind traveled back to Aidan. Those amazing lips. His skillful hands working my slick flesh. His cock filling me up and—

"What are you doing?"

I yelped and jerked, twisting my head around to find Aidan behind me, bending over with his head near mine. A faint smile curved his lips and that playful gleam twinkled in his eyes.

"Don't sneak up on me," I said, and lightly slapped his arm. "You scared me half to death."

"At least it was only halfway."

"Not funny." I grumbled out a sigh. "Why are you spying on me?"

"You seemed absorbed by whatever you're doing."

"And scaring the shit out of me sounded like a good plan?"

"Didn't mean to frighten you."

I swiveled my chair sideways to the desk, laying one arm on the desktop. He stayed right there, bent at the waist, his face a foot from mine and his smile turning wry.

"You can tell me," he said. "Whatever it is. I'm good at keeping secrets."

Gazing into those crystalline blue eyes, I was tempted to tell him everything. Keeping secrets gave me heartburn at best and turned me into a neurotic mess at worst. For five years, I'd concealed a big, damning secret. Sharing a non-secret—something I simply hadn't told him yet, something that couldn't get either of us thrown in jail—might ease a bit of the stress.

Aidan placed the pad of his thumb on my lower lip and pressed down. My lip popped free of my teeth. I sat up straighter, clearing my throat, surprised to discover I'd been biting my lip.

"Don't be anxious," he said. "I won't think less of you, no matter what it is."

I glanced at the computer, clicked a mouse button to bring up the job search screen, and faced him again. As I drummed my fingernails on the desktop, I realized I was biting my lip again and released it a second before his thumb would've touched my mouth. He withdrew his hand. I groaned in resignation. "I've been looking for a job. I'm unemployed and have been for months. My savings will run out very soon and I have zero prospects for employment."

One of his eyebrows hiked up. "That's your shameful secret?"

"It's not a secret. I hadn't gotten around to telling you is all. 'I'm an unemployed pauper' isn't something I tell everyone I meet."

"You don't need to be ashamed of having no money."

"I'm not ashamed of being poor. Not being able to find a job, that's another thing altogether." I drummed my fingers on the desk. "I have a master's degree in library science, but I've never had a job that required it, even when I worked in a library. Today, I'm considering a part-time secretarial position in Alaska. It's nobody's fault, but it sucks and it's demoralizing. Not the kind of thing I'm dying to share with the world."

Aidan dropped into a crouch beside me. "I know how you feel."

"Guess you do."

"Why not ask your family for help? Surely, they'd be glad to step in."

"The man who balked at accepting his brother's help is encouraging me to accept the aid of my family."

"I'm twice a hypocrite, eh?" He shrugged and sighed. "Donnae mean to be. But you did trick me into taking Lachlan's charity, so…"

"I owe you a personal humiliation of my own?" I puckered my lips, struggling not to smile. "We sure have a strange relationship, don't we?"

"But it works for us, doesn't it?"

"Suppose it does."

He stared at me for a few seconds, the intensity of his gaze making my skin itch. Finally, he said, "You called this a relationship."

"No, I—" *Oh damn.* I had. "I meant in the general sense, not like we're in a relationship."

"Ah, of course." His gaze flicked to the computer screen and back to me. "The job search seems to be making you tense."

"Duh."

He rested a palm on my thigh, skating it up to the juncture of my hip. "I can ease that tension and make you very relaxed."

"Um…" *Flashback alert.* "Thanks, but I need to focus on my job search right now. I can't keep living here past next month unless I find work. You'd be better off hunting for a financially solvent American girl."

"Don't care about money." Aidan moved his hand to my inner thigh. "I'm bankrupt, remember? We have more in common than I knew."

"Oh great. Two broke people." All of a sudden, keeping secrets from the man who'd given me mind-blowing orgasms and treated me with nothing but kindness seemed idiotic. I couldn't believe I'd worried about telling him I was jobless. Maybe I could share the rest.

No, not yet.

"Listen," I said, "can this stay off the MacTaggart grapevine for the time being?"

"I won't tell. You can trust me."

"You know I do." I'd told him as much, and hell, I must've trusted him from the start. Why else would I have let him do the things he'd done to me? I'd loved every second of it, even while anxiety about this whatever-it-was between us gnawed at my gut.

He leaned in, his face near mine, those kissable lips millimeters from mine. "My offer to distract you is an open one. Take me up on it anytime."

The hairs all over my body shivered erect from the heat of his gaze and the sultry tone of his voice, not to mention the nearness of his body. We'd had sex quite a lot, but this seemed like far more than a flirtatious offer for a roll in the hay.

"Maybe later," I said.

"Aye," he said, his voice a sensual rumble. "Later. I'm always ready for you."

"Likewise."

He traced a fingertip down my jaw. "Feel free to sneak into my room in the dead of night."

My traitorous body thrummed with excitement at the possibility. "Since you've been sleeping in my bed, that's pretty much a certainty."

"Tonight, I'll sleep in the guest room." His fingertip skimmed across my lips. "Just so you can sneak in and crawl under the sheets with me. We've never made love in the dark."

Hard to breathe. Hard to move. Hard to think or focus on anything except his lips. I imagined tiptoeing into his bedroom at two a.m., slipping beneath the sheets, crawling down his long body to close my mouth around his penis while it swelled into a raging erection.

"You like the idea," Aidan said.

I sank into my chair. "Oh yeah, I really do."

"Then I'll be waiting for you tonight." He brushed his lips against mine, straightened, and said, "I'm having a shower. Care to join me?"

I needed a couple seconds to shake off my erotic fantasy. "Not this time."

"My sister's coming tomorrow, so this may be our last chance to rattle the house."

"As much as I'd love that, I can't. Gotta continue the fruitless job search."

"You'll find something eventually." He kissed the top of my head. "I believe in you."

"Thanks." *I believe in you too*, I wanted to say. For some reason, I couldn't speak the words. They sounded too intimate, too much like something a woman in love might say.

Aidan padded off toward the bathroom.

I couldn't keep from thinking about him in the shower. Naked. Wet. Muscles flexing. Water cascading over his shoulders and down his chest and back. I could run my hands over that body and lave every inch of him with my tongue as I'd done so many times before. Couldn't get enough of it—of him.

The doorbell rang.

I jumped. My hand flew to my chest as the doorbell sounded again. I hurried across the living room and swung the door open.

Gavin frowned at me. "Why aren't you answering your phone?"

Chapter Twenty-Two

M y phone?" I stared at my brother, all six foot one of him, slightly cowed by the stern expression on his face. Pale gold eyes bored into me, demanding answers. I ratcheted my spine straight, squared my shoulders, and met his gaze head-on. "I've been busy."

Since Aidan and I had been on daily trips out into the wilds of Upper Michigan, we'd likely gone out of cell range a lot of the time. Plus, I'd been a little distracted by my new companion. That body. Those hands. Those lips. I lost track of everything else whenever he took my body, whispering Gaelic phrases in my ear while he drove me to the heights of ecstasy.

Oh lord, Aidan. I glanced at the hallway, down which the sizzling Scot had disappeared a little while ago heading for the bathroom. I couldn't hear the shower running. And more than anything in the entire universe, I did not want to explain Aidan to my brother.

Gavin squinted at me with stoic disapproval, the way only an ex-military man could. "Are you going to tell me, or do I have to tell you?"

"Tell you what?"

He angled toward me a smidgen, still squinting. "I talked to Tara."

Cold rushed through me, but I fought to camouflage my discomfort. I hadn't asked Tara not to tell Gavin about my houseguest, hadn't occurred to me I should. Feigning innocence, I asked, "What'd she say?"

Lips compressed, he hissed a breath out his nostrils. "You're living with some foreign guy."

"I'm not living with him." My fingers ached, probably because I was gripping the doorknob like the whole house might float away without me holding it in place. "His motel room was damaged by a burst pipe and he couldn't find anywhere else to stay."

"You've got a strange man in your house, not a stray puppy."

My mouth fell open, but no words emerged. My brain couldn't piece together a coherent syllable, much less a whole sentence.

Gavin took hold of my shoulders and turned me sideways, then strode into the house.

Mandy and Misty came tearing through the dog door, made a beeline for Gavin, and leaped up on him with such glee that he staggered backward a step. As the puppies slopped their tongues on any exposed skin they could reach, he tried to calm them with a hand on each of their heads. After a moment, they returned their front paws to the floor, content to have their heads scratched.

Kneeling to pet the furry girls, Gavin leveled his gaze on me again. "I don't like this one bit, C."

I let Gavin get away with calling me C because he was my big brother and big brothers got special dispensation. I would've hated it if anyone else called me that.

Shutting the door, I folded my arms over my chest. "I'm a grown woman, Gav. I can do whatever I want, without your permission."

"Without any sense either."

The puppies jerked their heads up, ears pricked, and took off for the hallway.

I would've preferred to believe they got a sudden urge to bounce around on my bed and ball up the quilt so they could pounce all over it. Unfortunately, I heard the faint click of the bathroom door opening. The puppies had taken off to lavish their attentions on Aidan.

Panic iced through me. Overbearing, ex-Marine brother meets hot Highlander who's ravishing his little sister on a regular basis. Nothing good could come of this.

I snagged Gavin's arm and tried to pull him toward the door, but he wouldn't budge, solid and immovable as a two-ton granite statue.

"Please," I said, "let's go outside and talk. It's a beautiful day."

His eyes narrowed again. "What don't you want me to see?"

And of course, that's when Aidan sauntered out of the hallway half naked and damp, a towel in one hand.

I clamped my lips between my teeth, wincing.

Gavin turned around, coming face to face with my houseguest. His eyes seemed to go flinty, narrowed to the merest slits and zeroed in on the Scotsman. My brother didn't fist his hands, but his fingers tensed and curled toward his palms just enough to convey his desire to throttle someone. Probably me. Maybe Aidan too.

"Hello," Aidan said, his smile friendly and wide.

My brother clenched his jaw. His gaze darted from Aidan to me.

Aidan had donned his low-slung jeans, but he wore no shirt. His bare chest glistened with lingering dampness from his shower. His wet hair was wild, and when he lifted the towel to scrub his head with it, his hair got even wilder. The trail of hair down the middle of his chest tapered into a line that dived beneath the hip-hugging waistband of his jeans, like an arrow pointing straight to his privates.

He couldn't have looked more like a sex god if he'd tried.

My brother lodged his hands on his hips. "Who the hell are you?"

"Aidan MacTaggart." The Scot held out a hand to my brother. "And you are?"

Gavin glanced at Aidan's hand, his lip curling an eensy bit. "I'm the Marine who's about to kick your ass from here to Mexico."

That did it. I stomped between the two men and rounded on my brother. "Stop acting like a caveman. Aidan is not the enemy and I can take care of myself, thank you very much." I leaned toward him and whispered, "Remember who took care of you after Mom and Dad died."

At the mention of our parents, the anger evacuated his body. He pinched his forehead between his thumb and forefinger, sighing as if the weight of the world resided on his shoulders alone. It had been a low blow, I knew, but all I could think of to defuse the situation.

"Should I leave?" Aidan asked, running a hand through his hair to comb it out. "Seems like the two of you have things to discuss."

"You don't have to leave," I said, casting him an over-the-shoulder glance. "This is my brother, Gavin."

Aidan smiled again, his curious gaze aimed at Gavin. "Your brother? That does explain it."

"Explain what?" Gavin asked.

"Why you're concerned about her welfare. I have three sisters and I wouldn't like to find a man I'd never met staying in any of their homes. Especially not my younger sister."

Gavin's face blanked. He didn't move or speak for a minute, maybe more. Then, as one side of his mouth ticked up, he said to Aidan, "Maybe I should go move in with your little sister."

"You could try," Aidan said, "but Jamie lives with my older brother Rory at the moment. He's not as friendly as I am."

Grasping the back of his neck, Gavin frowned. "I still don't like this, but...Calli's an adult. She can do what she wants."

I wanted this conversation to end, but that seemed unlikely. At least my brother was conceding I had the right to make my own decisions. Of course, that didn't mean he'd relinquish his right to critique my choices.

Gavin took a step toward Aidan, bypassing me, and offered his hand. "Might as well make peace, huh?"

"Aye." Aidan shook his hand.

"Just so you know," Gavin said, "I was in the Marines and I served in Afghanistan. Not only could I kill you with my bare hands, but my buddies from the Corps would help me dispose of your body so no one will ever find it."

"I don't doubt it." Aidan slung the towel over one bare shoulder. "I would never hurt Calli or let anyone else hurt her."

"Damn straight. If she gets hurt, I'll hunt you down and take you out."

"You could try."

Gavin stared at Aidan for a long moment, then slapped his shoulder. Hard. "I think we understand each other, don't we?"

Okay, this was all the bravado and male bonding I could handle. I waved my arms, to remind them I was there. "Your bromance has begun, congratulations. Should I leave you two alone?"

Gavin's mouth twisted into an exasperated expression. "Real funny, C. But you and me still need to have a serious conversation."

"There's nothing to say. Aidan's staying here, you don't like it, I don't care, end of discussion."

Aidan started for the hall, tiptoeing away.

"Where are you going?" I asked.

My brother snorted. "I hope he's going to put on a shirt."

I covered my face with my hands. This was going to be a long day. Very long.

As the Scot disappeared into the guest room, I turned back to my brother. "How long are you planning to hang around and scowl?"

"Depends." He crossed his brawny arms over his chest, fixing me with his military-man glare. "How long is your new friend sticking around?"

I hated to think about Aidan leaving, it made me sick to think about it, but I could hardly tell my brother that. Instead, I asked, "Where are you staying?"

"Here."

My stomach dropped through the floor, straight into the earth's core. "You can't. Aidan's in the guest room."

"You mentioned once there's a hunting shack on the property."

I blinked rapidly. "You want to stay in the shack that has no electricity and no bed? You'll need to buy a sleeping bag or something and—"

"Stop. I'm staying and that's that." He lowered his arms but gritted his teeth. "No way am I leaving till I figure out what's going on with you. Besides, I can handle roughing it."

"But—"

Gavin marched out the door, calling over his shoulder, "Going to get my stuff. Back in a tick."

As the door clicked shut behind him, I let my shoulders slump. *Oh, wonderful.* My bossy big brother planned on sleeping in the shack about two hundred feet from the house in which Aidan and I were having sex on a daily basis. Gavin intended to figure me out. Aidan intended to convince me to marry him.

If ever someone invented a recipe for thermonuclear disaster, this was it.

Chapter Twenty-Three

I woke the next morning in Aidan's bed, his warm body molded to the backside of mine and one of his arms hanging over my hips. Yep, I had sneaked into his bed last night—but only to sleep nestled in his arms, dressed in my nightie. He slept naked. Always. I knew because he'd told me so when I asked if he'd really expected us to have sex after spending the whole exhausting day with Gavin.

Aidan had mumbled, "Sleep naked every night. Not trying to have a poke at ye."

"Is 'poke' a strange Scottish term for sex?"

He'd mumbled again, an incoherent noise.

My brother and Aidan had circled each other all day, each sizing up the other in hopes of winning the argument about their opposing ideas of what I should do. Eventually, they'd reached a kind of detente—not friends, not enemies, but something in the middle. Gavin had even ribbed Aidan the way tough guys liked to do, which meant he'd accepted Aidan at least a little bit. By that time, I was too exhausted to laud their newfound peace. At least Gavin had retreated to the hunting shack, though not before commenting that he was within earshot of the house.

Could he really hear what went on in this house? The woods tended to mute sounds, making them seem farther away than they were. I'd noticed the effect with the puppies' barking. Still, having my brother ensconced in the shack not far from the house made me uneasy.

Oh yeah, thermonuclear disaster on the way.

Aidan had worked hard to make my brother feel better about my living situation and generally acted like a perfect gentleman. Despite the rocky start to their acquaintance, things had thawed a bit, and I was glad for it.

Rocky start? I shook my head, recalling Aidan's emergence from the bathroom. We were lucky Gavin hadn't kidnapped me to get me away from the Don Juan shacked up in my guest room.

The Scot in question was snoring softly behind me. I would've loved to stay here, wrapped up in his body, until he awoke. But I really had to pee.

I crawled out of bed and slunk from the room, shutting the door as quietly as I could. After relieving my needs in the bathroom, I meandered into my bedroom to look for the puppies, but they were nowhere in sight. Outside already, no doubt. The canines rose and shone with the sun. I snagged my robe from the chair, threw it on, and hurried out the door into the hallway intent on whipping up a sumptuous breakfast for me and my Highland lover. By the time I reached the living room, I could hear someone rapping on the glass doors to the backyard. Halting, I peered across the room.

Gavin was standing outside the doors, one hand in his pants pocket and the other rapping on the glass. The puppies leaped around him, with Misty bouncing up and down. Boing, boing, boing went the puppy. When Gavin spotted me, he waved—though his face was cinched into a grimace.

Pulling the robe tighter around me, I hurried to the doors and pushed them open. The slider whisked along its track.

"Morning," I said, with a bit too much cheeriness. "Are the girls being pests?"

"No, they're fine." He shooed them with his foot, but his gaze remained glued to mine. "You planning to let me in? Or is what's-his-name walking around buck naked?"

An image of a nude Aidan lying in bed at this very moment flashed in my mind. I squared my shoulders, determined to ignore the image and its effect on me. "Of course you can come in, Gavin."

I stepped aside to wave him in.

He shuffled over the threshold and threw me an odd sidelong glance. The puppies bounded after him as he headed for the kitchen bar, muttering something I couldn't make out. With an annoyed sigh, he perched on the nearest stool, facing me.

Mandy and Misty's ears perked up. Their heads swiveled toward the hallway and they took off in the direction of the spare bedroom. Where Aidan was naked. Gloriously, completely naked. What if he strolled out of the bedroom in that state?

"You're blushing," Gavin said, sounding surprised.

I laid a hand on my cheek, the coolness of my palm easing the burn. The effect didn't last, though. I clasped my hands over my belly but couldn't think of a damn thing to say.

Gavin forged ahead anyway. "Why are you blushing?"

Ah, the inquisition had begun. In lieu of strapping me to a rack, he speared me with his penetrating gaze. He couldn't know about me and Aidan and our carnal activities.

Unless it was glaringly obvious to everyone.

Gavin rested one arm on the bar, drumming his fingers. "You're sleeping with him, aren't you?"

I marched toward him, targeting him with my stare. "Do you really want to talk about my sex life?"

He turned a little gray, as if he might throw up. "No, I don't."

"Then accept that it's none of your business."

My brother frowned and began thumping one finger on the countertop. "What's wrong with you, C? For years, you didn't even date—as far as I know. When I called a week ago, you didn't say anything about a guy and now you're shacked up with him. I don't understand, that's all."

I didn't understand either, but I'd given up worrying about why I liked having Aidan around. He made me feel good, period. Didn't I deserve to feel good for a little while? Sure, the other night I'd thought I might be falling for him. That was crazy, though, and I'd convinced myself it couldn't be true.

Convinced myself. Yeah, that didn't sound at all like self-delusion.

Gavin hunched his shoulders. "I'm sorry, okay? Maybe it is none of my business. But I love you, Calli, you're the only family I've got—besides Tara, who's a good kid but kind of ditsy. You're supposed to be my level-headed sister, the one I can count on to make sense."

I supposed I couldn't blame him for being taken aback by my recent behavior. For five years, I'd had virtually nothing to do with dating or men. I might as well have joined a convent. Then one day, my brother stopped by to check on me and found his sister in flagrante with a stranger from another country.

"Sorry I disappointed you," I told Gavin, "but you're acting like I committed a capital offense by getting involved with a man. I like Aidan. You've been spending time with him, do you really think he's a Euro-trash gigolo taking advantage of me?"

Gavin sank back in his stool, slumping and gusting out a sigh. "No. I don't think that."

The gleeful yips and barks of two puppies worshiping my lover echoed from down the hall. At the thought of Aidan, the tension relaxed out of my shoulders.

"Now you're smiling," Gavin said, with a hint of wonder in his voice. He glanced at the hallway. "I may not like you sleeping with him, but I have to admit

I've never seen you this happy before. Ever. When you look at him, you get… gushy."

I stared at my brother. Gushy? No. Did I really gaze dreamily at Aidan? In front of other people? In front of my brother?

"Yep," Gavin said, in a knowing tone, "that's right. You moon over him and I'm guessing you don't even realize you're doing it. Man, you've got it bad, don't you?"

Got it bad? Noooo, oh no-no-no. I did not have it bad for Aidan.

Except every time I thought of him, my insides went warm and gooey.

I clamped my lips between my teeth and shifted my gaze to the kitchen cabinets.

Gavin laughed softly, not mocking me, just expressing a growing understanding of the situation. "At least promise me if you marry him, you won't move to Scotland."

My attention snapped back to my brother. "I'm not marrying Aidan."

"No?" Gavin's brows knit together over his nose. "You say that like there's no way in hell you'd even consider it. You always wanted to get married. I remember you acting out fake weddings between your Barbie and Ken dolls."

"That was a long time ago."

"What's happened to you, C?"

His question stabbed into my heart. What had happened to me? I married a foreigner so he could get a green card and then citizenship. I was trapped in a marriage I'd never wanted, struggling to break free but hampered by legal hurdles. If I went to the authorities, I'd get arrested for marriage fraud. Jail time, hefty fines, ruination. Who on earth would hire a convicted criminal?

"Whatever's going on with you," Gavin said, "you can tell me."

But I couldn't. I wouldn't involve him in my criminal mistake.

I opened my mouth to speak, having no clue what I'd say, but footfalls padding down the hallway spared me from bumbling through a lie.

Aidan sauntered into the living room dressed in khaki pants and a blue button-down shirt. The long sleeves only served to accentuate the impressive muscles in his arms. The top two buttons of the shirt were undone, granting a glimpse of the toned flesh beneath.

Out the corner of my eye, I noticed Gavin's smirk. He might as well have stuck his tongue out and said *I told you so, you moony idiot.*

Because yeah, I was mooning at the Highlander. The scent of his cologne wafted toward me, and with his wavy hair brushed back, he looked so good I wanted to run right over and lick him like a lollipop.

"Good morning," Aidan said, smiling at my brother. "Are you joining us for breakfast, Gavin?"

"Sure," Gavin said, still smirking. "You guys must be starving after all that…driving."

I shot my brother a sharp look. Aidan had told him about our road trips yesterday, but Gavin seemed to have guessed our activities involved more than sightseeing.

Gavin's lips warped as he tried not to laugh.

"Better have a quick breakfast," I said. "We have to pick Jamie up at the airport."

Gavin and Aidan began discussing breakfast options while I headed to my bedroom to get dressed. At least one secret was out. The other one, the big one, had to remain a secret. I wouldn't tell Gavin. But the longer Aidan stuck around, the more I longed to confide everything to him. Why should I want to confess my lawbreaking to a man I'd known for eleven days?

I didn't dare consider the answer. No matter what my heart might want, no matter what my body craved every second I was in Aidan's presence, this relationship could go no further than sex.

When you look at him, you get gushy.

Shutting the bedroom door behind me, I leaned back against it. I couldn't afford to fall for Aidan. But could I prevent it?

Chapter Twenty-Four

idan threw the front door open and his sister tumbled into the house, oohing and ahhing as she spun in circles, traveling across the floor without paying any heed to the obstacles in her path. When she veered toward the end table, Aidan took hold of her shoulders, bringing her to a stop. Her long, golden-brown hair whooshed around her shoulders.

Mouth open, hazel eyes wide, she said in a hushed voice, "This is beautiful. Can't believe I'm in America. I want to see it all, every bit of it."

"Easy," Aidan said, giving her a tolerant, slightly amused look. "You just arrived, Jamie. Give yourself time to adjust to the jet lag."

"But I want to see everything." She spun again, the sunshine streaming through the windows igniting green sparks in her pale gold eyes.

Though I hated to admit it, since the moment I'd met Jamie today I'd envied her. She was so full of innocent joy, so free of worries. Of course, everyone had something that bothered them, and I'd known her for a matter of hours. I shouldn't assume she was worry-free, but I still envied her ability to thrive in a completely foreign environment. I would've been nervous about my first trip to another country.

An explosive *thwap* announced the arrival of Mandy and Misty, who rushed at the newcomer in their home. Misty slapped her big paws on Jamie's tummy, struggling to stretch up tall enough to slather wet kisses on her face but unable to reach that far. Meanwhile, Mandy licked Jamie's ankles, bared by her sandals and knee-length skirt.

Jamie giggled. "That tickles."

I moved to shoo the puppies away, but Jamie shook her head.

"Don't worry," she said, "I love animals. Dogs are my favorite."

She knelt to let the furry girls maul her with their tongues and climb all over her.

Right then, Gavin entered through the glass doors at the back of the house. He stopped a few feet inside, watching the spectacle taking place on the floor with a bemused expression.

My enjoyment of the situation had been tempered by the call I'd received earlier at the airport. While Aidan had helped Jamie retrieve her checked bags, I'd stepped aside to answer my ringing phone. From the caller ID, I knew who it was. "What do you want, Rade?"

"To speak with my wife."

"Sign the papers. There's nothing else to say."

"I need to speak with you in person."

A hand on my forehead did nothing to quell the headache sprouting there. "I have guests. There's nothing more to talk about, anyway."

"Please. A few moments is all I ask."

"No, sorry."

He fell silent for a few seconds, the dull roar of traffic in the background. "I've already made arrangements to fly there. When we see each other, you will realize we should talk. If you don't, then I will leave again. You have my word."

"All I want is for you to please-please-please take the divorce papers and stop trying to put the skids on the whole process."

"I will you see in a few days. Have a good afternoon, Calli."

Before I could balk, he'd hung up.

The here and now swam back into focus around me.

"You can love me more later," Jamie told the puppies. She straightened, smoothing out her skirt, and turned toward Gavin. "You must be Calli's brother. I'm Jamie, Aidan's sister."

At the sight of Jamie—so perky and cute, full of life and armed with that MacTaggart charm—my brother grinned and hustled over to shake the hand of our newest houseguest. "Hey. Nice to, uh, meet you. I'm Gavin. Douglas. Calli's brother, Gavin Douglas."

Was my brother nervous? Or, heaven forbid, smitten at first sight? After the way he'd reamed me for letting Aidan stay here. After accusing me of going gushy for the Scot. Oh, I'd have lots of fun exacting Gavin's comeuppance for this.

Jamie's cheeks dimpled, she giggled again. "Nice to meet you too, Gavin."

Aidan grasped Jamie's wrist and urged her hand free of Gavin's. "Let me show you to your room."

Though she allowed her brother to haul her out of the living room, she glanced back to smile at Gavin, who—swear to God—mooned at her.

Hands on my hips, I shook my head. "Gee, Gav, looks to me like you're going gushy over Aidan's sister."

"What?" His eyes flared wide for a second before he regained his hold on stoicism. "I was being friendly to your guest, that's all."

"Uh-huh. Flirting is a requirement for proper etiquette?"

He spluttered, attempting to seem offended but failing. "All I said was hello."

Grinning, I pointed out, "No, you said 'uh, hey, nice to meet you, can I please shave your legs for you.' Right before you mooned at her."

And my brother's mouth fell open. Wide open. He flapped a hand as if trying to pump the shock out of his brain. "I did not say that."

"Okay, maybe I ad-libbed the shaving part. But you were stammering and gaping at her like you'd never seen a pretty girl before."

Gavin clapped his mouth shut. "I'm not the one getting naked with somebody I barely know."

"But you'd like to make time with Aidan's sister. His little sister."

I could tell by his chagrined look he hadn't missed the double standard. Him, ogling the younger sister of a man he'd criticized for ogling his little sister.

"Well—" Gavin jammed his hands in his pants pockets, assuming his stoic demeanor once more. "You're a grown-up, you can do what you want."

Ah, of course. Now that he had eyes for Jamie, suddenly I could do whatever I wanted.

I compressed my lips, struggling to hold back a smile. "Gee thanks, Gav."

With a grunt and a roll of his eyes, he stalked out the glass doors and toward the yard gate, heading back to his little haven in the woods.

Jamie and Aidan emerged from the guest bedroom, returning to the living room. Aidan looked harried while his sister seemed quite chipper and pleased with herself.

"Sooo," Jamie cooed, "we should get to know each other, Calli. Since you're going to be my sister-in-law."

Aidan raised his hands, mouth open, and shook his head. "Didnae say a word to her."

Jamie studied us both, her lips quirked. "Didnae have to, Aidan. I have eyes and I'm not an eejit. Besides, you told everyone you were coming to America to find a wife like Lachlan did."

Aidan gave me a pleading look.

I took pity on him and refrained from telling his sister I wouldn't marry him. Instead, I told her, "It's a bit early to think about that."

"Aye," she said, "but Aidan has a way of convincing women to do almost anything."

"Does he now." I arched a brow at Aidan, who hiked up his shoulders, showing me his palms.

If his sister only knew the things he'd convinced me to do. I hadn't needed much convincing. Making love with Aidan gave me more pleasure than I'd dreamed possible, pleasure both physical and emotional.

Making love? Emotional pleasure? My stomach plunged through the floor. If I was thinking in those terms...

Thankfully, I had no time to ponder the end of that thought.

"Where's Gavin?" Jamie asked, glancing around as if he might be hiding behind the bar.

"He's staying in the hunting cabin out in the woods," I said. "We'll see him again at lunch."

Did Jamie seem disappointed by the news? Maybe Gavin would be the one moving to Scotland.

"Mind if I have a shower?" Jamie asked. "Airline travel makes me feel grimy."

"Go right ahead." I gestured toward the hallway. "Bathroom's on the right."

"I know, Aidan showed me." She started to turn away, then looked at me. "Thank you for letting me stay here, Calli."

"No problem."

Jamie MacTaggart disappeared down the hall.

When the bathroom door clicked shut, Aidan approached me and slipped his hand into mine as we faced each other. I laced my fingers with his, loving the warmth and roughness of his palm on mine. The hands of a man unafraid of hard work. He gazed into my eyes for a long moment, his expression unreadable.

At last, he sighed and said, "Quite a full house, eh?"

"Definitely." I canted toward him a tiny bit. "Your sister and my brother seem rather smitten with each other."

"I'd like to tell Gavin to stay away from my sister, but I suppose that would be, ah..."

"Hypocritical?"

"Yes."

I rose onto my tiptoes to peck a kiss on his lips. "You MacTaggarts are a gorgeous bunch. Can't blame us mere mortals for falling to our knees before you."

"You haven't gone on your knees before me." He slid his free hand around to the small of my back, tugging me into his body. "But it's an intriguing idea."

Flattening my palm on his chest, I gazed up into those hypnotizing eyes. "Have you forgotten? I dropped to my knees and took you in my mouth."

A slow, naughty smile curved his mouth. "So you did. I have some other ideas for getting you on your knees, though, ones I'd love to try out tonight."

"Sounds good." I glanced toward the hallway. "We have two visitors within earshot of our screaming orgasms. How do we keep them from hearing?"

He gave a short, airy laugh. "Jamie won't care how much noise we make."

"I care." Realizing I sounded like a prude, I added, "I like my privacy."

"Don't worry." He brushed his fingers across my cheek. "We can be quiet."

"Not sure I can manage it. Not with you driving me out of my mind."

Aidan moved his hand in lazy circles on my back, bending his head to skim his lips over mine. "Trust me, I can make certain no one hears your screams."

"No gags, please."

He shook his head slowly. "No gags. I wouldn't do anything like that to you. But I will swallow your screams with my mouth on yours."

I imagined him doing that, our open mouths fused and muffling my cries of ecstasy, and my nipples hardened at the mere idea of it. "Just making sure." I eyed him with a touch of suspicion. "How exactly do you plan on keeping anyone from hearing us?"

"You'll see."

Releasing my hand, he wrapped both arms around me and lifted me onto my toes. His lips found mine, exploring with light sweeps that grew firmer the more he kissed me. I threw my arms around his neck and thrust my tongue between his lips, moaning at the feel of him. He coiled his tongue around mine with a moan of his own.

And just like that, I didn't give a damn who heard us.

He pulled back, frowning as if an unpleasant thought had occurred to him. "I brought my sister here to keep her out of trouble. And what happened? The minute she arrived, she found an American man to captivate."

"Poor Aidan." I skated my fingers over his cheek. "You can't catch a break, can you?"

With a devious gleam in his eyes, he ran his tongue across my lips. "After a day with your brother and my sister, I will be needing some physical therapy." He dropped one hand to cup my behind. "A lot of it, in fact."

"Here to serve."

As we began to kiss again, I tried not to think about what everyone else seemed to know. Jamie assumed we were seriously involved with marriage not far in the future. And Gavin, well…

Not gushy, not mooning.

The only one I seemed likely to fool was myself.

Chapter Twenty-Five

Aidan flopped onto my bed on his back, right on top of the covers, his arms spread wide and his head on one of the pillows. He groaned, eyes closed. "No one should have that much energy, bouncing around like a little bird. It's no wonder your dogs love Jamie, she's as energetic as they are."

I sat on the bed's edge, with his hand at my hip, and patted his chest. "Oh, poor Aidan. You have a sweet, happy sister who adores you. Must be awful."

"Hm." He cracked an eyelid to peek at me. "Thought I'd get more sympathy from you. After all, your brother was turning you into a bampot."

"You called me that in the club. It means crazy?"

He nodded. "You're not literally insane, but sometimes you act like it when you're stressed."

"I don't mind if Gavin makes me a little crazy. I'm glad to see him having a good time. After the way his wife left him, I didn't know if he'd ever show interest in a woman again."

Aidan lifted his head. "What did his wife do?"

Oops. I tried to salvage the situation. "Sorry, that shouldn't have slipped out. I doubt Gavin would want me telling you the story, but I'm wiped out and my brain filter isn't working properly."

He dropped his head onto the mattress with a grunt. "I'll have to ask your brother."

"You wouldn't."

"No?" He rolled his head to the side, giving me a mischievous smile. "Maybe I would. Or you could tell me, and I'll keep it a secret so he'll never know I know."

"Oh, you are wicked. Devious and canny, in bed and out."

He walked his fingers up my hip. "I'm in bed at the moment."

"So you are." I crawled on top of him, on all fours, my hair feathering around my face. "Wouldn't you rather have sex than hear about my brother's failed marriage?"

Aidan rubbed his eyes with his thumb and forefinger. "At the moment, no. I'm exhausted from spending an entire day with Jamie and Gavin. Siblings are a right trial."

"But we love them anyway, don't we?" I lowered my head to nibble his lips.

"Mm, aye." He inserted a hand between our mouths, thwarting me. "I'm genuinely exhausted."

I fell onto the bed beside him and rolled onto my side, cuddling into my pillow. "Aidan MacTaggart is too tired for sex. Does this mean the world is spinning backwards?"

He pulled me closer to tuck me under his arm. "Maybe I am ravenous, but it's your fault. I've never needed to make love to a woman this much before. Cannae get enough of you."

"Likewise. I'm addicted to the feel of you inside me."

"Thought it was the earth-shattering orgasms that had you hooked."

I slid my arm across his chest as I nestled my cheek against it. "That too. I've got it so bad, I'm giving serious thought to offering to try whisky again if you'll have sex with me right now."

"Are ye now." He chuckled. "Can't let ye suffer, can I?"

"It would be rude of you." His heartbeat thump-thumped under my ear, the rhythm of it soothing, even as the feel of his firm muscles awakened my body. "I've loved every minute with you."

He buried his face in my hair, inhaling deeply. "I loved every minute of it too. Plan to keep on loving every minute with you."

The puppies came barreling into the room and leaped onto the bed with us. Naturally, they both cuddled up to Aidan. The little turncoats.

A moment later, as my lids fluttered shut, a soft female voice inquired, "Want the door closed?"

I peeked through my lashes to find Jamie in the doorway, looking uncertain, as if she'd disturbed us in an intimate moment. In a way, she had. Aidan and I were curled up together on a bed—though fully clothed and half asleep.

He waved a hand at his sister. "Best shut it. Otherwise, the pups will paw at your door and whine until you let them in."

"Yeah," I said, " and then they'll assault you while you're vulnerable."

Flashing us a bright smile, Jamie laughed and said, "Good night."

We offered our good-nights to her, and she retreated, shutting the door with a soft click. Soon, Aidan was snoring beside me as I listened to the steady thumping of his heart slowed by slumber. Ensconced in his arms, I let my thoughts wander back through our days together, from the night we met to this day spent with his sister and my brother. Though we'd known each other barely more than a week, I'd spent more time with Aidan than I'd spent with anyone in a long time. I'd shared personal things with him. I'd laughed with him and slept with him and invited him into my life.

Crazy as it was, I felt like I knew him, like I could trust him. Hell, I'd told him I trusted him, and I meant it. I didn't know everything about him, but I'd met his cute little sister and overheard him talking to his bossy older brother, which made me feel like I'd met Lachlan as well.

A chill of doubt slithered through me, winding around my heart. How well did I really know Aidan? How well could I really know anyone? After two years of friendship with Rade, I'd believed I knew him and could trust him—yet after years of sticking to our agreement, he was determined to change the rules, which meant I'd misjudged him. Even my parents had kept major secrets from me, hiding their financial woes and leaving a giant mess for me to untangle after their deaths. For all I knew, Gavin and Tara kept devastating secrets too.

Shit. I couldn't do this. Couldn't keep second-guessing my instincts and suspecting everyone of having nefarious intentions. My parents didn't conceal things from me out of malice. They'd done it because they believed, wrongly, they were protecting me and Gavin. But then there was Rade.

And what about Aidan?

I raised my head to gaze at his sleeping face. My throat ached, constricted by an alien emotion, a kind of longing I'd never experienced before. A longing to believe in him. To trust him. I already did trust him, and it scared the hell out of me. I'd believed in one man who wanted to marry me, a man I thought cared about me as a friend. Here I was trusting another charming man intent on marrying me, a man who claimed not only that he would love me, but that I would fall for him. Did he want something from me, something as damning as a fraudulent marriage?

Watching him sleep, his lips forming a small smile, I couldn't believe it.

I pressed my cheek to Aidan's chest again and tried to banish those thoughts. They kept prowling the edges of my mind, keeping me awake until late into the night, when at last the weariness overtook me.

Chapter Twenty-Six

The next afternoon, I walked into the house through the sliding doors to find Aidan lounging on the sofa, one ankle crossed over the opposite knee. He had one arm draped over the sofa's back. A slight smile lifted the corners of his mouth as he gazed at the TV. On the screen, a black-and-white movie played. The two stars, whose names I couldn't remember, spun around on a dance floor in perfect synchronization, seeming to float in each other's arms. Lovely music weaved a spell around them.

"Jamie and Gavin are taking the puppies for a walk," I said, coming up behind the sofa. My gaze flicked to the TV screen. "Do you like old movies?"

Aidan tilted his head up and back to look at me. "I like good movies. Don't care about the age."

"Me too. I like good movies, I mean."

He watched me for a moment, as if measuring me up, then rose from the sofa and strode around the sofa to me. Offering a hand palm up, he said, "Dance with me."

"Now? Here?"

"Yes, Calli, now. And here in the living room."

"Why?"

"You're here and I'm here and there's music." He waggled his fingers. "Give it a go. Please."

One thing I'd learned about myself of late? I couldn't resist a Scottish man pleading with me to do almost anything. It was probably just *this* Scottish man. Either way, I placed my hand in his.

He drew me to him, one hand on the small of my back and the other cupped around my hand, raising our melded hands the way people usually did when dancing. With that palm on my back, he urged me closer until our bodies were molded together, snug and intimate.

"The last time we danced," he said, "you wore a bonnie green dress. You're even sexier now, wearing everyday clothes and smelling of soap and honey."

"It's my shampoo."

He lifted me off my feet and twirled us in a circle.

As my feet touched down again, my heart did a ridiculous little stuttering thing. I swallowed, my gaze inexorably pulled to his. "Don't think this is regulation ballroom dancing."

"Forget regulations." He began to move his hips and feet, encouraging me to move with him. "We're moving together, that's all. Casual, not formal."

Stiff and awkward, I shuffled along with him as we made our way around the open expanse of floor behind the sofa. My feet bumped into his. A thread of anxiety inside me snapped taut and my muscles followed suit.

"Relax," Aidan said, his tone patient, his expression tinged with affectionate humor. "I want to dance with you, nothing else."

"Nothing else?" I felt one corner of my mouth crimp. "We've gone more than twenty-four hours without sex. How long can you hold out?"

He combed his fingers through my hair, his gaze warm and soft. "I like having you in my arms, with or without sex. So please, take that steel rod out of your spine and tell me what's bothering you."

"Sorry. Didn't mean to ruin the moment." I hauled in a deep breath and released it little by little, with no measurable effect on my nerves. "Hard to melt steel, though."

"Close your eyes."

I stared into his jewel irises, into the depths of their deep blue color. Part of me longed to relax and simply take pleasure in this moment, in the pleasure of being held by a sexy and oddly sweet man who made me feel…worthy.

Sighing, I shut my eyes and gave in to the rhythm of our movements, the soothing melody of the movie music, and the warmth of Aidan's body.

He started to hum softly.

Without examining the reasons why or considering the implications at all, I rested my cheek on his chest. My body went soft, pliant against his. He held our hands to his heart, near my face. I barely noticed when we stopped moving across the floor, our feet now stationary but our bodies moving as if we still glided over the wood beneath our feet. I nestled into him, slipping my hand out of his so I could wrap my arms around him, relishing the feel of his body and the beating of his heart.

He combed a hand through my hair again, the touch feather-light and soothing.

A breathy moan whispered out of me. "You're so nice."

"Nice?" he said, faint laughter lightening his voice. "Thought I was wicked."

The sensations he evoked in me had my mind weakening, my will too, and I could no longer control the words tumbling from my lips. "You are wicked, but you're also nice. And sweet. You're all of it."

"Don't spread that rumor, please. I have a reputation to maintain."

I lifted my head, my chin propped on his chest. "I want to tell you everything, but there's a chance you could get in trouble if I do. Legal trouble. You might become an accessory or something."

"Tell me. You're worth any risk."

Nestling my cheek against his chest, squeezing my eyes shut, I explained the whole story to him.

"I told you the basics about Rade and me," I said. Though acid churned in my gut, I forged ahead anyway. "I mentioned how kind Rade was after my parents died. He offered to go with me to the funeral home, the probate lawyer's office, whatever. I was grateful for the offer, but I couldn't let him do it. He'd never met my parents and…well, I felt I needed to do it on my own. Still, he was there to keep me company and bring me food, little things like that. But when he proposed marriage, he offered me a kind of help I couldn't turn down. I should have, I realize that now. But I was grieving, and I made a horrible decision."

Aidan spread his hands over my lower back, stroking with his fingertips. "What sort of help?"

I took a deep breath. "Remember I said my parents had hidden their financial problems from me and Gavin? I'm sure they were embarrassed and thought they were protecting us, believed they'd get back on track and we'd never have to know. After they died, Gavin and I had to shell out our own money for the funeral expenses and neither of us had much to start with. What little was left of their estate went to paying their debts and we had to sell their house to pay off the mortgage, since neither of us could afford the monthly payments. I'd gotten student loans to pay for college and Gavin was fresh from the Marines, trying to find a job while recovering from the things he'd been through in Afghanistan. Our parents' deaths hit us both hard, but him more so than me. We were wrecked, emotionally and financially."

"Calli…" Aidan brushed wayward hairs from my forehead with his free hand, while his other hand remained entwined with mine. "I'm so sorry."

"Believe it or not, that isn't the worst part." I swallowed hard, my throat dry and tight. "Two months after my parents died, I had to cut back my college classes to part-time and get a job to stay afloat. This meant my student loans would become payable in six months' time. No way could I get back on my feet before that happened, and I couldn't afford the payments either."

"Your good friend intervened, I'm guessing. With an offer."

"Rade said he would pay off my student loans and give me the money to finish college. He knew I wanted to go to grad school to study library science, and he offered to pay for that as well. If I did him a favor."

Aidan's hands tensed on my back. We'd stopped moving our bodies, though we lingered in each other's arms.

"He'd help me out of my jam," I continued," if I helped him out of his. Rade's student visa was running out. He wanted to stay, he had plenty of money he inherited when his parents died. I could have my financial problems wiped out in one fell swoop—if I married him."

Aidan made a noise somewhere between a huff and a sigh. "He wanted you to marry him so he could stay in the country."

"Yes. A green card marriage, so to speak." I hugged him tighter, desperate to cling to his anchoring presence while I rocked on a sea of memories. "I was still reeling from my parents' deaths and Gavin was still a mess. I was frantic about the money problems. What Rade offered me sounded like a generous, compassionate offer. And when he told me about his parents, how they died and he was devastated, how he understood what I was feeling...I agreed to marry him."

Aidan swirled his palms over my back, the gesture calming and imbued with a gentle compassion.

"You have to be married for three years," I said, "before the non-citizen spouse can apply for citizenship. Rade swore once he got his citizenship, we'd wait six months for good measure and then get divorced. It's been five years. He got his citizenship a year ago."

Though Aidan said nothing, I saw the question on his face.

"Rade promised to file for divorce," I told him. "Kept saying he'd do it soon, he was busy, just be patient. Two months ago, I realized he'd never do it and I filed myself. Couldn't afford a lawyer, so I did it myself and paid all the fees. Then I had to pay a process server to deliver the papers to Rade, but he manages to always be gone when the server shows up at his house. I can't afford to pay the server anymore."

A scowl etched lines on Aidan's face. "Why won't this *bod ceann* let you go?"

I raised my head to look at him. "*Bod ceann?*"

"Dickhead."

I almost smiled—almost—but couldn't quite make my lips form it. "Rade claims he wants to have a real marriage, asked me to move in with him. After all these years of sticking to our agreement, suddenly he wants to change it. I don't understand. We lived separate lives by mutual agreement, I can count on one hand how many times I've seen him in those years. Sure, he sent me flowers and cards on my birthdays. I thought he was being polite, being a good friend and all. Now I'm not so sure, but I can't figure out what he wants."

"This has some bearing on why you don't want to love me, I gather. Confused about how, though."

I buried my face against his chest, inhaling the masculine scent of him. "Too many people have turned out to be the opposite of what I thought they were. My parents deceived me by not talking about their problems, leaving a mess when they died. Gavin and Tara married people who changed later on. And my husband is suddenly singing a different tune after years of promising to set me free."

Aidan rested his chin on top of my head. "All I want is you, however I can have you. And I willnae give up because one bastard has a hold on you."

"Rade's not a bastard. But you'd be better off going back to Chicago to find another American girl."

"Cannae." He exhaled, ruffling my hair and tickling my scalp. "I want you."

He wouldn't accept this. He wouldn't give up. And still, I could not make myself tell him to leave. Having him around gave me more than spicy interludes with a man who made me feel alive and sexy, it also gave me solace in ways I couldn't understand or explain. His sweetness, his earnest determination, his heady sexuality…How could I give up those things?

"You haven't wanted to tell me," he said gently, "but it would help to know what happened with your cousin and your brother. With their marriages."

"Tara's first husband seemed like a decent guy, but he turned out to be emotionally abusive, putting her down all the time and making her feel worthless. She left him after fourteen months."

"And Gavin?"

I pulled away from Aidan, hugging myself. "His wife up and left one day for no good reason. Said she was bored and needed to find herself in New York. He was like a zombie for weeks after. Leanne seemed like a nice enough girl, but she betrayed Gavin."

Aidan settled his hands on my upper arms. "You worry I'm not what I seem. That later, after we're married, I'll change into a selfish prick or I'll keep important things from you."

I hunched my shoulders. "That's the problem. I can't know if what I see now is the real you. I've known you for twelve days, Aidan. Twelve days."

"Asked you to give me four weeks."

"Even that isn't enough. No amount of time will be enough."

His hands tightened on my arms, no more than a smidgen but enough to reveal his frustration. "You can never be certain of another person. I wish

I could promise you nothing will ever change, but it would be a lie. I won't lie to you. All I can promise you is that I will do everything in my power to make you happy and keep you safe."

I studied his face, anxious to find some kind of answer there, some kind of magic cure-all for my fears. He couldn't cure me. I had to do that myself and I had no frigging idea how to accomplish the feat.

He drew me a little closer, maintaining a gap of a few inches between our bodies. His hands moved up to my shoulders. "You can ask my sister what kind of man I am. Or call Lachlan and he'll tell you. If you need references outside my family, I can give you the names of a dozen people who'd be happy to tell you I'm not a bastard."

"That's not necessary." I shut my eyes for a moment, seeking a composure that eluded me. "The problem is inside me. In my head and my heart. There's nothing you can do to fix this."

"I know," he said, with a note of resignation in his voice.

When he pulled me into his arms again, I didn't fight it. Being close to him gave me more solace than I'd known in a very long time and I needed it today more than ever. With my head on his chest, I could almost forget why I was trying so hard not to love him.

He laid a hand on my head and began to caress my hair while his other hand cradled my back.

"You remind me of Rory in some ways," he said, "since he doesn't want to fall in love either. But I won't give up on you because you're afraid. I'll fight for you, Calli."

He would, I knew that. He'd fought for me since the night we met.

With his fingers stroking my hair and his strong hand on my back, I couldn't hold back the weariness anymore. It had seeped into me for days and days, triggered by the strain of keeping Aidan close while struggling against my growing feelings for him. Yes, I had feelings for him. I could admit that in the privacy of my thoughts, safe in the cocoon of his embrace. Should I give in to whatever was blossoming between us? Could I risk it?

My lids had grown heavy, too heavy to stay open. I peeked at Aidan through the ever-narrowing slit of my eyelids.

"Someone needs a nap," he announced, and swept me up in his arms to carry me down the hall to my bedroom.

Aidan set me on my feet, pulled back the covers, and picked me up again to deposit me on the mattress. He tucked the covers over me. "Should I undress you?"

"No, but thanks for the offer."

"Anytime." He straightened. "I'll leave you to it, then."

"Stay. Please."

Without a word, he ambled around the bed to crawl across it and snuggle up behind me. He draped one arm over my belly, his face pressed to my neck. I felt…protected. Contented. Happy, in spite of everything.

Did I love him? Not yet. But the slippery slope had morphed into an easy slide down a warm and welcoming path that led straight into Aidan's arms.

Chapter Twenty-Seven

The next afternoon, the four of us—two Douglases and two Mac-Taggarts—sat around the picnic table in the backyard finishing up the last bits of our meal. Aidan and I had escorted Gavin and Jamie on a tour of the local area this morning, which mostly involved visiting gift shops where Jamie could pick out souvenirs for her siblings and parents. Gavin had helped her choose gifts for her brothers while Aidan and I observed the pair's flirtatious interactions.

Did I look like that with Aidan? Giggling, smiling, touching his arm.

I didn't giggle, not in public. As for the rest, I couldn't be sure. Gavin had assured me I mooned over Aidan and went gushy at the sight of him. Gushiness had become an epidemic among the four of us.

Aidan's hand settled on my thigh under the picnic table, pulling me out of my thoughts. He massaged my flesh gently, seductively.

My breaths quickened when his hand glided higher.

He announced, "Calli and I are going for a drive. Alone."

Might as well have said we were sneaking off to have sex somewhere away from my brother and his sister. Because that's what we were doing. Aidan had confided his escape plan to me while we prepared lunch, and I had agreed by saying, "Oh God, yes, please. As soon as possible."

Two entire days without Aidan inside me had made me antsy.

Gavin aimed a hard look at Aidan. "I'm watching you."

The slight twitch of his lips belied his vague threat. My brother was teasing my lover. Couldn't decide if that was good or bad.

Aidan removed his palm from my thigh to take my hand. He glanced at his sister, then back to Gavin. "Got my eye on you too."

The squint of his eyes was more humor than threat.

Male bonding accomplished, Aidan led me across the yard and through the house, out to the convertible waiting for us in the driveway. Before I had time to ask about his specific plans, he was whisking me away on a mysterious drive down the highway.

As the scenery zipped by and my hair whipped around me, I gazed at him with an adoration I could no longer deny. "I'm all for a sex getaway, but where exactly are we going?"

His smile was smug and secretive. "It's a surprise."

"Since you're new to the area, do you even know where you're going?"

"You doubt me?" He feigned taking offense, then added, "I researched it online. And I've got supplies in the boot."

"In your boot?" I leaned over to peer down at his feet. "You're wearing tennies."

He rolled his eyes. "Not in my boot, in the car's boot."

"What's the boot?"

"The trunk." He hooked a thumb over his shoulder, toward the trunk in question. "What are tennies?"

"Tennis shoes. Sneakers." I gestured at his feet. "Those."

"Ah."

I relaxed into my seat, one arm on the center console, the other on the door's armrest. "Guess the culture clash has hit us at last."

"No, it hit us when I spoke naughty Gaelic to you."

"Oh yeah, how could I forget that?" I smiled at him, recalling the day he'd arrived in Michigan. "You can talk dirty to me in Gaelic again if you want."

"Best wait until I'm not steering a fast-moving vehicle." He threw me a sidelong glance, complete with a suggestive smirk. "Talking dirty to you tends to get me excited."

"Doesn't seem to take a lot to get you excited."

"You either, *mo chridhe*." He winked.

"Three times you've called me that. What does it mean?"

"My heart."

I had no response to that. He called me his heart? Way too serious, better to ignore it.

We passed the remainder of our trip in casual discussions of our respective siblings, the scenery, cultural differences, and countless other things. After two hours, we reached our destination.

I surveyed the motel as Aidan parked the car. "This was your great plan? A motel?"

"Told you I wanted you alone so I could have my way with you."

"Sure, but I kind of assumed there'd be romantic gestures involved."

"Why?" He gave a stellar impression of a clueless man. "You said we're not dating and you won't fall in love with me. Why would I bother with courtship?"

He kept up the clueless act a little too long, so long in fact, I almost started to believe it. Finally, he grinned and kissed my cheek.

"We're here," he said into my ear, "because I wanted privacy. Your surprises are in the trunk, remember."

"Surprises? Plural?"

"Aye."

He hopped out of the car, coming around to my side to open the door and usher me out, offering me his hand. I accepted it. He led me to the motel's office, where we checked in—he'd made a reservation this morning—and then made our way to our room. It was situated on the far end of the long, one-story building. Aidan let me into the room, then hurried off to move the car.

When he returned, he was carrying an insulated cooler bag and a plastic grocery sack filled with items I couldn't make out. He set both on the table near the window. Closing the curtains, he sat down on the bed next to me, buttressed with one arm on the mattress behind my butt. He leaned in close.

"Your surprises," he said, "come in stages. Just like you will."

"What does that mean?"

"Means I'm going to make you come for me over and over, harder every time."

Excitement shimmered through me. My skin came alive as if he'd skimmed his hands over every inch of me. "Will any part of this plan involve me on my knees? You did promise."

"And I keep my promises." He curled his tongue around my earlobe. "But I'm not giving anything away. You'll need to be patient, *mo leannan.*"

Had no idea what that last part meant, but right now I didn't care. All I could think about was how much I wanted his hands on me, his mouth on me, his cock inside me.

Aidan kicked off his tennies and laid back on the bed, propped up on his elbows. "Strip."

"Excuse me?"

"Strip, Calli." His smoldering gaze settled on me. "It means take off your clothes."

"I know what it means. Not used to being commanded to undress."

"You like it when I command you."

Heaven help me, I did. Which meant I trusted him. Which I'd already told him. The reality of it hadn't quite sunk in, though, until this moment.

I rose from the bed and began to undress. "You've seen me strip before. This is hardly a novel experience."

"But I love watching you unveil that luscious body."

He watched me with glittering eyes and parted lips, his gaze tracking my every movement. By the time I got to my underwear, a lump had started to swell inside his jeans. When I shed my bra, he reached one hand down to stroke himself through the denim. A hunger erupted within me, a desperate need to unzip his pants and free his erection so I could swallow it whole. My mouth watered.

I shimmied out of my panties.

Aidan exhaled a ragged breath. His hand stroked more firmly as his cock swelled bigger and harder before my eyes.

On impulse, I knelt between his knees and took hold of the zipper on his jeans. My hand brushed against his. He moved to push mine away but then hesitated and withdrew his hand to support his body on both elbows once again.

I dragged the zipper down with exquisite slowness, loving the rough and strangely erotic sound of it. My breasts tightened, but at the sight of his erection revealed inch by inch, the peaks shot hard.

"Christ," he said, his voice rough, "I want to suck those little nipples until you shudder."

"My turn first." I spread the flaps of his jeans, freeing his cock. It waved over his belly, the tip red and glistening. I closed my fist around the base, thrilled by the feel of silken skin and the tiny ridges of veins. I pumped his shaft slowly, relishing the way his breaths grew shallower and quicker. Emboldened by his response, I pumped harder and faster, my palm gliding up and down his cock as I took in the expression on his face. Lust. Awe. And a tenderness that plucked at my heart even as it amped up my own arousal. I worked him harder, bending to lap the moisture from his crown. When he gasped, I grinned. "Mm, I do love the way you taste."

The awe overtook his entire face. "Calli Bethany Douglas, you are a goddess."

"You've earned your Viking name." I pressed my lips to the head of his penis as I milked him with my hand. "You are magnificent."

Letting out a long and resonant groan, he fell back onto the bed. His fingers clenched the bedspread.

My hand still on his cock, I swept my tongue over the tip in one long lick.

He sprang up, hugged me tight, and flipped us both over so I wound up on my back beneath him. Breathing hard, his face pinched, he stared at me for several seconds. My heart raced, my skin tingled, and I couldn't tear my gaze away from him. He crushed his mouth to mine, forcing me to open for him, his tongue invading my mouth with searing, demanding thrusts until my sex pulsed and wetness rushed over my folds.

He jumped to his feet.

I gasped, the breath stolen from me.

He stripped off his clothes in a rush, then fell to his knees at the bedside, between my legs. Both of his hands grasped my hips, pulling me closer until the edge of my ass lay on the bed's edge. He frisked his hands down to my inner thighs and pushed my legs apart.

"My turn," he said in a silky, sizzling tone that matched the fire in his eyes. Moving his hands to the bed at either side of my legs, he angled in until his mouth hovered millimeters from my sex. "Taking it slow this time. You'll beg me to hurry up, but I willnae."

His mouth descended on my clitoris, surrounding it with his ravenous lips and tongue. He suckled with such gentleness I was on the verge of begging him already, but when his tongue lapped at my rigid nub I lost all capacity for speech. He lapped in languid strokes, maddening strokes, while his teeth nipped at my sensitized skin. One strong finger found my opening, teased it, then slid up my cleft with aching slowness, only to glide back down at the same speed.

"Aidan," I whimpered, desperation triggering my voice. "Faster, please, faster."

He groaned against my clit and an electrical jolt fired through it. Rather than speeding up, though, he pulled my flesh into his mouth to lick and suckle it as if in slow motion. Pleasure coursed through me, almost an orgasm, but not quite. Not quite. Oh God, not quite. My knees pulled up on their own as if a wire running the length of my body had been cinched tight. His tongue rasped over my flesh in a ferocious lash and I thrashed my head, my hands fisted in the covers, my breaths sharp whimpers.

Aidan shoved a hand under my ass and boosted it up. The angle gave him better access, letting him rake his tongue up and down the length of my cleft once, twice, before he thrust his tongue deep inside my sex. Every muscle inside me tensed in anticipation, spurred by the ever-increasing pressure of an impending release. His tongue flicked inside me, tormenting my flesh.

My back arched, and I let out a wailing cry.

He withdrew his tongue, scraping it up my swollen skin. Just as his mouth consumed my clit and his tongue lashed it fiercely, he delved two fingers inside me.

Ecstasy rocketed through my body, making me shudder and convulse under him. I shouted and whimpered, overpowered by the climax, while my sex clutched at his fingers in undulating spasms. When at last I fell limp on the covers, he sat back on his heels to drink me in.

With a lust-darkened expression, he slid his tongue over his glistening lips. "You taste so good I could feast on you all night. But this was only stage one."

I gaped at him, panting from the release he'd coaxed out of me. "You'll make me come harder than that?"

His smile was devilish, his chuckle dark and full of erotic promise. "Yes. I. Will."

Chapter Twenty-Eight

O n your knees," he said. The way his lips kicked up at the corners belied his commanding tone, and the rock-hard penis curving up toward his belly made it difficult to take him seriously. He turned one hand palm up and lifted it in a *get up* gesture. "Donnae lie there, love, being lazy and satisfied. We're not done yet."

I pushed up onto my elbows and stuck my tongue out at him.

He moved his hand upward again. "Knees. Now. Or do I have to spank you?"

"Like to see you try."

He gave my thigh a playful slap. "Get up."

I got up. On my knees on the bed, inches from the edge, I reached out to fondle his chest. He flapped his hands, wanting me to back up. I dutifully waddled backward on my knees until he held up a staying hand.

He retrieved a cardboard package from the plastic shopping bag he'd brought. A box of condoms. He ripped open the box and plucked out a single foil packet.

The cool draft from the air conditioner tickled my skin, but it wasn't the chill making my nipples harden again. It was the fully aroused Highlander stalking around the foot of the bed, climbing onto his knees on the mattress, jostling the bed as he moved behind me.

Excitement stirred low in my belly, a sweet current of desire and anticipation. Already drenched from his oral ministrations, my sex burned for more.

Aidan slipped his hands around my waist, skimming them up my belly, pausing when they brushed the undersides of my breasts. "Turn your head."

I rotated my head to the right, toward the wall.

"No," he said with laughter in his voice. He laid a hand on my cheek and gently urged me to look the other way. "See us."

My gaze fell on the mirror attached to the dresser. It provided a full view of us on our knees together, our naked bodies separated by a matter of inches, his erection almost touching my backside. I drew in a deep breath, captivated by the sight and the knowledge of what he intended to do next.

He pushed the hair away from the left side of my neck with his long fingers, feathering his warm, damp lips over the skin at the hollow of my throat. "I want you to watch while I take you. Watch yourself come."

Breath, stolen. Pulse, racing. I tipped my head back a little, silently begging him to touch me more, more, more. When his cock grazed my backside, I threw my head back against his muscled chest.

"Will you watch?" he asked.

"Yes."

With my head still on his chest, I turned it to the side far enough that I could glimpse the mirror. My gaze became riveted to the vision of him sheathing his engorged shaft with a condom. When he caught me looking, he gave himself a long, languorous stroke.

I couldn't take my eyes off of him. Big and brawny. Tanned skin seeming to glow in the golden light from the bedside lamp.

He took my waist in both hands, rocked his hips back, and drove into me in one fluid thrust. His cock consumed me, penetrating so deep and filling me so thoroughly I gasped. As I gazed at the mirror, transfixed by the sight of us—his intense and determined expression, the need and pleasure on my face, my breasts quivering as his hips rocked into me and he found a steady, firm rhythm. His shaft sank deeper inside my body, awakening hidden places within me, stimulating a passion so fierce I shuddered from the bliss of it. He splayed one hand over my belly, holding me to him, while his other hand drifted up to cup and squeeze my breast, making me arch against him, my mouth falling open on quick, shallow breaths.

Dimly, I noted the hush in the room—broken only by the susurrations of our breaths, the faint creaking of the bed, and the brushing of skin against skin.

I focused on the mirror again, observing in rapt delight as he pinched my nipple between his thumb and forefinger, sending a shockwave down the nerve that connected to my clitoris, stunning a gasp from me.

Our gazes connected in the mirror.

There in his eyes, I glimpsed my raw lust reflected in those beautiful blue irises. More than passion, though, I saw an aching tenderness, a deep yearning for more than a physical bond. And in my own eyes…the same longing, the same tender and almost painful need for connection.

He tore his gaze from mine to dip his head to my neck, nuzzling my throat and grazing his teeth over my skin, as his cock thrust harder.

I flung my arms over my head, locking my hands behind his nape, but I couldn't wrench my focus away from the mirror. My need mounted higher, the pressure built, spurred by the image of our writhing bodies and of his cock sliding out a few inches only to slam back into me. His measured thrusts escalated into a pounding that made my breasts bounce.

My gaze gravitated to his face. He turned his head toward mine, his expression full of a sweet longing that made my heart ache even as my body tensed in anticipation of release. I couldn't look away from the mirror, from his face, trapped by the emotion in his eyes and the matching pang in my chest. I wanted to stay with him. To be with him.

I couldn't hold on to that thought, or any thought. The climax overtaking me erased everything else, obliterating reason with a stunning ecstasy that sent my head spinning and unleashed a wild cry.

Even as the orgasm faded, I clung to him, reveling in his frantic thrusts as he barreled toward his own release. In the mirror, he threw his head back as he plowed into me one last time. I felt his cock pulse, and for a crazy moment, I wished he hadn't worn a condom, so I could experience the full force of his climax deep inside me.

He pulled out, panting, but held me against him with his hands linked over my belly.

"You did it," I said. "You made me come harder than the first time."

"Mirror helped, eh?" He murmured the words against my throat as he trailed little kisses down my skin.

Oh, the mirror had turned me on. But the reason for my head-spinning orgasm had nothing to do with observing his gorgeous body taking mine. It stemmed from the dizzying mishmash of emotions whirling through me even now. I wanted to be with him, to marry him, to have his children.

I glanced down at his hands on my belly, right over my womb. The back of my throat hurt. My eyes stung, but I blinked back the nascent tears. No matter how much I wanted to stay with him, it did not mean I was falling for him. I'd known him for *thirteen days*.

How long was long enough to be sure?

Aidan swept a fall of hair away from my face, his fingers skating over my cheek. "What is it? You look about to cry."

"Tears of sexual pleasure," I said in a breezy tone I didn't feel. "You give me such incredible orgasms, I can't help but weep from the sheer bliss of it."

"Bollocks." He turned my face toward his. "What is it?"

"I got a little overwhelmed by the intensity of this. I like being with you. A lot. I'm—" *Not falling for you.* "— glad you're not leaving yet. That's all."

"You like being with me?" His fingers caressed my cheek, soft and tender. "Sounds personal and…intimate."

Oh shit. Had my subconscious gotten the better of me? No, I'd misspoken. Nothing more. "I meant I like having sex with you."

His triumphant smile lit up his face. "You like me. A lot."

"No," I said, elongating the word for dramatic emphasis. Which one of us was I trying to convince? "I do like you, but not that much. Don't get all excited and misinterpret what I said to mean I'm in love with you. I'm not." I scooted away from him to flop onto my back atop the covers. "I couldn't fall for someone I met a couple weeks ago."

"Never said you were in love with me. But you must be afraid you might love me, else you wouldn't have said it." He chucked his condom in the little trash can by the bed and settled onto his side next to me, his head held up on one bent arm, cradled in his large hand. "If you like me a lot, that's enough for the moment."

"You can't hold me to statements I make right after experiencing a brain-scrambling orgasm."

"All right, I won't." He spread a hand over my belly, just below my breasts. "But I like you very much too. And it's not coming inside your exquisite little body that makes me feel this way."

Jesus, we really needed to get off this topic. "What happened to my surprises?"

"Ah, those." He hopped off the bed to retrieve the plastic sack and insulated bag. Both items he placed on the bed next to me as he perched on the edge. "First, something to remember me by."

I sat up, tucking my legs under me in cross-legged fashion.

From the plastic sack, he produced a mug emblazoned with bold, red letters that spelled out "Scots do it better." He placed the mug on my knee.

Laughing, I picked up the item and turned it in my hand. "Where did you find this?"

"Had it made special, by a shop in town. Picked it up this morning."

"So that's where you disappeared to for ten minutes when the rest of us were browsing souvenirs."

"I slipped away to a shop down the street." He smiled, lips closed, clearly proud of his surreptitious shopping.

I set the mug on the bedside table. "Jamie said you were in the restroom."

"She was my accomplice." He tossed the empty sack onto the floor and unzipped the top of the rectangular, insulated bag. Reaching inside, he paused to look at me. "I've pulled together a kind of picnic for you, but I was limited to the items available in your kitchen."

"Then I'm sure I'll like whatever it is. Seeing as it's my food."

"One item was not from your kitchen." He brought out a plastic travel cup with a straw sticking out of it, filled with a light-brown liquid. "Try this? You said you would if I gave you sex."

"Uh…What is that?" I asked, eying the liquid askance. My brain at last digested what he'd said, and I added, "Whisky?"

Aidan sighed, offering me the cup. "Don't curl your lip. Ahmno giving you poison, and this is Atholl Brose, a blend of whisky, oatmeal, honey, and cream. Give it a go is all I ask." His tongue darted out to moisten his lips. "Though not even Atholl Brose can compare to the intoxicating taste of you."

He unscrewed the cup's lid to show me the contents. A creamy liquid sloshed inside the cup, its white color tinged with a rich shade of caramel.

Rolling my eyes up to look at him, I said, "Well, I did promise."

"Do you trust me?"

"I do."

He reattached the lid, tilting the cup so the straw angled toward my mouth.

I closed my lips over the straw, taking a tentative pull. The liquid flowed over my tongue, creamy and sweet with a dark undertone from the whisky. "Mmm, this is good."

"Maybe whisky isn't so horrid after all."

"Not when it's drowned in cream and honey."

"I know, you still hate whisky on its own." He bent forward to steal a slurp of the rich concoction. "But you like Atholl Brose and you like me. I'll settle for that."

The thought flitted through my mind that the Atholl Brose might've been another idea ripped straight from the headlines of his brother's romance.

Aidan's mouth warped into a rueful smile. "You're wondering if Lachlan did this with Erica. I can see it on your face."

Damn. Could he read minds or what?

He began to rummage in the insulated bag, his gaze focused on the items inside it. "No, Lachlan did not feed Atholl Brose to Erica. This was my idea."

"Good. That's probably why I like it."

"I have more for you." He brought out a plastic, sandwich-size container and set it on the bed, then continued his rummaging. "Glad I redeemed my-self with you. I was supposed to be the MacTaggart who seduces the lasses and Lachlan is the uptight one who cannae be romantic if his life depends on it. I was starting to worry I'd lost my touch."

"No chance of that." I took another sip of my drink. "But I don't think this is genuine sibling rivalry. Ever since you told me about Seona, I've had an inkling you feel guilty about something and I think that's the real reason you feel like a failure."

He slumped, his gaze shifting to the bedspread. "You're a clever lass. Should've known I couldn't hide the truth from you for long."

"Guess the question is do you trust me enough to tell me."

Those brilliant blue eyes rolled up to drill into my gaze. "I trust you. Completely."

My stomach fluttered, and my pulse sped up. Why should I be excited because he said he trusted me? It was dumb.

I took a long pull on my straw, flooding my mouth with sweet-and-spicy goodness, giving me a moment to compose myself. Clearing my throat, I said, "Are you going to tell me?"

"Aye." He shoved both hands into his hair and scratched his scalp furiously. With a groaning sigh, he began. "I told you about my casual-dating arrangement with Seona."

"You were sleeping with her."

He glanced away and nodded. "Six months ago, she invited me to go rock climbing with her. I've never been interested in sports, though Lachlan and Rory like to do the Highland games. Hammer throw, caber toss, anything to impress the lasses."

"You don't care about impressing us females?"

"I'd rather prove my manliness in other ways." A hint of the familiar sensual grin surfaced for a second, then faded. "But Seona, she did all sorts of extreme things like rock climbing. I agreed to go with her. I'd done a bit of climbing with my brothers, so I understood the risks and the basic techniques."

A shadow seemed to fall over his face, a dark veil of memory. The sadness in his eyes made my heart hurt for him, and I laid a hand over his where it rested on his thigh.

He slid his hand out from under mine and moved my hand to my knee. "She took us to Glen Nevis, a mountain near Loch Leven not far from Ballachulish, and we set out along her favorite trail until she found a spot she liked for climbing. The terrain is difficult and not for casual hikers, only for people who want a challenge. We didn't get around to scaling the cliffs. I donnae know what happened, but all of a sudden the ground came out from under us and we were falling." He squeezed his eyes shut. "Next thing I remember is waking up in hospital."

I almost couldn't bear to ask, but I had to know. "How bad was it?"

"I got off easy. Cracked ribs, dislocated shoulder, various cuts and bruises. Seona…Her injuries were more severe. Besides broken bones, she hit her head on a large rock. She blamed me for the accident."

"Why? Did anybody figure out what happened?"

"There had been rains the day before, and as best as anyone could tell, that softened the mountainside enough to make part of it come loose. Our weight must've triggered it. No one's fault, they said, nothing but a freak accident."

"But you still blame yourself."

"I was in front with Seona behind me. Maybe I could've spotted the danger if I'd been paying more attention. But I was too busy flirting with her."

"That doesn't make it your fault."

"She blames me, and I can't help agreeing."

I moved my hand, wanting to touch him, but realized he'd only reject it. I folded my hands on my lap. "Why does Seona keep calling you and demanding money?"

"For her pain and suffering." His fingers dug into his thighs, his jaw clenched. "She seems all right overall, but she's become fixated on the accident and very bitter about the fact I wasn't injured worse."

"Aidan, I'm so sorry. No wonder you feel guilty, with her hammering it into your head."

He moved to the side of the bed, swinging his legs over to set his feet on the floor. With his profile partly in shadow, he looked even more forlorn. "She'd always been hotheaded, but now she seems to want revenge on me. I can't understand it. I may feel guilt over the accident, but I don't have the money she wants. Spent it all on coming here, finding you."

"Guess that makes it my fault she's hounding you."

"Not what I meant." He jammed a hand into his hair. "I wasted money on this trip because I was desperate to change my life, to stop being selfish and settle down to start a family. Be responsible."

I scooted across the bed to sit beside him, one leg tucked under me, turned partway toward him. With his hand still in his hair, his arm blocked his face. I grasped his forearm, gently urging him to lower his hand. After a few seconds of stalwart refusal, he let his arm drop.

"Aidan," I said, laying a palm on his cheek. "Regret is pointless. It was an accident and you can't know why it happened, no matter what Seona says. You have to let it go. Stop giving her that kind of power over you."

"Power?" He looked at me finally, his forehead wrinkled in confusion.

"Yes." I took his hand in both of mine. "She's using your guilt against you. You know she has problems, and she's obsessed with you. Why are you accepting it's all your fault just because she keeps telling you it is? The woman is trying to extort money from you. Nothing she says can be believed."

He stared into my eyes for a long moment. "Maybe you're right, but it's not so easy to get rid of guilt. Or fear. You should know about that."

Of course, he was right. How could I urge him to dump his guilt when I clung to these old fears? But I couldn't stand by while some bitch harassed him. There had to be a way to expose her real motivations.

"I have an idea," I said. "Why not have Lachlan or Rory—maybe both of them, actually—go and talk to Seona? They can find out what she's really after."

Aidan's expression grew thoughtful, and after a moment of contemplative silence, he gave me an appreciative nod. "You are very clever, *mo chridhe*. Seona lives in Ballachulish. I could ask Lachlan or Rory if they'll have a talk with her. Lachlan might be best, he could bring Erica along as a buffer."

"Sounds like a plan." I raised my brows and smiled. "You're going to ask Lachlan for help? I seem to recall a certain someone refusing any kind of assistance from—"

"Aye, well, I've changed my mind. You convinced me." He scrunched his mouth up as if annoyance and humor warred in his expression. "Don't need to remind me I'm fickle."

"You're not fickle. You finally wised up to the fact overbearing brothers can be useful on occasion."

Aidan turned toward me, bending one knee and reaching for the sandwich container. He offered it to me. "Let's have our picnic in bed and forget about the rest for tonight."

"But you'll call Lachlan?"

"In the morning." He tapped a finger on my nose. "Happy?"

"Yes." I took the plastic container, popped the lid off, and gazed down at the sandwich nestled inside the little box. With a quick peek into the insulated bag, I said, "Ham and cheese? And potato chips?"

"The selection in your kitchen was rather limited."

"But I was kind of expecting something Scottish."

"Couldn't find haggis around here, anyway." He grinned at my wrinkled nose. "So, you don't want Scottish food after all, eh? Turn your sweet little nose up at my whisky and now you look fit to vomit from the mention of haggis. I think I should be offended at your disrespect for my cultural heritage."

"I do love plaid," I offered in conciliation, then leaned in until our faces were a breath apart. "Especially when you're wearing a kilt."

"You like my legs."

I slid a hand down his naked thigh and back up to his hip. "Among other things."

He sneaked his tongue out to graze my lips. "Why donnae we put off the picnic for a wee bit longer?"

"Oh yes, please." I shifted my hand to his swelling cock. "And I can think of something Scottish I'd love to devour."

Chapter Twenty-Nine

Aidan and I arrived back at the house around ten the next morning, relaxed and satiated like nobody had a right to be. After learning about his accident, I felt like I knew him so much better—which triggered a frightening, warm fuzziness in my chest. I'd sworn I wouldn't fall for him. The more time we spent together, the more we opened up to each other, the harder it got to pretend I wasn't falling.

Hand in hand, we walked up the path to the front door. I glanced at Aidan just as he glanced at me, and we both grinned like idiots.

Oh, I was in so much trouble.

Movement caught my eye through the window beside the door. The curtains hung slightly parted, with a space of about an inch revealing a sliver of the interior. I leaned forward, squinting at the scene inside until it coalesced into a clear picture. I blinked quickly, sure I must be hallucinating.

Nope. I was seeing what I thought I was seeing.

There on the sofa, Jamie and Gavin sat side by side facing each other. Gavin had one arm stretched across the sofa's back as he kissed Jamie. Passionately. With tongues. She had one hand thrust into his hair, cupping the back of his head as they ravished each other's mouths.

"What is it?" Aidan asked.

I shuffled backward a step. "Why don't we go for a walk? The puppies must be in the backyard playing, so if we go around the outside of the house we can—"

"What don't you want me to see?" His voice rang with a certainty that I had a reason for steering him away from the house.

"No reason," I said, my voice pitched a little higher than usual. *Damn*. I could keep a major secret from my loved ones for five years, but I couldn't deceive Aidan about his sister making out with my brother.

He leaned over my shoulder to peer through the gap in the curtains. His jaw tensed, a muscle ticked there. Eyes narrowed, he emitted a faint growl.

"Calm down," I said, turning around to lay my hands flat on his chest in a vain effort to urge him away from the window and the house. "They're adults. If they want to—"

Aidan grasped the knob and shoved the door open.

Jamie and Gavin jumped. Her hand flew to her mouth, but he adopted a look of confused innocence. Didn't look fake at all. No sirree.

I rushed inside, shutting the door, and grabbed Aidan's arm to stall him as he stalked toward the sofa. He halted, eying me sideways.

"Let's not overreact," I told him, but he snorted out a breath.

Gavin pushed up off the sofa. "Hey, didn't think you'd be back so soon."

"Duh," I said. "Figured you wouldn't be sucking face with Aidan's sister if you thought he was about to come home."

Aidan's gaze rotated toward me again. He mouthed, "Home?"

Shit. Had I implied this was our home? Like we were a couple? A serious, in-a-committed-relationship couple?

My hopes of no one else noticing disintegrated when Gavin said, "You two are living together. I knew it."

"Not the way you mean. He sleeps here."

"With you."

"Honestly, we've already had this conversation." I tugged at the hem of my shirt. "Aidan is not my boyfriend."

Three smirking people snickered.

Hands on my hips, I tried to scowl at them—but they all smiled at me and I lost my indignation. Slumping my shoulders, I let my arms go limp at my sides.

Jamie hopped up and aimed her bright, dimpled smile at me. "Gavin's not my boyfriend either, then."

I sighed. "Are all you Scottish people so snarky?"

"You like it," Aidan said, slipping an arm around my shoulders. In a low and sexy voice, he murmured, "From me, at least."

My body softened, and I couldn't help relaxing into him. The man knew how to brush aside all my defenses with no effort at all. I wanted to hate him for that, but I couldn't. I enjoyed it too much, even while it scared the hell out of me.

"Would you mind," Jamie said to me, "if Gavin was my boyfriend?"

The sneaky little lassie had hit me with a trick question. If I said no, I'd sound like a jerk and a hypocrite. If I said yes, Aidan would feel betrayed. I genuinely liked Jamie, though, and I couldn't begrudge the two of them a chance at happiness. And yet, I didn't want to hurt Aidan.

He grumbled, as if reading my thoughts. "It's all right. Let them have their fun."

Gavin raised a brow at Aidan. "Fun? I like Jamie a lot. It's more than fun. Not like you and my sister, having sex while she says you're not her boyfriend. At least I'm upfront about it."

Ouch. He'd aimed that barb at me, for sure. Well, Aidan a little too. Mostly me.

"Upfront?" Aidan said, tensing against me. "You snogged with my sister while I was away."

"You want I should do it in front of you?" Gavin had a mischievous gleam in his eye. "All right, I will."

He pulled Jamie into his arms and mashed his mouth to hers. She dissolved in his embrace, despite the audience of two watching them.

I could relate. Aidan's kiss made me forget everything else.

Aidan pulled away from me, scowling. "Why donnae ye just tear her clothes off right in front of us?"

Gavin released Jamie, a look of self-satisfaction on his face.

Oh yeah, he'd done that solely to tick off Aidan. *Men.* They acted like adults when necessary but reverted to schoolyard tactics when their egos got involved.

Jamie's cheeks flamed a bright red.

I hurried around the sofa to her, placing a protective arm around her shoulders. "Both of you, stop harassing the poor girl. Gavin, quit trying to annoy Aidan. And you Aidan, let your sister live her own life. At least she's not in Chicago trolling the clubs. My brother is a good man." I threw Gavin a chastising look. "Most of the time."

Both men turned their gazes to the floor, suitably chagrined.

Jamie murmured in my ear, "Will you be my honorary sister?"

"Wouldn't that make me Aidan's sister?"

"Not at all." She got a canny glint in her eyes. "But if you marry him, you could be my sister-in-law. Even better than honorary sister."

I glanced at Aidan, but he was still fixated on the floor. If he'd heard his sister, he didn't let on.

A breath gusted out of Aidan and he raised his head. "I'm sorry. Won't happen again."

Gavin looked up as well. "Me too. Sorry."

"I suppose," I said, "we will accept your half-assed apologies."

"We will," Jamie concurred.

My brother looked at her, then at me, a question in his eyes.

I waved a hand. "Go. Take Jamie to dinner, make out with her in the car, whatever. You're adults, and we—" I shot Aidan a pointed look. "— will not interfere. Will we?"

Aidan's gaze zeroed in on mine. "You have my word."

He'd infused the phrase with a depth of meaning I couldn't quite plumb. What he was trying to tell me, I couldn't figure out. No, I did understand. He meant that I could trust his word, trust him not to change into someone else later on, trust him to be honest and faithful forever.

Maybe I could. Maybe...

Gavin turned to us girls. "Calli, I am sorry for being such a jerk."

"I know."

He took Jamie's hand, guiding her toward the sliding glass doors. As the doors whisked shut behind them, I moved to Aidan and slid my arms around his waist.

"What shall we do now?" I asked.

The dog door whacked open as Mandy and Misty blasted through it. They swarmed around our legs, leaping and licking and whimpering with glee.

Aidan hugged me closer, glancing at the puppies. "Take the furry lassies for a walk, it seems."

Chapter Thirty

We meandered back from our walk in the woods, tired puppies trotting alongside us with their tongues lolling. I held Mandy's retractable leash while Aidan gripped Misty's, a task that required the muscles of a strong man given Misty's tendency to pull with all her considerable strength. Aidan had done the impossible, taming my puppy so she walked without yanking him off his feet. As the house came into view behind the trees, an odd noise caught all of our attention.

Mandy and Misty pricked their ears, canting their heads in the direction of the hunting cabin.

Trees screened the cabin from our view, where it lay a few hundred feet away. The noise originating from that direction sounded farther away than it likely was. The woods could deceive a person's ears. The keening noise grew louder and quieter in a ululating rhythm and I noted another, less obvious sound beneath it, a noise that resembled grunting.

"Is that a fox?" Aidan asked, squinting in the direction of the noises.

A throaty, wordless shout reverberated through the woods. The keening escalated into a high-pitched scream.

Realization tingled over my skin. "No, that's not a fox."

Aidan scrunched his brow at me. "What is it..."

He trailed off as a second, louder shout echoed among the trees and a female voice screamed, "Gavin!"

Aidan's eyes went so wide I thought they might pop out of his head. "He's fucking my sister, the bastard!"

The puppies started barking and pulling on their leashes.

"We better go," I said, "before they hear the dogs."

He tried to frown, but it wound up as a rueful smile. "Guess this is my punishment for seducing you."

I patted his cheek. "Your sister's an adult, this was bound to happen sometime."

"Would've rather not heard it."

"You'll get over the trauma." Clasping his hand, I led the way back to the house.

The noise from the cabin ended with another scream as Aidan and I entered the fenced yard. We released the puppies from their leashes and they took off, racing around the yard barking and jumping. Soon, a squirrel high up in a tree snagged their attention. The puppies crouched at the base of the tree, their gazes locked on the critter beyond their reach.

"They'll be occupied for a while," I said.

Aidan was staring in the direction of the cabin, his face blank.

"Don't torture yourself," I said. "They had sex, it's not the end of the world."

He turned away from the fence and what lay beyond it, hidden in the woods. "I understand how your brother felt when he found us living in the same house."

"Gavin's not sleeping with your sister as revenge. He wouldn't do anything so petty and sleazy."

"I know he wouldn't." Aidan folded an arm around my shoulders, hugging me to him. "Jamie wasn't a virgin. She'd been engaged a few years ago and sometimes sneaked back into our parents' house in the early morning, getting caught a few times. That's why she lives with Rory at the moment, for privacy. I don't think she's been with anyone for a good while, though."

As we strolled across the yard toward the house, I looped my arm around his waist and leaned my head against him. "I was a virgin when I slept with you, but Gavin had no idea about that. We don't talk about sex."

"I only know about Jamie because I saw her buying condoms." He cleared his throat. "I may have gotten slightly upset about it. She threw the box at me and said she hadn't been a virgin since she was nineteen."

"She wouldn't have told you if she hadn't been ticked at you?"

"No. I don't talk about sex with my sisters."

"You talk about it with your brothers?"

He pulled the sliding doors open, and we entered the house. Without letting go of me, he pushed the door shut and turned us both until we faced each other. "I talk about sex with my brothers, but I don't share details."

"No kiss and tell?"

"Absolutely not." He screwed up his face in fake disgust. "I don't want to hear about the adventures of Lachlan and Rory and their women."

I linked my arms around his neck. "Enough about our families. I'd rather talk about what you're going to do to me."

He cupped my buttocks in his hands, tugging me into his groin—and his hardening penis. "Tell me what you want this time."

"I have an idea, but it might be silly."

"Got no problem with silly." He ground his erection into me, its rock-hard length a delicious pressure. "Say it and I'll make your fantasy come true."

"I know you will." Boosting up onto my tiptoes, I leveled our gazes. "Even though it's daytime, I want you to go into the bedroom, take your clothes off, and get into bed with the lights off. Oh, and shut the curtains too. Make it as dark as possible in there."

"You want to crawl into my bed in the dark and have your way with me."

"Because you invited me to do it." I coiled locks of hair around my fingers, toying with the silken strands. "And it's my bed, technically."

"Our bed. We both sleep in it."

"True. Our bed, then."

Aidan stepped backward out of my arms, whipped off his shirt, and tossed it onto the sofa. "Be waiting for you."

He strode toward the hallway, disappearing around the corner. When I heard the click of the bedroom door closing, I kicked off my shoes. While I was hopping on one foot to get my socks off, a soft knock sounded at the front door.

With one foot bare and the other socked, I hurried to the door and peeked out the window beside it, parting the curtains with two fingers.

Rade stood there, eyes on the door, arms slack at his sides. Dressed in a suit without the jacket and with his tie loosened, he looked like a CEO who'd come from the office after a long day of corporate wheeling and dealing.

I let the curtains flutter back into position and glanced down the hallway. A naked Aidan waited for me down there. But my husband waited outside, and he wouldn't leave until he'd said whatever he planned to say to me.

Besides, my car was in the driveway, so he knew I was home.

Pulling the door open, I frowned at Rade.

He smiled. "Calli, I've missed you."

"What do you want?"

"May I come inside?"

Considering the naked Scot lounging on my bed at this moment, admitting my husband into the house seemed like a bad idea. "Tell me what you came here to say. And make it fast, I've got things to do."

Someone to do, actually.

"As you wish," Rade said. He leaned against the doorframe, his expression affable. "I had intended to honor our agreement and give you a divorce, but

I realized I can't do it. I don't want to lose you. We've known each other for seven years and it would be a shame to throw away our entire history. Give us a chance."

"Us?" I had a sinking feeling in my stomach that told me he meant what I thought he meant, but I had to know for sure. "Spit it out, Rade. What exactly are you suggesting?"

He cast his gaze down to his feet and for the longest moment I worried he wouldn't answer. Then he aimed his dark eyes at me and said, "I love you, Calli."

I blinked. Swallowed. Blinked some more.

"You love me?" I said. "Since when? Sure, we knew each other for two years in college, but for years we've hardly had any contact."

"I've called you twice every month."

Had he? I didn't keep track, what with more important things to worry about—like jobs and money and family. "We had brief chats about nothing of consequence."

"I sent you cards and flowers for your birthday and holidays."

That I did remember. I'd assumed it was friendly gestures, nothing more. "You can't be in love with me."

"I loved you in college. My feelings have never changed." He fiddled with his tie, doing nothing in particular with it. "I'd hoped living together for six months would reveal your feelings for me, but you still seemed un-interested. I then hoped these years apart would make you realize we need each other, but then you filed for divorce. After everything I've done for you in the past, is it such a terrible imposition to ask for one last chance to win your heart?"

And there it was. A reminder I owed him.

"When you paid my debts and my grad school expenses," I said, "you swore there were no strings attached, other than helping you get citizen-ship."

"This is not a string. It's a simple request."

"Simple?" I straightened, one hand on the jamb and the other on the door. "You expect me to fall in love with you. After seven years, don't you think I would have if it were possible? I don't feel that way about you. It's time to let go and move on with your life."

I glanced down the hallway, wondering why Aidan hadn't come out to see what happened to me. Maybe he had peeked out but decided to stay out of the way instead of coming to my rescue.

What did I expect Aidan to do? Punch Rade? Beat him senseless and warn him to stay away from me? I could handle this on my own. I had to. Relying on Aidan was a mistake, since he wouldn't be around forever.

But I wanted him to stay forever.

"Calli?" Rade said. He'd stepped away from the doorframe, his questioning gaze directed at me. "Are you all right?"

"No." I swung my focus back to him. "You informed me you want to rewrite the rules of our arrangement. But you can't make me love you, because I'm in love with someone else."

He jerked as if I'd smacked him. "You can't be."

"I am. Might as well give me the divorce because I'll never be with you."

"But..." His head drooped, his entire body sagged. "You might never have loved me anyway, but if I hadn't been such a coward, we might've had a chance at least."

"Would you really want a relationship built on indebtedness? It wasn't love to you, it was obsession. I'm grateful for everything you did for me, more grateful than you'll ever know. But I've given you five years of my life and it's time to go our separate ways."

He nodded, his head still bowed. "You are right. I'm sorry for my selfish behavior, for holding on when I should have let you go. Give me the papers, I will stop fighting the divorce."

"By law, someone other than me has to give you the papers. I'll call the process server."

"Be assured I will accept the delivery. Have your server come to my house tomorrow morning."

I touched his shoulder. "Goodbye, Rade. I hope you find what you need."

As I eased the door shut, he raised his head. The resignation on his face tugged at my heart. He wasn't evil, just misguided and confused.

The door clicked shut, severing him from my life.

I watched through the curtains until he'd driven off down the long gravel road, dust pluming up behind his car. I grabbed my phone and called Tanner Pierson, arranging for him to deliver the papers after Rade arrived home tomorrow. After ending the call, I leaned against the desk gazing into the emptiness of the hallway.

It was over. A lightness rushed through me, as if my head floated high above my body.

Not over, something inside me whispered. Not over unless he kept his word and accepted the papers. Unless he stopped fighting the divorce. The lightness disintegrated, and I slammed back down to earth. It wasn't over until the divorce was finalized.

Deflated by the weight settling onto me again, I shambled to the bedroom. The door hung open about six inches, the room beyond steeped in shadows. I eased the door further open, stole inside, and shut the door. The curtains, though thick, permitted a hint of sunlight to filter into the room and reveal an outline on the bed. A long, Aidan-shaped outline.

The shape moved, and the bedside lamp clicked on, spilling golden light over the bed and onto his body, burnishing his suntanned skin. He lay with one leg outstretched, the other bent so the sheet had slid off to expose the nakedness of his entire leg up to the hip. The sheet covered his privates, draping over his other leg, but the rest of his gorgeous body was on display. He linked his hands behind his head, gazing at me with a tight expression. Despite his casual pose, he was not at ease.

"That was your husband," he said.

I nodded. "He claims this time he'll accept the divorce papers. I've decided to believe him and let the process server try one last time."

"What makes you think your husband will keep his word?"

"He seemed sincere." I shuffled to the bed, perching on its edge, angled toward Aidan. "Rade said he loves me and wants a chance to win my heart."

Aidan's arms plunked down on the bed. "What did you say?"

"No, of course. I don't love him, and I never will. He's done a lot for me and I'm grateful, but gratitude isn't enough to make me feel that way about him."

Aidan watched me, unmoving, unblinking.

"There's a bigger reason I can't love him," I said, scooting further onto the bed. "I'm in love with someone else."

"Who might that be?" No hint of sarcasm or playfulness. He spoke the words with no inflection, not the slightest hint of emotion. Hiding behind a stoic mask, like I'd seen Gavin do so many times.

I crawled across the bed on hands and knees to crouch beside him. "I love you, Aidan."

No reaction. Couldn't breathe. Couldn't move.

A smile stretched across his face, widening and brightening until a grin of pure joy lit up his entire being. "I love you too, Calli."

I gave his arm a half-hearted slap. "Why did you say nothing for so long? I thought you were going to reject me and I'd have to sick my vicious puppies on you."

"Rather get a tongue bath from you." He picked up my hand and splayed it on his bare chest. "Didn't pause to make you worry. I was in shock. After two weeks of working hard to seduce you and make you love me, I finally succeeded."

"Oh, poor Aidan. Two whole weeks you had to wait." I patted his cheek. "Think of it this way. Lachlan needed an entire month to get Erica to love him."

"You're right. I outdid Lachie."

"Sure did." I leaned in to whisper in his ear. "Turn off the lamp. It's time for your tongue bath."

When I sat back, I noticed the sheet had tented over his groin.

I clambered off the bed as he shut off the light. Disguised by the false twilight, I stripped off my clothes and slithered under the covers, my head beneath the sheet. I found his legs, running my hands up and down the corded lines of his muscular thighs. He was so sexy, so good, so amazing.

"There's a succubus in my bed," he purred. "Will ye drink the life from me?"

"Mmm, I think I'll leave you just enough to keep this hard." I closed my fist around his erection. "I've got plans for it."

Positioned between his legs, I took his cock in my mouth, working it with my tongue and hands, my body stirred to tingling life by the salty flavor of him and the sensation of his cock whisking in and out of my mouth. He writhed beneath me, making desperate noises deep in his throat.

I released his shaft and laved my tongue over the moist head of his erection.

"Fuck," he growled.

"Oh no, we haven't gotten to that yet." I flung the sheet off of us. The fabric billowed and settled down at the foot of the bed with a soft rustling sound. "Condom?"

"What?" He sounded drunk, or at least dazed.

"Hand me a condom, please." I rose to my knees, walking forward on them so I knelt astride him. "Unless you want to keep lying there fully aroused and on the verge of coming."

A big, warm hand seized mine and flipped it upside down. Something scraped across the bedside table. He slapped the condom packet into my palm.

"There," he grumbled. "Hurry, love."

"Feeling pressured?"

"If ye donnae hurry, I'll lose my—"

"Verve?" I tore open the packet and unrolled the condom onto his engorged penis. "Can't let you suffer, can I?"

"Bloody hell, would ye—"

I plunged my body down onto his cock. Seated astride him, with the full length of his erection buried within me, I slanted forward to lay my palms on his chest. He'd slouched down onto the silky sheets with his head elevated on a plump pillow.

He let out a groan of such depth, such intense relief, that it resonated in his chest. His hands found my buttocks and gripped them. "Please, *mo leannan*."

"I love it when you beg."

My hands on his chest, anchored to him by his palms clamped on my ass, I lifted my hips and slid back down onto his cock. He cried out, hoarse and sharp. I rocked my hips, riding him at a leisurely pace, loving the feel of him inside me and the blissful friction of our bodies melding and separating amid the slapping of our flesh. The darkness made it hotter, our joining charged with an erotic electricity, the power of the unknown wildly seductive. When I could stand it no longer, I worked my hips with mounting vigor, my breasts bouncing in his face, as my own pleasure escalated into a burning need, an inferno that consumed me from the inside out. He thrust up each time I slammed down on his cock, our movements in sync, and I felt his heart pounding beneath my palms even as my heart pounded, the blood thundered in my ears, and the nerves in my sex throbbed.

"Aidan, oh God!"

He sputtered something in Gaelic and flipped us both over with me pinned beneath his sweat-sheathed body. His hips pistoned even faster. He shoved his hands under my hips, hoisting them up as he drove into me with frenzied force and speed. The squeaking of the bed mingled with his grunts and my strangled shouts. I clutched the slats of the headboard, my fingers aching from the strength of my grip on the wood.

I threw my head back, my back arched, and I screamed. "Yes-oh-God-yes!"

The world seemed to vanish, there in the dark, while I came with convulsive force and flung my legs around his hips to ride out the magnificent fury. He punched into me again, so deep he almost penetrated my soul, and I let out a whimpering cry as my climax pulsated on and on. One more thrust and he came apart inside me, bellowing from the ferocity of his own release.

My breaths heaved so hard and fast I couldn't speak. The joy of our love, of declaring it to each other at last, had fueled a passion more exquisite than any we'd achieved before. At least, any I'd achieved.

Aidan collapsed beside me with a thud that rocked the bed. He nuzzled my ear, his breaths blustering over my skin and ruffling my hair. "Are ye mine?"

"I'm yours, always."

"Ahm yours too, *mo chridhe*. Yours forever." He hooked an arm over my belly. "That was the best sex I've ever had. And I thought making love to you couldn't get any better."

"Same for me. I love having sex with you almost as much as I love you."

He chuckled, enfolding me in his arms, cradling me to him in the twilit serenity of our room. We lay like that for several minutes, silent except for our breathing, our hearts slowing with every passing second. The world seemed to have telescoped down to this room, this bed, the two of us entwined.

A noise roused me from my trance. It sounded like bagpipes. Distant bagpipes.

"My phone," Aidan mumbled. "Forget it."

"It might be important. Maybe Jamie needs you to rescue her from my ravenous brother."

Sighing, he heaved his body off the bed, turned the lamp on, and rooted around on the floor until he found his jeans. He dug the phone out of a pocket, answering with a groggy hello.

He jerked ramrod straight, his eyes wide. "What happened?"

I could hear the tinny, indistinct sound of someone talking from the other end of the call.

Aidan's expression went as stony as his stiff posture. He responded to the caller with grunts and the occasional half-growled "aye."

He hung up, tossing the phone onto the table. It clacked onto the wood surface.

"Everything okay?" I asked, pushing up onto my elbows.

Aidan scrubbed his face with both hands, then flopped onto the bed on his back. The mattress bounced, and the frame squeaked. Staring up at the ceiling, he said, "Lachlan and Erica spoke to Seona."

"Okay." I rolled onto my side facing him, braced on one elbow. "Did it not go so well?"

"She told them why she wants money. She needs it for the bairn."

"The what?"

He covered his face with both hands again, letting them slowly slide down. The anguish on his face made my gut clench.

"A bairn's a baby," he said, without looking at me. "She's pregnant, and she says it's mine."

Chapter Thirty-One

A weight crashed down on me with such mental force I felt I might plummet straight through the bed and the floor, down into the depths of the earth. With shaky arms, I pushed up into a sitting position. I couldn't speak. Had no clue what to say. The man I loved might be having a baby with another woman.

Might be. Should I cling to the hope it wasn't true?

"They're sure," I said. "Lachlan and Erica are sure it's true. Seona is really pregnant."

"Yes." Aidan kept his gaze glued to the ceiling, his hands on the bed, his body stiff and motionless except for the rising and falling of his chest. "Seona is very pregnant. Hard to tell for sure, but Erica guesses maybe six or seven months along."

"Is that—Does the timeline match up?"

"Sounds like it. The last time I slept with her was the night before the accident, about six months ago. I was sure I used a condom."

I felt like such a creep for asking, but I had to know. "She could've slept with someone else, couldn't she?"

He pinched the bridge of his nose, eyes shut. "I suppose so. We were casual, not exclusive."

"You didn't ask her if she was with someone else."

"Calli." He swiveled his head to look at me, his face the picture of grief. "How can I ask that? If she says it's mine, I have to take her word unless I find out otherwise."

A coldness had infiltrated me from my skin all the way down to the core of my being. "What will you do?"

"She nearly died, and for all I know, it was my fault. If the bairn's mine, I won't leave her out in the cold. I'll take care of them both."

"You'll marry her."

"Donnae know."

He didn't know? Aidan was an honorable man, and I loved him for that, but now his honor would tear us apart. After two weeks of pursuing me, making me love him, I could lose everything and I didn't even have the option of resenting it.

As everything he'd told me percolated through my mind, the suspicious part of me woke up and demanded some answers. "She didn't admit she's six months pregnant until today? That woman's been harassing you for money but failed to mention the baby. Doesn't that seem suspicious to you?"

"Donnae know."

I pulled the sheet over me, suddenly cold, while I considered my next words. "Did you ask for any kind of proof it's yours?"

"That's why I'm flying home tomorrow. To find out." He levered himself off the bed, sitting with his arms limp at his sides, his body slumped forward. "Any sort of paternity test will take time. If she fights it, I suppose I'll have to try for a court order."

Which would take more time. I'd waited so long to be free of Rade and with that endpoint finally in sight, Aidan and I got punched in the face by Seona's revelation. Maybe this thing with Aidan had been a huge mistake. How well could I know him after fourteen days? Maybe the universe was sending me a message that marrying him would lead to more trouble.

Maybe this wasn't meant to be.

"I need to talk to Jamie," Aidan said. "She's coming home with me, whether she likes it or not."

He stood and collected his clothes. I watched in numb silence as he dressed and headed out the door. I sat there, unable to move, while he staggered down the hallway. The sliding doors zipped open and shut.

Tomorrow he'd be gone. Would I ever see him again?

I wrapped my arms around myself. If Seona was having his child…

This just wasn't meant to be.

The morning arrived and flew past, hurtling toward the afternoon. The afternoon when Aidan would leave me and fly back to Scotland, possibly forever. An ache had sprouted in my chest this morning, when I rolled over in bed to gaze at Aidan's sleeping form, and the ache hadn't eased up since. His head had been turned toward me, cradled by the pillow. His lips were curved upward at the corners in a contented smile.

My beautiful Scot. Sweet, considerate, intelligent, funny Aidan.

He wasn't mine, though. Seona could lay claim to him with a tie much stronger than any I'd forged with him. She might be having his baby.

Now, hours later, I lay on the bed again. On my back this time. Fully clothed. I stared at the ceiling while Aidan gathered his things, stuffing clothes into a suitcase. My gaze drifted to the foot of the bed and the two puppies curled up there, observing Aidan with solemn faces, as if they sensed he was abandoning us. They loved him almost as much as I did.

The *zzzt* of a zipper being pulled shut snapped me back to the moment. Aidan had closed up his suitcase. He slouched near the bedside table, morose and silent, his gaze on the blank screen of the phone in his hand.

He didn't know what to say. Neither did I.

So, I said the only thing I could think of. "I'll pack you a snack in case you get hungry at the airport."

Crawling out of bed, I hustled down the hallway and across the living room into the kitchen, desperate to get some distance from Aidan. The puppies trailed after me, yawning. I shoved my hand inside the open cardboard box on the kitchen counter, tucked under the overhead cabinets, and pulled out a handful of little dog biscuits. As I began tossing them to the puppies one biscuit at a time, even their enthusiastic little leaps to catch the biscuits in midair failed to make me smile.

Aidan was leaving. Today. In a matter of minutes.

When the last biscuit had been devoured, Mandy and Misty raced out the dog door to tear around the yard in big circles.

If only we humans could recover from heartbreak so easily.

I turned toward the refrigerator, and though I hadn't eaten anything since breakfast, I couldn't summon the slightest bit of hunger. The thought of food made me queasy. I had to make Aidan a snack of some kind, I'd said I would. But my eyes stung, blurring more every second. Determined not to cry, I sucked in a breath through my nose and swiped away the tears pooling in my eyes.

"What's wrong?"

Aidan's voice made me jump. I shuffled around to face him across the bar.

He stood with his hands on the back of one of the stools, his expression unreadable.

"Nothing's wrong," I said, but the tightness in my throat made my voice strained. "We don't have much time left."

The import of those words struck me the instant I uttered them. He was going away, and I might never see him again.

"Aye," he said, sounding weary. His posture was slumped too, as if he could no longer hide the truth. "I...don't want to go."

"You have to. It's time."

"Do I have to leave?" His sapphire gaze drilled into me. The tone of his voice intensified too. "We could be together. If you come with me."

"I can't marry you."

"Not yet." He leaned forward, desperation tightening his features. "Stay with me. Live with me. I donnae care about the circumstance as long as you're with me. We can marry after your divorce comes through."

"I have to be here for that."

"You can fly back when the time comes."

"Aidan—" His statement a moment ago flared in my mind, bright as lightning. "What do you mean if I come with you?"

"Back to Scotland."

I scuffled backward a step. "You assume I'll go with you? Why don't you stay here?"

"Do you want me to?"

"If I did, would you do it? Would you stay here to be with me?"

"You know I have to go home to see Seona." He lowered his eyes, his mouth cinching into a tense line. "Besides, I don't belong here. Scotland is my home and I want to share it with you. I know you'd love it."

"You know? How, exactly?" I raised my hands as if I might ward off the fear shivering through me on a cold wave of dread. "Let me get this straight. You assumed from the start that if you could make me fall for you, I'd happily trot off to a foreign country and leave my whole life behind."

"What life? You've got no job, no money—"

"I have a brother and a cousin I love."

"Gavin lives in Minnesota and Tara's in Chicago. You hardly see them."

My hands fisted at my sides, I stared at him with a sick feeling in my gut, like I was seeing him clearly for the first time. And in that moment, he looked an awful lot like someone else I knew. *This is Aidan, not Rade*, my logical brain insisted, *and Aidan is a good man*. He wouldn't trap me like Rade had. But he had worked damn hard to make me love him, the way Rade had wanted to do.

Aidan hadn't forced me to love him. No one could do that. I'd fallen for him because of his strength, his integrity, his humor, his sensuality, and so much more. Despite realizing the truth of it, I could not shake the bone-chilling fear. He'd assumed I would move to another country. He never asked me if I'd do it but made it a foregone conclusion.

I should've seen it coming. All his talk about wonderful Scotland. His cagey answer when I'd asked him two weeks ago on the beach what he would do with his American wife when he found one. Would he expect her to move to Scotland? He'd hedged his answer, saying he hadn't thought that far ahead. How could I have missed the signs?

I backed up to the counter, grasping its edge with both hands. "If Seona's having your baby, this is all moot anyway."

"We can still be together, even if the bairn's mine."

My fingers had gone so cold I had to stuff them in my armpits. I shook my head. "You're not the kind of man who could do that. You'll marry her."

"I want you, that's all I know right now."

"You want a wife. Why does it have to be me? Seona can give you a family right off the bat. Why do you still want to marry me?"

"Donnae love her. I love you."

I was shaking, not entirely from the chill. "You wanted an American wife, and I was handy. It was an accident we met, you were only interested because you found me in the same stupid club where Lachlan and Erica met. Why marry me?"

Aidan opened his mouth to speak, then shut it. He studied me with a piercing intensity and I could practically see wheels and gears turning in his mind, clicking into place as he figured me out.

"Not for a bloody green card," he said with a bitter edge to his voice, "that's for certain."

"I didn't mean…" Couldn't finish the statement, because he was right. I assumed the worst. Disaster mode had become my default position. Yet I kept coming back to one question. After two weeks, how well could I know Aidan?

He straightened and strode around the bar into the kitchen, straight to me. Positioned in front of me, no more than a foot away, he said, "I'll do it. I'll stay here. To keep you in my life, I'll do anything."

"What about Seona?"

His features contorted as he hissed, "Shit."

"Right, you have to go home and see her." I rubbed my temple where the beginnings of a headache pulsed. "Besides, you just said Scotland is your home and you'll never belong here. That means you won't be happy here, so if you stay, you'll resent me for making you do it."

Aidan leaned forward, bracketing my body with his hands next to mine on the counter. His body surrounded me, his breaths blustered over my face. "What do you want of me? I will do whatever you say, if you'll only tell me what I have to do to make you happy."

I've never seen you this happy before, Gavin had said. And the irony was, Aidan had made me feel happy and normal and free.

Until everything got ripped away by one phone call.

My pulse raced, from more than anxiety. Aidan's nearness, his determined expression, the plea in his eyes…It all ratcheted up my pulse and squeezed a cold sweat from my brow. My palms had grown clammy too.

"Aidan," I said, "go home. Take care of Seona and the baby."

He ducked his head down and his lips scraped across mine. "Donnae want to go. I love you. I need you with me."

"Doesn't matter what we want." I sucked in a breath, fighting to stave off a fit of wrenching tears. "This was never meant to be. It's time we face the truth."

His lips, so close to mine, stretched into a tight scowl. "You're wrong. We are meant to be. I went to that club because it's what Lachlan did, yes. But you mistook me for someone else, like Erica mistook Lachlan for her blind date. I didn't make that happen. We took a road trip, which was your idea, and I didn't realize that's what Lachlan and Erica did too. Lachlan only told me a few days ago. Erica had legal problems and so do you. Erica had a dog and you've got puppies."

"What's your point?"

He splayed a palm over my lower back, drawing me nearer, his eyes blazing into mine. "I didn't do any of that, couldn't have planned it if I tried. Fate brought you to me and me to you. We belong together."

I turned my head away, but his lips scraped across my cheek. "I don't believe in fate. This is a crock of shit and you know it."

He placed one finger on my chin, compelling me to look at him. "I will come back for you."

"You seem to be forgetting one important part of the Erica and Lachlan story. They broke up. We had a fling, like they did, and it's time for you to go home."

"Not a fling." He rubbed the pad of his thumb over my lips. "And you're forgetting Erica and Lachlan got back together."

"Then I guess you'd better leave it to fate to decide what happens to us."

Aidan stared into my eyes, his thumb on my bottom lip. The silence stretched on and on, broken only by the muted barking of puppies outside. At last, he lowered his hand.

"I love you, Calli. I always will."

He pressed his lips to mine, softly exploring them, his mouth warm and yielding.

I longed to give in, but I couldn't. Not this time.

Aidan stepped away from me, turned, and marched to the front door. His bags rested on the floor there. He picked them up, and with one hand on the doorknob, he hesitated.

"I know you're afraid," he said, glancing over his shoulder at me, "I understand why. And honestly, I have no idea what's going to happen with Seona. All I know is I don't want to live the rest of my life without you. Maybe that's why I believe in fate, because it's my last hope for a happy ending with the only woman I've ever loved."

Aidan MacTaggart walked out the door, out of my life.

When the door clicked shut, I shambled out of the kitchen and over to the window beside the door. I couldn't hold back the tears any longer. They streamed down my face in hot little rivers of pain, even as I peeked between the curtains to watch Aidan go. Jamie and Gavin waited by the Mustang, holding hands. Seeing Aidan, Gavin gave Jamie a quick kiss and said something to her, his expression so affectionate and tender it made my tears flow faster.

At least one good thing came of this mess. My brother had found happiness.

Jamie and Aidan piled into the rental car with their luggage. The engine growled to life.

I stood paralyzed with my hand holding the curtain open, crying in mute despair while the sound of the engine and the ticking of wheels on gravel faded into silence. Then I crumpled into a heap on the floor and sobbed, my back against the wall.

The door opened, and Gavin walked into the house. He hissed a curse under his breath, shut the door, and crouched in front of me.

"Jesus, Calli." He reached out as if to touch me but pulled his hand away. "What can I do?"

I shook my head, crying too hard to speak.

He sat down beside me and tugged me to him, slinging an arm around my shoulders, murmuring sounds of sympathy. When he rested his chin on my head, I crumpled against him and sobbed even harder.

"It'll be okay," Gavin said. "One day it'll be okay, I promise."

"He's gone," I croaked. "I lost him."

Chapter Thirty-Two

I hugged my knees to my chest, slouching deeper into the corner of the sofa. Two weeks had dragged by since Aidan left, two weeks of boredom and anxiety and a yawning emptiness inside me. Rade had accepted the divorce papers, as promised, and we'd both attended our pretrial conference during which he'd insisted on giving me a financial settlement. He seemed to feel guilty for delaying things for so long and for taking advantage of my bad situation to talk me into marrying him. After all these years, he'd finally accepted the truth. I would never love him. Now I had to wait for our final hearing, when the divorce would become final.

Seven more weeks to go. Then I'd be free.

Aidan called every day. Our conversations were awkward and painful, both of us having no idea what to say to each other. Seona was indeed very pregnant, but she refused to have any paternity testing done. She still wanted money, of course. When Aidan had threatened to seek a court order for the test, she relented and agreed to it.

The last time I'd talked to Aidan, the day before yesterday, he'd sounded exhausted and harried. I glanced toward the kitchen and the clock on the microwave, its numbers glowing in the oncoming twilight. It was a little after nine o'clock. I hadn't heard from Aidan in more than forty-eight hours. Dozens of times today I'd picked up the phone intending to call him. Dozens of times, I chickened out. What if he'd learned the baby was his? He would marry her, I knew. I loved his nobility, but I couldn't stand to hear the news of him marrying someone else. Not knowing ate me up inside yet knowing might hurt even worse. Maybe that's why he hadn't called, because he realized I'd be devastated. Aidan would never hurt me if he had a choice in the matter.

The whole mess had turned me into a bundle of anxiety, my stomach twisting into knots every time I thought about it. I'd told Gavin and Tara everything. Absolutely everything. Gavin had wanted to "beat the holy living shit" out of Rade for convincing me to marry him, but I'd talked my brother out of that idea. I loved him for offering, but since I was on my way to divorce court anyhow, I didn't see the point. Tara labeled my soon-to-be ex-husband "a slimer of the first degree who should be chucked into a volcano." My loved ones had to hate him on principle, but I couldn't. I pitied him. Rade had been so afraid to declare his feelings for me that he'd wasted years of both our lives on the belief I would someday love him. Though he'd gotten his citizenship, he would never have me.

The horrible irony of it all was that I'd found a man I could love, a man I wanted to marry, only to lose him. Aidan had claimed fate brought us together, and I scoffed. Lately, I'd begun to wonder if fate had played a hand in our relationship, though not for the better. We'd ignored the signs we didn't belong together, and fate had slugged us in the gut.

I must have lost him, otherwise he would've called. What if he'd made up with Seona and realized he loved her? I wanted him to be happy. I had to accept it if someone else gave him what he needed.

My ricocheting thoughts kept bouncing back to one fact. I'd known Aidan for two weeks before he left the country. How well did I know him? Could we really be in love after such a short time? Maybe we were deluding ourselves, drunk on hot sex and the dizzying high of our whirlwind relationship.

My phone rang.

Surprised, I almost dropped the phone when I plucked it off the coffee table. It rang twice more while I fumbled to get it flipped right side up and swipe the screen to accept the call. "Hello?"

"Calli, it's me."

Aidan's voice flowed through me like Atholl Brose, sweet and spicy and warmly welcoming. So unlike the last time we'd talked on the phone. Good news? Oh God, I prayed for that.

"How are you?" I asked, striving for an equanimity I didn't feel.

"Exhausted but fine." He paused for a heartbeat, then said in the sultry tone I remembered so well, "I've missed you."

"Oh Aidan, I've missed you too." The mere sound of his voice had me melting into the sofa cushions, relief overwhelming the anxiety for a blessed moment. "No wonder you're exhausted. Why are you awake? Isn't it two a.m. there?"

"It is. Planned to get some rest and call you in the morning, but I cannae sleep."

I sat up, straight and stiff, my hand tightening around the phone. "Is there news?"

"Aye." He paused again, hauling in an audible breath. "The baby's not mine."

Every muscle in my body went weak. I collapsed against the sofa again, my head falling back, my gaze on the ceiling. "Did she lie?"

"No, not quite. After the results came in, she admitted she'd slept with someone else while she and I were together. She couldn't know which of us was the father."

"You're always very careful to use condoms."

"I am, but no protection is perfect. Mostly, she wanted me to be the father because this other man was a one-night stand. She doesn't know his name, much less how to contact him."

"What about her demands for money?" I asked. "What excuse did she give for that?"

"Desperation. She's alone and running out of money. Her family moved to Australia last year, and she's been embarrassed to tell them about her troubles."

I had no clue what to say to all of this. What was the appropriate response? Seona had behaved in a despicable manner, but had she done any worse than Rade had done to me? If I didn't hate him, I supposed I couldn't hate her either. Desperation made people do stupid, selfish things.

"Seona doesn't want money anymore," Aidan said. "My sister Fiona has a friend in social services who's helping Seona. Her mother's coming to be with her until the baby's born, and after that, they're all going to Australia."

"I'm glad she's getting what she needs."

"This means it's over. We can be together, Calli."

Could we? Yes. Should we? A month ago, we'd been strangers. Two weeks together had seemed like enough until he returned to Scotland and I had two more weeks to consider the ramifications of leaping into a relationship.

"Are you there?" he asked.

"Yeah, I'm here." I drew my knees up, hooking my free arm around them. "I don't know if it's a good idea."

"What?"

"Us. We haven't known each other long. A couple weeks, really, and I'm not sure that's enough."

His sigh huffed through the phone. "How long would be long enough? A month? Six months? I love you and you love me. More time won't change that."

"I thought I loved you. Maybe we've both been blinded by two weeks of incredible sex."

"What we have is more than sex and you know it." He groaned, a sound of frustration and weariness. "You've had too much time to think and come up with reasons we don't belong together. I know you worry you don't know me, but you do. What happened with Rade, the problems Tara and Gavin had, those have nothing to do with you and me."

"I thought I knew you. Then you announced we were moving to Scotland."

"Wasn't an announcement. I'm sorry I upset you, but I didn't mean it as an order. We can talk about the options."

"My home is here. Your home is there. What's to discuss?"

"Why won't you come visit me here," he said in a reasonable tone, "and at least see what it's like before making up your mind."

"If I don't want to move there, what then?"

"Told you before," he said, "I'll live in America if that's what you want."

"And you'll hate me for making you leave your beloved homeland."

"For Christ's sake, Calli. What do you want me to say?" Silence followed, with lots of deep-breathing noises. Regaining his composure, no doubt. "We can work it out. Please stop looking for excuses to end this."

As much as I longed to teleport myself to Scotland and crawl onto his lap, to let him soothe me and convince me everything would work out, something inside me wouldn't let go of the fear.

"Bad things happen," I said. "Life has taught me to expect them. Good things are rare, and I can't risk it on the hope we might beat the odds."

"Please don't do this. I'll fly over there, and we can talk in person."

And he would change my mind. We both knew it. But eventually, reality would flood in again and I'd be trapped in another country. "I'm sorry. You'll never know how much knowing you has meant to me, but I can't do this. Goodbye, Aidan."

I disconnected the call.

And cried until I fell asleep, slumped on the sofa with the phone still in my hand.

On this warm and sunny morning, three days after I'd told Aidan it was over, I would've preferred to wallow in private. Instead, my cousin and my brother had knocked on my door—without any advance notice, determined to cheer me up.

"You okay?" Gavin asked. He sat next to me on the sofa, half turned toward me.

Tara sat forward in the armchair kitty-corner to where I hunched on the sofa, her worried gaze locked on me. In her dainty hand, she held two sheets of paper.

My chin on my knees, I sighed miserably and at last answered Gavin's question. "No, I'm not the least bit fine."

"You love him," Gavin said, "so call the guy and tell him."

"He knows, and it doesn't matter." I buried my face between my knees, wrapping my arms tighter around them. "I can't marry a man I knew for two weeks."

"Spend more time with him. Get to know the guy better."

"Won't make a difference. I can't trust my judgment where he's concerned, I get swept up in the romance of it all and forget to be rational."

"Love isn't rational, C. You've got to take a chance." Gavin pointed at the piece of paper Tara held. "He's not giving up. Can you really walk away from this?"

I rubbed my arms, uneasy at the sight of the papers covered in handwritten words. Aidan's letter. It had arrived yesterday by FedEx, but I'd mutated into a coward who couldn't open a frigging letter. Instead, I'd burst into tears when I saw the return address with Aidan's name in it. This morning, I'd finally summoned the courage to rip open the envelope and read the letter.

I cried for three hours after that. No one had ever written me a love letter, much less one so beautiful and tragic.

I'd let Tara and Gavin read the letter because Aidan had concluded his two-page missive with the statement that I should "let Tara and Gavin read this because you need their support." Aidan had told me before he went home that he would fight for me. I assumed he meant I'd need support to realize I was being an eejit.

Which I was. An idiot and a coward.

The first few sentences of his letter would've made me smile, if I didn't feel like my insides had been hollowed out.

"In the name of transparency," he'd written, "I should tell you Lachlan sent Erica a note after their breakup. That's not why I'm writing to you. Lachie only managed two words and I have much more to say." After that, he'd talked about our two weeks together and how much they'd meant to him, how much he missed me, how much he wished I could be there with him. "I know you're afraid but staying away from me won't make you feel any safer. Don't give up on us. Come see me, or I'll come to you, and we'll take as long as you want getting to know each other. Please give us another chance."

Recalling his words, I felt the sting of tears once again. God, I missed him. What the hell was I doing? I loved him. He'd treated me better than anyone in my life.

The last line of the two-page letter echoed in my mind. "I'll love you for the rest of my life and the whole of eternity."

I swiped at my eyes, sniffling. "Even if I wanted to, how could I run back to him now? After the way I hurt him?"

"He'll forgive you," Gavin said.

"Maybe, but he shouldn't. I'm bad news."

"Bullshit."

"Let's review," Tara said, holding the letter up so she could peruse it again. "How does Aidan MacTaggart feel about Calli Douglas?" She scanned down the letter, following the path of her gaze with one fingertip on the paper. "'I've never loved anyone but you, he says. Those weeks with you were the best of my life and I believe with all my heart we will be together one day. You are the love of my life.'"

Tara lowered the paper and gave me an empathetic look.

I clamped my bottom lip between my teeth. The love of his life. He was the love of mine, for sure.

"But here's my favorite part," Tara said, reading from the letter again. "'I should've told you I wanted us to live in Scotland, but I honestly didn't think about it. I was consumed with the need to win you. The moment we met, I knew I wanted you and only you. Please believe me, mo cree—crid—'" She struggled to pronounce *mo chridhe* but gave up with a shrug. "'Please believe me, I will go anywhere you want. Just come back to me.'"

Gavin laid a hand on my arm. "We all know what he wants. And we know you want him back. The question is, are you willing to take the risk and go after him?"

Did I have the courage to fix what I'd broken? If he rejected me, despite his letter…Well, at least I gave it my best shot.

Tara shook her head. "Don't be a chicken, sweetie."

"Jamie says he's heartbroken," Gavin told me, "but he's trying to hide it. You're the same way, and if you don't get your ass on a plane right away, I'll hogtie you and send you to Aidan in a FedEx box."

I lifted my head, which felt like it weighed fifty pounds. "Thanks for the stern encouragement, but I don't know if I can do it. Move to another country? You guys would be so far away."

"He says you can work that stuff out," Tara said. "The man adores you and would do anything for you. Isn't that worth an airline trip to find out if you can be together?"

"What if I don't know him after all?" I said. "Mom and Dad kept secrets from us. Gavin's wife up and left him for no good reason. Then there's your first husband, Tara."

My cousin rolled her eyes. "If we're over our past traumas, you should be too. These are lame excuses and you know it."

Gavin folded his arm around me and pulled me into a hug. "I get why you're scared. After everything that's happened, it's easy to think nothing good could ever come. But good things do come. Look at me and Jamie."

She and Gavin kept in touch by phone, text, and any other modern convenience available to them. They were the cutest couple on earth, and I wished them nothing but happiness—even if I didn't have any for myself. Maybe I still had a chance to reclaim mine.

"And there's me and Blake," Tara said. "Two sickeningly happy couples."

"Three," Gavin corrected. He gave me a quick squeeze. "If this idiot will get off the sofa and go to Scotland."

I pulled away from him, unbending my legs. "Scotland? I can't pick up and go there. What about the puppies?"

My gaze traveled to the backyard where, as usual, Mandy and Misty were frolicking.

"I'll stay here," Gavin said, "and take care of the pooches for you. If you marry Aidan, I can bring the girls over there when I come for the wedding."

I shook my head. "Planning the wedding is a little premature, don't you think?"

"Go, Calli."

Thanks to the settlement from Rade, which he'd paid me already, I could afford the trip. I could see Aidan again. Touch him. Kiss him. Beg him to take me back. Excitement rushed through me, electrifying every nerve, tingling over my scalp, lightening my psyche. Gavin and Tara were right. I had to try.

So he neglected to tell me he wanted to live in Scotland. He was willing to go wherever I wanted, and besides, I hadn't thought to ask where we'd live if I fell for him. It hadn't been a lie, just an oversight.

A realization struck me like a meteor. I would risk anything to have another chance with him.

I leaped off the sofa, standing up straight. "I'm going to Scotland to get my man."

Tara grinned and squealed, leaping up to suffocate me in a bear hug. Gavin joined in and I found myself enveloped by the two people I loved second most in the world. Aidan came first—and I would get him back, whatever it took.

I bolted for the bedroom to pack my bags.

Chapter Thirty-Three

I climbed out of the rental car, keeping the door in front of me because the wussy side of me had reared her head higher the closer I got to my destination. My first stop after a two-hour drive from Inverness had been Aidan's house, a quaint old cottage in the village of Ballachulish. He hadn't been home. Luckily, his next-door neighbor took pity on me after spotting me on his doorstep, my shoulders slumped and my head hanging. The elderly woman gave me directions to the house on the outskirts of town where Aidan's parents lived. They'd been kind, and though I got the impression they knew I'd hurt their son, they told me I'd find him at Lachlan and Erica's place.

And so, here I stood. On their property. Staring at their house. Hiding behind a car door with fingers clamped over its top edge hard enough to cause a twinge of pain. *Coward.*

Tilting my head back, I studied the puffy white clouds that scudded across the blue sky. The color of the sky paled next to the lustrous sapphire of Aidan's eyes. His face flashed in my mind and my chest ached. I'd crossed an ocean to get here. I would not chicken out now.

I shut the car door and marched to the front door of the quaint farmhouse. Niall and Sorcha MacTaggart, the lord and lady of their little clan, had told me Erica and Lachlan owned a farm. I'd thought they meant in the general sense of living in the country on acreage. Nope. I glanced around as I approached the house, taking in the barn and the chicken coop, inside which I could hear the critters clucking away. A green tractor sat parked alongside the barn, its newness evidenced by the gleam of its paint job.

At the door, I hesitated with my hand raised to knock. What if Lachlan hated me for wounding his brother? Aidan said his eldest brother was super protective. He might toss me out on my ass. And I would deserve it.

Ugh. I had to get a grip right this instant. No more self-flagellation. I came here to get my man, and dammit, I was going to do it. Or try to do it. *Double ugh.*

I rapped three times.

A dog barked from inside the house, and a deep male voice shouted something, probably an admonition for the dog to be quiet. Aidan had been so sweet with my furry girls. My eyes burned for the millionth time since Aidan's departure and I hauled in a long breath, determined not to cry before I'd even seen him.

The door swung inward, revealing a mountain of a man. *Holy mackerel.* He was taller than Aidan, with darker hair and paler eyes, but the resemblance was unmistakable. I gulped against the tightness in my throat as I gazed up at Lachlan MacTaggart. One side of his impossibly broad shoulders bunched when he leaned against the door, his hand perched on its top corner. A black T-shirt stretched taut over his torso, jeans hung low on his hips. He was barefoot, his hair unkempt—kind of spiky, the way Aidan's hair looked after I raked my fingers through it while in the throes of passion.

I straightened, rolled my shoulders back, and said, "Is Aidan here?"

Lachlan squinted at me, canting his head. "Who's asking?"

"Me." I squelched my groan of disgust at the stupid response.

"Thanks for the clarification." His lips curved up the slightest bit, and he arched his brows. "Who are you, lass?"

"Oh. Right." I started to offer my hand, but the trembling in my fingers made me shove both hands in my jeans pockets. "Um, I, well…I'm Calli Douglas."

"Ah." He eyed me up and down like a man sizing up his enemy before a battle. His eyes had narrowed again, and his mouth had compressed into a line. When his focus shifted to my face, his gaze bored into me and made me squirm. "What do you want with my brother?"

My skin went cold. He *was* going to kick my ass.

A woman appeared behind Lachlan, her chestnut hair as mussed as his. Her hazel eyes drifted to me, and in one quick scan she seemed to learn everything she needed to know. Smiling, she held out her hand to me. "Erica MacTaggart."

I settled my hand in hers, surprised by the firmness of her grip. "Uh, Calli—"

"Yeah, I heard your little tête-à-tête with Lachlan." She aimed a reproving look at her husband. "Be nice, honey. Remember how you felt after you ripped my heart out and threw it in Lake Michigan?"

She smiled brightly at him.

Lachlan slouched a little, gazing at his wife as if the entire universe existed in her eyes. My gut twisted. Aidan had looked at me that way once upon a time. Before I ripped his heart out.

Erica kissed Lachlan's cheek. "Why don't you let us American girls have a chat?"

"All right." He threw me a tight smile. "Nice to meet you, Calli."

His wife smacked the back of her hand across his chest. "Be nice."

Jaw slack, he spread his hands wide and shook his head. "I said it was nice to meet her."

"Uh-huh." Erica shooed him away from the door. A baby cried from somewhere deeper inside the house and she pointed in the direction of the sound. "You take care of Nicholas and I'll take care of our guest."

Lachlan dashed off and Erica gestured for me to go inside, then shut the door behind us. Locked in with people who must hate me. *Ich.* Part of me itched to run far, far away from all this. My less-wussy side won, urging me to see this through no matter what humiliations I must endure.

Erica led me into a living room where two matching armchairs stood in front of the fireplace with a sofa behind them. My hostess took a seat in one chair and I took the other, perching on the chair's edge with my hands clasped on my lap. I wrung my hands, chewing the inside of my cheek.

I said the only thing I could think of. "Your son's name is Nicholas?"

"Lachlan wanted to call him Uilleam, a Gaelic name I can barely even pronounce. I nixed that idea."

Nodding, I watched the empty fireplace. Yeah, I was avoiding eye contact. Wussdom was a tough place to escape from. I scratched my arm, fidgeting in the chair.

"Relax," Erica said, leaning back in her chair. "Nobody's going to jump on you. Lachlan's worried about Aidan, that's all. He's very protective."

"Aidan mentioned that." I dared to meet Erica's gaze. "You must think I'm a horrible person."

Her smile was gentle and...motherly. "Not at all. I'm sure Aidan told you how Lachlan dumped me. I made him wait two months before I forgave him."

Christ, if Aidan put me off for two months I didn't think I could handle it. I realized with a start my fingers had moved up to my throat, one finger tapping a manic beat.

Erica leaned forward and stretched out a hand to touch my knee. "Aidan's nowhere near as stubborn as me. Though, to be fair, I had been framed for embezzlement by my ex. Kinda hard to trust after that."

How exactly did one respond to such a confession? *Gee, sorry your ex was such a douche.* It hardly seemed adequate.

Sitting back, Erica rested her arms on the chair's arms and crossed her ankles. "I think you and I will be good friends."

"Your husband might not approve."

"He will once you and Aidan work things out." A playful gleam glinted in her eyes to match her mischievous smile. "Besides, I have a certain…influence over Lachlan."

I could guess what she meant by that. Aidan had influenced me, for sure. I'd ditched all my rules, one by one, helpless to resist my hot Scot.

"You're brave to come all this way," Erica said. "I admire your conviction."

"But?" I heard the word in her tone, even though she didn't speak it.

"You have to understand, Aidan's never had his heart broken before. I don't think he's ever been in love either." She leveled a somber expression on me. "He's a sweetie-pie, but he's been through a lot this year."

The accident and the stuff with Seona. I couldn't blame his family for being protective, but the revelation he'd never been in love before had left me reeling. Somehow, I had to stick it out through this conversation.

"I would never want to make him feel worse," I said. My throat ached, my stomach roiled, and the sting in my eyes told me I'd cry if I didn't rein in my anxiety. What if he'd changed his mind about me?

As if she'd read my mind, Erica said, "Aidan loves you, and when a MacTaggart man loves, he never gives up on it."

"But I—broke his heart."

"Broken things can be mended."

Footsteps clumped nearer from somewhere deeper in the house. A little smile curled Erica's lips, and she hopped up from her chair. She shooed me out of my chair and toward the living room doorway. As we crossed the threshold, she stopped me with a hand on my arm. "I'm going to tell you something you can never let anyone, especially Lachlan, know I told you."

"Okay," I said carefully, not at all sure I wanted to be the keeper of a secret like that.

She glanced around as if looking for her husband, who wasn't in sight. Then she whispered, "Lachlan's a manly man too, but he fell to his knees and cried when he begged me to forgive him. And I mean *really* begged. Don't assume Aidan's too proud to take you back."

"I hope you're right." The memory of his letter flashed through my mind. He'd poured his heart and soul into the words he scrawled on those two pages. Maybe that had been his version of falling to his knees for me.

He didn't have to beg. I was the one in need of forgiveness.

Lachlan emerged from a room down the hall carrying a steaming mug. He hesitated when he noticed us huddled in the doorway. One of his dark brows lifted. "You two look secretive. Must be talking about Aidan."

"No." Erica grinned. "We were gossiping about you."

His mouth opened, then closed. "I don't want to know, do I?"

She shook her head. "But you should wish Calli luck. She's heading out to get her man."

Lachlan, expression thoughtful and eyes on me, took a sip of his hot drink. "She doesn't need luck."

I glanced at Erica, who nodded.

"He's right," she said. "Now go."

She hustled me to the door, swung it open, and gave me a gentle shove. Her smile broadened when I turned around to blink at her. "Try the barn first, then the garden. You can't miss the former and the latter is behind the barn."

Lachlan came up behind his wife, linking his arms around her waist. "Go left, take a right at the end of the house."

I stared into space for a moment, imagining all sorts of horrible ways this could go, then gave myself a mental smack and headed out. Erica and Lachlan watched in silence, their smiles encouraging, and I prayed they really knew more about how Aidan might react than I did. I had the whole scared-witless, angst-ridden thing going on, making me think nothing could possibly work out. As I reached the end of the house and angled right, I glanced back at my hosts.

Erica waved.

I waved back and marched toward the blue barn, a squat building with windows and Dutch doors, which had their top halves swung open. I leaned over the closed half, peering into the gloom. Sunlight coming in through the windows cast a gentle glow on the interior where two cows munched on hay. I could see a wide-open back door, larger than the one before me, that opened onto a pasture full of pink heather blossoms.

No Aidan.

For a moment, I just stood there staring at the cows. *Such a coward.* I cleared my throat and called into the barn, "Aidan?"

No answer. I hollered again but still got no response. He either wasn't in the barn or he was ignoring me. I decided to think positive and assume he wasn't in here. To the garden, then.

As I walked around the barn, acid churned in my stomach and swelled into my throat. I realized I was wringing my hands and stuffed them in my jeans pockets. In a few more steps, I cleared the barn and caught sight of the garden, a large plot the size of the house and barn combined, with a wooden fence around it and a gate that hung ajar. Between the slats of the fence, I glimpsed a figure crouching amid the rows of neatly sewn seedlings.

A mixture of excitement and terror tingled over my skin, raising every hair. It was him.

He faced away from me, but I recognized Aidan's golden-tinged, wavy brown hair. An ache started in my chest, a pang so intense I lifted a hand to my breast. My feet refused to budge. I crossed my arms over my stomach, swallowed against a lump in my throat, and studied his backside for so long my eyes started to water from the sun burning into them.

Now or never, Miss Chicken.

I would not be a coward any longer. I came here to take a chance and stop fearing the future, fearing what might happen, and to embrace the possibilities for good things.

And the best thing that ever happened to me was him.

Exhaling a shaky breath, I straightened, lowered my hands to my sides, and strode across the distance to the garden.

Chapter Thirty-Four

At the gate, I hesitated. Aidan knelt straight ahead of me, bent forward as he placed seeds in their little holes with exceptional care. He'd treated me with care too, like I was a precious flower in need of his tender touch. God, had I needed it. Needed him. I always would.

I settled a hand on the gate post, my other hand clenched over my belly. "Aidan."

His entire body went rigid. He uncoiled his spine until he crouched there upright, his head still aimed away from me. With a slow and deliberate motion, he set down the spade he'd been holding and set his palms on his knees. Though he remained silent, his shoulders rose and fell as he took deep breaths.

Seconds ticked by, bleeding into minutes.

Uncertainty trickled through me, cold and insidious. Maybe I'd made a mistake. *Run*, an instinct urged, but that was the old me talking. I would not hide this time. "Aidan, it's me."

At last he spoke, his tone gruff. "I know. Ye think I wouldn't recognize your voice?"

Oh shit. This sounded bad. Really bad. Angry or hurt or something worse.

He rose to his full height, unfurling that muscular body inch by inch. Rolling his shoulders back, he turned to face me. His expression unreadable, he aimed his glimmering eyes at me but just stood there. Silent. Unmoving. Unmoved? I prayed not.

My throat felt thick, a sour taste infiltrated my mouth. I walked up to him, halting an arm's length away.

"Hi," I said. Could I have thought up anything more lame to say? "Erica said you were out here. I was hoping we could talk. No, that's not right. I need to talk, and I hoped you would listen. Please."

No response. He watched me, giving away nothing.

"I know I screwed up," I said. "I know you have every right to tell me to go to hell. No one's ever been as good to me as you are, and I let my stupid fears come between us. I used the past as an excuse to keep you at a distance, to keep from falling for you. It didn't work."

His gaze searched my face, his eyes glinted in the sunlight.

I shuffled one step closer. "I made so many mistakes in my life. I thought I didn't deserve happiness, didn't deserve someone as good as you. God, you are so good. You make me feel like I'm not a criminal, like maybe I could have someone who loves me and treats me with respect. A man like you." My voice broke. I moved a little closer, gazing into the eyes of the only man I'd ever needed. "For years, I've hidden from life because I felt guilty for breaking the law to help Rade, sure I'd be found out and locked up. I couldn't believe anything good could happen to me, but then you barreled into my life and turned everything upside-down in the most incredible way. The whole thing with Seona threw me for a loop and you were right, I had too much time to think of lame reasons to stay away from you. The truth is, I love you so much it terrified me. But not anymore."

His lips twitched so minutely I couldn't be sure I'd seen it. An almost smile? Or a sign of disgust?

"What I'm trying to say," I told him, "is I am so sorry. I'll do whatever it takes to make up for hurting you."

I swore one of his dark brows lifted the tiniest bit and maybe, just maybe, he swallowed against a tightness in his own throat. My throat ached, my heart ached, my soul ached. If I couldn't fix this...

"You said you'd wait," I began, daring to light my palm on his chest, barely touching him, the sun-warmed fabric of his T-shirt soft against my skin. "Said you'd wait as long as it took. These two weeks felt like an eternity. But hey, at least I didn't make you wait two months. We've got one up on Erica and Lachlan, right?"

Did one corner of his mouth tick up a millimeter? *Please, please, please.* Time to go for broke.

Fanning both my palms on his solid chest, I leaned in and angled my head back to meet his gaze. Though he kept his chin raised, his eyes rolled down to gaze into mine. They were glossy with...tears? *Oh God, please.* I'd never prayed for another human being to cry, but I was frantic for any sign, however small, that my words affected him.

"I love you, Aidan."

His brows furrowed, his eyes widened a fraction.

"Please believe me," I said, powerless to hold back the words. "I love you so much I can't imagine my life without you anymore." I skated my right palm over his chest until it bumped over a small, hard shape beneath his shirt. I tapped one fingertip on the circular object. "What is this?"

He ducked his head, turning it to the side, eyes closing.

Diving my hand inside his shirt, I pulled out the object. A diamond engagement ring, dangling from a long silver chain.

I skated my finger over the shiny gold band. The diamond glittered in the sunshine as bright and perfect as the love Aidan had offered me. I yearned to believe the ring was for me.

Rubbing my thumb over the brilliant stone, I looked up at his averted face. "I'm not giving up. I'll come back here every day, ten times a day, to beg you to forgive me if that's what it takes. I'll stalk you until you either take me back or have me arrested. Hell, I'll strip naked and run down the streets of Ballachulish screaming your name. Don't care about dignity or pride anymore, all I care about is you."

He rotated his face toward me.

I waited, goosebumps of anticipation popping up all over my arms. Seconds elapsed. *Tick, tick, tick.* My mouth went dry, but my hands grew clammy. *Tick, tick, tick.*

He cleared his throat and drawled, "Well, it took you bloody long enough. Thought you'd never come to your senses."

"You mean—" I stared at him, uncomprehending. "Do you mean you forgive me?"

"Nothing to forgive. I knew you'd turn up eventually. You are hopelessly in love with me, after all." He smirked and winked. "Just like I predicted you would be."

A tiny sob burst out of me and all the fear and tension that had kept me upright rushed out. I slumped into him, my forehead falling to his chest. He wrapped his brawny arms around me, tucking me within his comforting embrace. I was home.

He crooked a finger under my chin and raised my face to his. "Did you think I'd give up so easily? A few weeks is nothing. Told you I'd wait as long as it took, because you're worth it."

"I know, but I told you—"

"Hush." He took my face in his hands, brushing my tears away with his thumbs. "If I learned anything from Lachlan and Erica, it's that second chances come along if you're patient. And when you get a second chance with the one person you love more than anything, you jump on it."

"Erica said I...broke your heart."

"You did." He held my face, preventing me from flinching away. "Easy, *mo chridhe*, I'm not a weakling. I can handle a broken heart." He tilted my head back, slanting his down to within an inch of my face, those gorgeous eyes shining with love. "Now it's your job to heal it."

My finger hurt. I glanced down to find I'd been twisting the ring around my fingertip, carving out a red line in my flesh.

"You spoiled the surprise," he said, and snatched the ring away. He yanked it, snapping the chain and letting the silver links plummet to the ground. He held the ring between his thumb and forefinger. "This belongs to you."

I couldn't breathe. "You still want to marry me?"

He shook his head, the picture of affectionate exasperation. "Havenae you been listening? Ahmno letting our second chance slip away."

"You're jumping on me?"

His lips curved into the sexy smile I adored. "That'll come next, you can count on it. First..." He dropped to one knee before me, proffering the ring, his face tilted up to behold me with undeniable love. "Calli Douglas, will you marry me?"

"Yes." I held up the appropriate finger, ready to accept the ring. "After my divorce is finalized, of course. That happens in less than seven weeks. Can you wait?"

"To marry you, yes." He slipped the ring onto my finger. "To make love to you, no."

"Get up so I can kiss you senseless, *mo chridhe*."

Aidan surged to his feet and pulled me into his arms. "I missed you."

"I missed you so much. Can't believe I took so long to come here."

"Thought you were going to kiss me."

I flung my arms around his neck and crushed my mouth to his, reveling in the softness of his lips, the way he yielded to me and opened for me, inviting me to plunder his mouth. I explored him with long, lazy strokes of my tongue, relishing the taste of him after two interminable weeks apart. He answered my every movement with his own, twining his tongue with mine, molding his lips to my mouth as if we were fused together. Inseparable. Inevitable.

Though we broke the kiss, his lips grazed mine as he spoke. "I love you, Calli. Would've waited forever, but I had no doubt it wouldn't take that long."

I combed my fingers through the silky waves of his hair. "We are meant for each other. No other man on earth could understand me like you do."

"Stopped thinking we don't know each other well enough, eh?"

"The letter changed everything. You have a real way with words."

"I wasn't sure you'd like what I wrote. Never said flowery things like that before."

"What you wrote made me cry." I trailed my fingertips down his cheek. "In a sad way at first, but later in a good way. I read the letter again on the plane. You amaze me, Mr. MacTaggart."

"You amaze me too, Mrs. MacTaggart."

I arched my brows. "Getting a little ahead of yourself, aren't you?"

"Always. Impulsive, remember?"

I could do nothing except laugh and kiss him and touch him—and love him, without reservation or inhibition. For the rest of our lives, for every second I had with him, I would love Aidan with all the devotion in my soul.

He glanced around, lips compressed and eyes narrowed, as if searching for something.

"What is it?" I asked.

"Looking for the closest place where I can strip you naked."

Desire rippled through me, hot and liquid. "Outside?"

"Not making love to you in my brother's house, when he's home with his wife and bairn." Aidan caught sight of something, smiled with satisfaction, and swept me up into his arms. "Found it."

He carried me toward a small grove of apple trees laden with ripe, red fruit and set me down on the grass beneath the largest tree, in the umbrella of its shadow.

"Growing apples in the Highlands," he said, settling in beside me, "is a difficult task. Almost takes a miracle to keep them growing and bearing fruit. Must be good luck to make love under the fertile bows of a Scottish apple tree."

"Are you implying this is a magic fertility tree?"

"Maybe it is." He dug a condom packet out of his pocket, holding it up. "I've been carrying this around so I'd be ready whenever you turned up. Should we use it?"

"What exactly are you asking me?"

He laid a hand over my lower belly. "Would ye like to start trying for a bairn today?"

A baby? I could've dreamed up a hundred reasons why we should wait, but none of them mattered anymore. The idea of having a child with Aidan made my heart swell.

I snatched the condom packet from his fingers and tossed it aside. "Does that answer your question?"

He chuckled. "Well enough, aye."

Lying stretched out on the green grass, elevated on my elbows, I admired the view as he shed his T-shirt. Acres of tanned skin tantalized my imagination with thoughts of tracing every line of muscle with my fingers and my tongue. My mouth watered at the prospect.

"By the way," I said, "Rade insisted on giving me a financial settlement to compensate me for the years I gave him."

Aidan paused with his jeans half unzipped. "Did he?"

"Yes. A hundred thousand dollars."

He gaped at me for several seconds, but then a grin lit up his face. "I'm marrying a rich woman."

"Does it bother you?"

"Not in the slightest."

I clasped my hands over my belly, my feet shifting in restless movements.

"What is it?" he asked.

"Even though we're not married yet," I said, "I'd like to give you some of the money, to get your business going again. We'll be sharing everything soon enough, and I don't want to wait."

He stood there in silence, hands lingering on the waistband of his pants, for a long moment.

"I could be a manly man and say no," he told me. "But I can tell you want to do this, and I can't deny my future wife anything."

"Thank you. I hope this doesn't wound your male pride."

"Donnae worry, love. Ahmno sensitive."

Yes, I'd learned that about him weeks ago. And it was one of a countless number of things I adored about him.

While he resumed unzipping and pushed his jeans down, revealing the sleek and beautiful length of his engorged penis, I observed with growing lust. "I do love watching you strip. Maybe I should stuff a few hundred-dollar bills in your waistband."

He kicked his pants away. "You get me for free. Donnae take my clothes off for money, remember?"

"Oh yes, you did mention that once upon a time."

My fiancé stood naked before me. Glorious, unashamed, towering above me like a Celtic god.

Aidan knelt over me, his knees straddling my thighs. "Time to unwrap my gift."

His gift. He was my gift too, the most precious one I'd ever received, the one I'd never asked for but couldn't live without. That night in the club, when he'd crashed into my life, I couldn't have predicted how much he would change my world. But he had known, always.

You will fall for me.

I'd keep falling over and over, every time he smiled at me or kissed me or made love to me. This wicked Highlander was mine.

Epilogue

Eight Weeks Later

I lay naked on a king-size bed inside our new home, a two-story farmhouse a five-minute walk from Lachlan and Erica's place, watching as my husband of two hours and forty minutes kicked off his shoes. A kilt swaddled his hips, cascading down his thighs. Beneath the plaid, his ever-stiffening penis tented the kilt. Like any proud Scotsman, my Highlander had substituted a kilt for the pants but had worn the rest of the tuxedo—including the shoes and socks.

Only Aidan MacTaggart could pull off a look like that.

Now he took hold of the kilt, and with one flick of his wrist, sent it plummeting to the floor. His erection waved in the air, thick and long, the tip reddened and already damp with a drop of moisture. As usual, he'd forgone underwear.

Aidan knelt at the foot of the bed. "Wish you'd let me take you to a posh hotel. It is our wedding night. Or afternoon."

He'd whisked me away from the reception early, at my request. I needed time alone with my husband.

"Rather start our life together in the home we'll share," I said, and tickled his knee with my toes. "You know I don't care about fancy stuff. I want you. That's all I need, today and every day."

"It's all I need too." On all fours, he crawled up my body until his hands and knees straddled me. He stopped with his head over my belly. "We are going on the honeymoon, even if Lachlan did pay for it."

"Lachlan and Rory. It was their wedding gift to us." Two weeks in the south of France, at a villa on the Côte D'Azure. "Can't wait to see the French Riviera. Sure you don't mind bringing the puppies with us?"

"Wouldn't be the same without the furry lassies." He ducked his head to swipe that agile tongue over one nipple. "Though I'm glad Jamie took them for tonight, so I can have you all for myself. Cannae wait to see you lying nude on a private beach, for no one but me to see."

"You have become rather possessive of my body."

He kissed my belly. "Let me show you how much I covet your body."

I bent one knee and grazed it against his cock. "I covet yours too."

He hissed in a breath as I hooked my leg around his hip. "*Thig mi air do mhuin.*"

"No clue what that means, but I'm game for anything."

"Means I'm coming to mount you." He laid a hand on my belly, gliding it lower and lower until his fingertips teased the hairs on my mound. "No need to *fannadh* anymore, unless you want me to watch."

"I want you inside me."

"*Dé an doimhneachd?*"

"You have got to teach me Gaelic. What's that one mean?"

"How deep."

Lifting my hips, I pressed his palm into my mound so his fingers skimmed my clitoris. "Deep as your *slat* can go. I want you so deep inside me I can feel you come, like you're a part of me."

"We are a part of each other, *mo leannan.*" He thrust his hand between my folds, caressing the skin, fondling my clit. When I arched my back and moaned, he grinned. "I'm impressed you learned a Gaelic word all on your own. *Slat?* Never taught you that one. Where'd you learn it?"

"Rory told me."

Aidan's hand stilled, his eyes went wide. "That bloody *bod ceann*—"

"I'm kidding," I said, helpless not to laugh at his adorably offended expression. "Your brother's not a dickhead. But I learned *slat* from the Internet."

"Did you now." That hand began to stroke me again with leisurely ease, stoking my need, making me wriggle against his palm and clench my fingers in the sheets. "I'm going to show you things the Internet cannae teach ye."

"No better teacher than Aidan the Magnificent."

He pulled his hand away, glided a palm to the inside of each of my thighs, and spread me wide for him. "We come together this time."

Joined hearts, joined lives, joined bodies. He'd always taken care of my pleasure first, before taking my body, though I invariably climaxed again when his impassioned love-making drove me over the edge along with him. But this time, on our wedding night, it seemed appropriate we find our pleasure as one.

He planted his hands at either side of me, his arms straight and his face above mine. "I love you with everything I am."

"I love you, Aidan, so much."

He slid inside me, slowly, delicately, filling me until it seemed we had merged. He, a part of me. I, a part of him. Forever.

I clung to him as he began to pump his hips, pulling his cock out of me and then driving it deep inside again, the pace languid and deliciously torturous. With my heels flat on the bed, I hoisted my hips up to meet his thrusts, my mouth open on a string of moans and gasps, the desperation to come mounting like a spring wound ever tighter. He pumped faster, harder, grunting each time he lunged into me and blustering out a breath when he retreated. I locked my legs and arms around him, begging him to never stop, to make me come, to never stop.

My body went rigid, my release hovered so close I could almost taste it, the promised pleasure like a bite of a decadent dessert hovering a breath away from my lips. His hips pistoned at a frantic pace as his cock pounded into me, making me cry out.

In the instant my orgasm wrenched my body, the ecstasy flooding over me, his release pulsed inside me and he threw his head back, shouting a long litany of Gaelic. I clutched him and cried out again and again, lost in endless waves of bliss. Aidan pumped into me twice more, then shoved a hand down to massage my clit, ever determined to see my climax through to the very last. When I thought my orgasm would never end, it at last faded away on a final, shuddering wave.

He collapsed beside me and pulled me into his arms, cradled against his powerful body. We both breathed hard, nearly breathless from the incredible rapture of our love-making. With my ear pressed to his chest, I listened to his heartbeat while it gradually slowed.

"The wedding was beautiful," I said, "but this was more fun."

My thoughts traveled back to the wedding and the two of us reciting our vows atop a hillside behind Lachlan and Erica's home, surrounded by a carpet of purple heather. It seemed appropriate we join our hearts and lives on the same hill where they had taken their vows. After all, I would never have met Aidan if he hadn't gone to Dance Ardor in hopes of re-creating his brother's journey to lasting love.

"Weddings are for the guests," Aidan said. "This was for us."

"I finally got to meet the infamous Rory, but I didn't see the caber."

"He was in a good mood today, because of the wedding." Aidan shook his head. "The man needs a strong woman to shake some sense into him."

"I'm sure he'll find the right girl someday."

"Not unless she ties him up and drags him away from his office."

"Let's not talk about your family anymore tonight."

"Anything my wife wants." He rolled onto his back, taking me with him, and I wound up sprawled on him. His fingers traced small, delicate circles on my back. "Should I worry about your brother's intentions with my sister?"

I laughed, recalling the sight of Gavin and Jamie engaged in a secret conversation. They'd slipped away from the crowd at the outdoor reception—held at Lachlan and Erica's, of course—to a spot off to the side where they could have some privacy. Aidan had spotted the pair and poked me in the ribs, his lips twisted as he nodded toward Gavin and Jamie.

"What are they up to?" he'd asked me.

I'd shrugged. "No idea. Maybe a quick tryst."

He'd looked so adorably horrified at the idea. "Bad enough he had her in a hunting shack in the woods."

"Young love. What can you do?"

Back in the present, ensconced in the arms of my wicked Scot, I propped my chin on his chest and said, "Gavin and Jamie may be the next couple to tie the knot. Do you have a problem with that?"

"Not so long as he treats her right."

I raked my nails down his chest. "You mean as long as he doesn't act like the two Scotsmen I know, who seduce us American girls at first sight."

"Exactly."

A phone rang, muffled but nearby. I sat up, trying to decide if it was my phone or his. "Sounds like mine."

"Let it go," Aidan said. "We're on holiday."

"Better check it, just to be sure."

He wriggled out from under me and marched across the room stark naked to dig my phone out from under my wedding dress, which had wound up piled on a chair. He glanced at the phone's screen and cursed in Gaelic.

"What's wrong?" I asked, sitting up.

"It's the surgery," he said, and tossed me the phone.

I caught it in one hand.

"My checkup?" A few days ago, I'd signed up with the MacTaggart family's GP, a prudent step considering we wanted to have a baby. "Probably calling to tell me the blood tests were fine. It was a standard physical, that's all."

"They called on our wedding day. Must be urgent."

"Don't turn into a worry wart. That's my job." I held the phone to my ear. "This is Calli."

"Miss Douglas—" The woman halted mid-sentence. I recognized the melodic voice of the surgery's nurse. "Pardon me. It's Mrs. MacTaggart now, isn't it? Congratulations, dearie."

"Thank you."

"We've got your blood results and there was a wee bit of a surprise. I thought you'd want to hear it right away."

"Surprise?"

"Yes." The woman made a delighted little noise. "You are pregnant, dearie."

"What?" I virtually screeched the word. "That's incredible. I thought it would take longer to happen, but this is such perfect timing."

"Congratulations, *gràidh*."

She'd called me darling. It would've been sweet, if I hadn't been overwhelmed by the news. "Thank you for calling. I have no idea what to say."

"Tell your husband, that's what you should do."

She said goodbye, and I said it back, not thinking anymore, acting by rote. I dropped my phone on the bed and looked at Aidan.

He grasped my face in his hands, searching my eyes. "What is it? Are you ill?"

"No, not at all." I laid my hands over his, unable to stem the tears trickling down my cheeks, and smiled. "We're having a baby, Aidan. I'm pregnant."

For a couple seconds, he stared blankly at me. Then he let out the loudest, most uproarious whoop I'd ever heard, head thrown back, arms flung wide. The whoop segued into laughter and he leaped onto the bed, bowling me over with him. Tangled in each other's arms, we laughed and cried and kissed. The kissing grew more heated, our hands began to grope, and his penis began to swell once more.

"This," he said, licking and nibbling his way down my neck, "requires another celebration."

"You mean sex."

"Would ye rather drink champagne?"

"Oh no. I want sex, right now."

He pushed up onto his knees. "I'd wager we made the bairn that day under the apple tree."

"The magic fertility tree? I think so too." My eyes fluttered shut as he skimmed his hands up and down my body, exploring every curve and dip, worshiping me with his rough but tender hands. "This might sound weird, but I'm looking forward to coming back after the honeymoon and getting to work. Cataloging your uncle's piles and piles of family papers and historical books is like catnip to a librarian."

"I'm looking forward to working with my new partner." He dipped his tongue into my belly button, swirling it there. "The best partner a man could want. My bonnie, clever wife."

He lay down beside me and settled his head on my belly, his ear to my womb and a blissful smile lighting up his beautiful face. "I was right again. Said you could give me everything I wanted, and you have."

"Don't get arrogant about it. You might be wrong at some point."

"Maybe." He kissed my belly and smirked. "Donnae hold your breath, though."

I grabbed a pillow and whapped him on the head with it.

He peppered kisses over my skin, up between my breasts, to the hollow of my throat. There, he breathed his words against the sensitive flesh. "I want you, but only if it willnae hurt the wee one."

Wee one? I needed a second to figure that one out. "If you mean the itty-bitty fetus growing inside me, nothing you do is going to hurt it."

"Good." He rolled us both over, with me on top. "But to be safe, you should take the reins this time."

"Oh, I see. This is for safety." I placed my hands on his chest and pushed up into a half-sitting position, my breasts dangling. "I thought you just liked watching my boobs bounce."

He waggled his eyebrows. "That I do."

I raised onto my knees, took hold of his shaft, and positioned the head at my opening. "You ready for hot, married sex?"

"We've already done that, *mo leannan*."

"But this time it's hot, married, we're-having-a-baby sex."

"Ah, that is different."

His crooked smile was the most wonderful thing I'd ever seen. He looked like a man overjoyed at the prospect of raising a bairn. With me. Our family.

"Aidan," I said, my hand still around his cock, "you've given me everything I didn't know I wanted. Let me show you how grateful I am."

I slid onto his cock, inch by velvety inch, until he was seated snug inside me.

He grasped my hips, that naughty gleam in his eyes. "I'm grateful I found a wife who's such a great fuck."

I slapped his chest. "Arrogant Scot."

"Cheeky American."

For the rest of the night, we demonstrated our gratitude and devotion to each other in more ways than I'd ever imagined, even in my wildest fantasies. Not only had I met a man who treated me with respect, one who appreciated my quirks and made all my fantasies come true, I'd also found the one man in the world who accomplished a feat I'd believed impossible.

He set me free—in every way.

And for that, I would be grateful for the rest of my life.

Love the

Hot Scots

series?

Visit

AnnaDurand.com

to subscribe to her newsletter
for updates on forthcoming books in this series
&
to receive a free gift for signing up!

Anna Durand is a bestselling, multi-award-winning author of contemporary and paranormal romance. Her books have earned bestseller status on every major retailer and wonderful reviews from readers around the world. But that's the boring spiel. Here are some really cool things you want to know about Anna!

Born on Lackland Air Force Base in Texas, Anna grew up moving here, there, and everywhere thanks to her dad's job as an instructor pilot. She's lived in Texas (twice), Mississippi, California (twice), Michigan (twice), and Alaska—and now Ohio.

As for her writing, Anna has always made up stories in her head, but she didn't write them down until her teen years. Those first awful books went into the trash can a few years later, though she learned a lot from those stories. Eventually, she would pen her first romance novel, the paranormal romance *Willpower*, and she's never looked back since.

Want even more details about Anna? Get access to her extended bio when you subscribe to her newsletter and download the free bonus ebook, *Hot Scots Confidential*. You'll also get hot deleted scenes, character interviews, fun facts, and more! You also get the short story *Tempted by a Kiss* and a bonus audio chapter narrated for you by Shane East. Visit AnnaDurand.com to sign up!